# WAVE AND DIE

*The second title in the Jordan Lacey series*

Sussex wives will be careless with their husbands and, in the sequel to *Pray and Die*, off-the-wall private investigator Jordan Lacey is on the trail of yet another missing spouse. Then she is accused of an arson attack leading to the death of the errant husband and starts to wonder whether sleuthing is her true vocation. There's a silver lining to every cloud however: Jordan no longer has to vie for the attention of the dishy DI James, since he's hounding her...

# WAVE AND DIE

*Further titles in the Jordan Lacey series by*
*Stella Whitelaw from*
*Severn House Large Print Books*

PRAY AND DIE

# WAVE AND DIE

Stella Whitelaw

**Severn House Large Print**
London & New York

This first large print edition published in Great Britain 2002 by
SEVERN HOUSE LARGE PRINT BOOKS LTD of
9-15, High Street, Sutton, Surrey, SM1 1DF.
First world regular print edition published 2001 by
Severn House Publishers, London and New York.
This first large print edition published in the USA 2002 by
SEVERN HOUSE PUBLISHERS INC., of
595 Madison Avenue, New York, NY 10022

British Library Cataloguing in Publication Data

Whitelaw, Stella, 1941 -
    Wave and die. - Large print ed. - (Jordan Lacey series)
    1.   Women private investigators - England - Sussex - Fiction
    2.   Detective and mystery stories
    3.   Large type books
    I.   Title
    823.9'14 [F]

    ISBN 0-7278-7151-X

Printed and bound in Great Britain by
MPG Books Ltd, Bodmin, Cornwall.

# One

There were only a few minutes left before closing time. I didn't want to spend the night huddled on a bench, shivering and hungry, and alone on the deserted pier. Yet I was still walking the pier at ten minutes to ten because I knew something was wrong. My seventh sense told me that all was not kosher, correct, genuine, legitimate.

'I know I'm right,' I muttered.

Today was Latching Pier's seventieth birthday. Happy Birthday, pier. The pier had in its time been wrecked by a storm, damaged by seas, blown up in the war. A display of faded sepia photographs and mementoes were on show by the entrance. Elegant Edwardian women with parasols and little dogs strolled the decks, now trans-fixed in time; jagged scraps of shrapnel from wartime shells were fixed on a board; news-paper cuttings of the fire that gutted the kiosks and booths in the fifties were pinned to the back.

The council had made it a jolly day for the

7

kids with clowns and jugglers, roundabouts and face-painting. Cockle and whelk stalls provided grown-up nibbles. The mayor and mayoress, festooned with regalia, paid a regal visit, doing the eight-minute circuit out to the sea end and back. The mayoress was visibly frozen in an unsuitable suit and tottering along the boards in strappy high-heels. She didn't come to the pier often, that was obvious.

'Aren't you too old for that kind of stuff?' I said to Sergeant Rawlings. He grinned at me from behind bright orange tiger-stripes and white whiskers painted on his ruddy face. He was out of uniform, fawn wind-cheater zipped to his throat.

'Grandson dared me. If anyone asks, I'm on surveillance.'

I'd known Sergeant Rawlings a long time. He'd been one of my silent supporters when I'd been kicked out of the force for criti-cising a superior officer's dubious tactics in a rape case that got off. My outspokenness got me suspended on full pay. I saved like mad for the future so when the Disciplinary Board, in their united wisdom, finally dispensed with my uncomfortable presence, I had enough capital to start my own busi-ness. First Class Investigations. The first private eye in Latching.

'How's Latching's most famous private investigator, Jordan?' Sergeant Rawlings asked. 'Found any more dead nuns on meat hooks?'

'Very quiet in the fatalities section, I'm glad to say. Rather too quiet in other areas. The highlight of the week has been a lost King Charles spaniel, neutered, called Fergie.'

Sergeant Rawlings cocked a tigerish eyebrow. 'Strayed?'

'Not far. I found it at a neighbour's house. Shacked up with a better class of dog biscuit. Followed the paw prints. Have you looked at the photographs of the pier taken seventy years ago? Someone dug them out of an attic and put them on display at the entrance.'

'No, I haven't. Should I? Are you trying to tell me something?'

'There's something wrong there but I'm not sure what.'

'Did you spot a corpse mouldering under one of the girders? Shall I radio for DI James? He'd love a corpse on the pier especially if you found it. He keeps a box file of your lost causes under his desk. Puts his feet on them.'

The wind at the end of the pier was making it hard to stand upright. I hung on to a rail and turned my head away to catch a breath. The fight was glorious. A skinny nine stone of human bone structure was battling against a Force 6 gale. The bunting

9

strung from lamp posts streamed ferociously, the plastic flags crackling like army percussion.

The sea was a dinosaur, thumping its mighty tail against the girders. How the seagulls flew in this degree of force was a minor miracle.

The mayoral party made a quick exit in an official car. Force 6 wind had not been on the itinerary for the day. Someone got it wrong.

I didn't want to talk about the subject of lost causes. DI James made loss seem like a big well and I was deep down inside that well, unable to climb out or find any kind of hold. No one wanted to give me a helping hand. Unkind people, remembering various mishaps, might say I was safer down a well or a mine, less prone to accidents and unfortunate coincidences. The kind of accidents that follow me round without the benevolent scales of the Chinese Dragon. Least, I'm told they are benevolent.

'So what's wrong with the photographs?'

'I don't know. That's what's so irritating.'

'Come on, Jordan. They're closing the pier. Look, the band's going home.'

His words were like a stab in soft tissue. The band had gone home from my life long ago. My musician – a top jazz trumpeter – was always making tracks for his slippers and king-sized duvet. He had a wife too. I

10

watched the bandsmen from the local Salvation Army packing away their instruments, the street lights glinting on the brass and the braid of their uniforms.

'OK. Let's call it a day. Nice to see you, Tiger.' I growled realistically.

He tapped his nose. 'Under cover. You won't get a word out of me, even if you torture me with your cooking.'

'Fat chance,' I said, combing my hair with my fingers. 'I don't entertain married men.'

Liar, there was one married man I would go for if I'd got the slimmest chance. I had nearly said older married men but I might need Sergeant Rawlings' help some day. My friends in the force were my secret weapon in the tough world of private investigations. Not that DI James could be called an old friend, more like a Holmes-type antagonist. He just about tolerated me on a good day and I could take a lot of him in any kind of weather, any hour, coming or going.

Tiger Rawlings strode off to his semi-detached at the back end of Latching's residential sprawl, his heavy beat-boot tread giving away his profession. I lived a pebble's throw away from the beach. I know the seagulls by sight. They take turns harassing me. The sea was my lullaby at night; the sand my endless carpet for walking; the waves my own brand of Prozac. If I lived any nearer, I'd be camping out inside one of the upturned fishing boats drawn up on the shingle.

Cancer folk love the sea. I'm a July person. I get withdrawal symptoms if I don't get to see waves for a few days. My skin starts to dehydrate and my eyes itch. Perhaps I ought to carry around a bottle of sea water to sniff on the quiet.

I was seriously looking for wheels. It was quietly humiliating to turn up to cases on my bicycle, even if it was a mountain bike with all the gears and right accessories.

This lack of transportation was brought home forcibly the next morning when a one in six hill climb up the South Downs had me gasping for breath. Exhaust fumes aren't good for asthma either but my sticky airways couldn't cope with uphill cycling.

Most of Latching is flat and I can zip round the streets without any trouble. But cycling doesn't look professional and I was keen that First Class Investigations should look as good as its name.

The call that morning at my office behind the class junk-shop cover was from a Mr Terence Lucan, owner of Latching Water Gardens out at Preston Hill. He sounded very agitated and upset.

'The police are not taking this seriously, Miss Lacey,' he said. I knew the feeling. 'I want them to send someone out now, immediately, but they say they can't come until late this afternoon. All the clues will have dried up.'

'What is the nature of the crime, Mr Lucan?'

'My flowers have gone. Stolen. My beautiful flowers.'

I could understand why the police were not sending a fleet of pandas, sirens blaring, lights flashing. A few flowers might be precious to flora and fauna-loving Mr Lucan but they hardly had priority status.

'This is a life-threatening situation. Can you come at once?'

I caught on. The flowers would die. 'I'll be with you right away. Give me your address.'

Right away turned out to be an hour later. I had closed the shop, put up the GONE FOR LUNCH SIGN, pushed my bike up that damned hill.

Mr Lucan was waiting at the end of the entrance drive. I half hoped he would be dapper, silver-haired, neat moustache, distinguished-looking, and I would have solved the disappearance mystery of the century. But he was small, wiry, red-haired and freckled. No amount of plastic surgery could have turned that trick.

'Hello, Mr Lucan. I'm Jordan Lacey, First Class Investigations.'

'You took your time.'

13

'I didn't know I'd have to climb Mount Everest.'

He grunted, taking in my hot appearance. 'It is a bit steep. Would you like a drink?'

'Thank you. That would be very kind.'

He turned to walk back down the drive. Trees of all kinds lined the way, their branches dipping and rustling a rural welcome. The sheer density of leaves isolated the gardens from the rest of the world. 'And don't ask me if I killed the nanny,' he added briskly.

'Never crossed my mind,' I said, wheeling my bike after him.

His office was a rustic portacabin, festooned with hanging baskets of flowering busy Lizzies, still sporting tiny red and pink flowers. I needed an oxygen-giving plant for my office. At least the thieves hadn't taken his busy Lizzies. Mr Lucan went over to a fridge in the corner of a chaotic office. There was so much stuff everywhere. Piles of catalogues, box files, spiked invoices, ledgers, stacks of addressed envelopes for mailing. I approved of his industry if not his disorder.

'Diet Coke?' he asked, waving a frosted can.

'Perfect,' I said. After a drink, I shed my helmet and took out my notebook. 'Tell me about these flowers.' I wondered if I was going to have trouble with the spelling.

14

'Nymphaea, they're called. The thieves must have come in the night. They knew what they wanted, and wore diving gear. It looks like they parked a van the other side of the wall.'

'Mmn ... diving gear?' Diving gear for gardening? My pen stopped in mid air.

'They went under the water to select the best plants. Not easy in the dark. Professionals, they were. Took all the best varieties. Known all over the world, my water lilies. International reputation.'

'Ah, water lilies,' I repeated, picking up the dropped penny. 'Could you put a value on your plants?'

'Every plant is worth between five pounds and thirty pounds.'

'And how many did they steal?' I asked, confident that he would not know.

'Something over three thousand. I've checked how many ponds they have cleared. It's heartbreaking. All that work. All that stock. Ten different varieties, all my best.'

I tried to look cool at the cost of lilies. Quite a haul in the middle of the night. Even I could multiply 5/3063,000.

'Will the plants survive?'

'Only if they are transplanted back into water immediately. They need sunlight and quiet water, otherwise they'll die.' Mr Lucan stared at an ancient photocopier in his office. On it stood a pot of African violets, the deepest of blues.

'Major lily murder,' I murmured.

'Sacrilege if they let them die. These are rare and exotic plants.'

'I don't think they will neglect them,' I said encouragingly. I don't like seeing potential clients upset. 'These aren't your usual out-the-pub, let's trample the council flower beds, type yobbos. They sound a professional bunch of thieves and they probably have a customer waiting. Maybe an Arab sheikh with a new pond to fill.'

'A pretty big pond. But an Arab sheikh could afford to buy them straight from me, and several do. Why buy them from a shady source? Do you think you'll be able to get them back for me? You'll have to work fast.'

'May I have a look around? I might spot something.'

'Feel free. I need some coffee. My nerves are shredded.'

I thought he deserved to feel shredded. A loss of nearly £90,000 was not exactly the petty cash. I wondered how I was going to work fast. Type quicker?

He said I was to call him Terence. I suppose he was sick of Lucan jokes. He made a good mug of coffee. Instant but nothing cheap. I wandered round the nursery, hugging the mug, enjoying the flowering shrubs, not sure what I was looking for.

16

There were a few varieties of exotic lilies unfolding their waxen petals on the water of a display pond near the entrance. They were beautiful. I almost forgot why I was there but then I spotted tyre marks near the decimated ponds and the marks of a make-shift ramp which had been used to lift the sodden plants over the wall.

I scoured the damp ground but there were so many overlapping footprints, it was impossible to find a single print. I found a squashed shred of tobacco – the kind some men and young girls roll for themselves. Disgusting habit. Then I found several more, very Sherlock Holmes. The bits went into a clear plastic specimen bag. I pressed the strip fastening. They could go far with DNA these days.

It was a mess. A lot of water had been sloshed about and ragged weeds and roots lay everywhere. All shades of petals had been trodden into the mud. How was I ever going to find a van dripping with wet plants?

Mr Lucan was looking upset, his face working horizontally, his hands clenched by his sides.

I told Mr Lucan my fees to cheer him up: £10 an hour or £50 a day plus expenses. He went for the day rate and signed one of my client contract forms which I had brought with me. This efficiency would be my ruin. I thanked him for the coke and the coffee and asked him if he rolled his own cigarettes.

'Never smoke,' he said. 'Too much pollution in the atmosphere already.'

I couldn't have agreed more. As I was leaving the water garden, an emotion hit me that I hadn't felt for a long time. It was solar plexus, mouth-drying, head-rocking stuff. I was shattered, earthquaked. I fell in love, totally.

DI James faded from my heart, lodged somewhere at the back, despite my, at times, desperate longing for the man. This was different. The love object was a small, crimson-red car, beetle-shaped, with shiny black mudguards and huge lamps. It also had spots. Seven huge and perfect, black spots.

It was an old classic Morris Minor, 1,000, J-registration. I stood and stared in complete adoration, hungry for possession, longing to touch the spots.

'Want a car?' said Terence, strolling around the love object. Words escaped me. 'She's for sale. Cheap, tough, good-looking. Runs like a dream. Only one owner, careful, like me.'

'I'll take it,' I croaked, not even asking the price.

'Lord Nuffield hated the design. Called it a poached egg. But it still sold a million. Stirling Moss had one; so did the Archbishop of Canterbury.'

'If it was good enough for Stirling, it's good enough for me.'

'Only one condition. You must never remove the spots.'

'Never,' I said. As if I would.

The altitude of Preston Hill must have made me light-headed. I'd bought a car I couldn't afford and taken on a case that would be impossible to resolve. Those water lilies might be half way to the Middle East by now.

# Two

'This ladybird must remain a ladybird,' Terence Lucan insisted. 'The spots should never be removed. She's absolutely unique.'

I swallowed. I wanted that car so much, a happy little red ladybird with bold black spots painted all over her bodywork. An eye-catching vehicle, hardly ideal for detection work, I groaned inwardly. I'd be spotted a mile off. Joke.

'The Minor is a piece of history. Designed by a Turk, Alec Issigonis. The first one cost £358 10s 7d.'

'I can meet that,' I said weakly. 'The criminals would never spot me on a dark night.'

Terence was not amused. Not many people do see my jokes. I know a very funny story about a rabbit wanting to buy a lettuce in a butcher's shop but no one ever laughs. Perhaps it's the way I tell it.

'How much do you want for the car?' I added, praying for a miracle. It was not forthcoming.

'Two thousand, three hundred and fifty pounds. Worth every penny. Lord Nuffield was furious when he saw the first designs. He called it a poached egg,' he said again.

Two thousand. He could have said two million and the despair would have been the same. My bank balance only registered in hundreds and even that was a strain. My income regularly ran into one figure.

'I can give you the three hundred as a deposit,' I heard myself saying. Had I gone mad? Were the men in white coats waiting at the end of the drive? 'The rest will have to be by instalment.' Very small instalments. It would take me about twenty years.

'If you find my water lilies, I'll give you the car.'

It was a challenge. 'I'll find them,' I said with confidence. I'm such a fraud.

I didn't know where to start with Mr Lucan's stolen water lilies. Following stray husbands and wives was much easier. You just keep them in sight and pray that they would do something stupid like pay for a room at a Travelodge with their credit card.

Cycling back to Latching was downhill and a breeze. The air was peaceful and car-free. Hardly a fume wafting. Not far away a treeful of speckled thrushes (rare) were practising to take on the three tenors. I had long ago planned to die with the voices of the three tenors soaring in my ears. I had bought the Rome video, all that silvery

21

moonlight, and was saving up for the machine. It was not as if time was running out. You could not find a healthier asthmatic in the whole of West Sussex.

The van and tyre treads were the only lead. Perhaps they had used a stolen vehicle. I went into Latching police station, brisk and efficient.

'Have you had any reports of finding an abandoned van, stolen sometime earlier in the week, the same said van now found in a muddy condition with bits of leaves and weeds everywhere?' I asked at the desk. 'Or abandoned diving gear?' I threw in. 'You know, helmet, goggles and breathing mask?'

'Also wet and covered in weeds?' the duty sergeant added without a glimmer of a smile. He was new and closely shaven. A bit of tissue clung to a nick. He did not know me. So no jokes about nuns or humming the *Jaws* signature tune.

'Your name please, miss.'

'Jordan Lacey.' I handed him my old photocopied card. He looked dubious despite the fact that I am a registered PI. Today was one of my close-on-sixteen-looking days.

'Is this work experience?' he asked suspiciously.

'Look, buster, I was running this police station when you were still having sweaty nightmares over your GSE results.' It was an exaggeration but who was checking?

'You used to work here?' He looked mildly interested. 'Why did you leave?'

'The hat didn't suit me. By the way, I have a special arrangement with my mates. You help me, I help you. It works. You know how the uniform can be a hindrance, Sergeant.' I gave him instant promotion. He nodded as if he was sent out on CID work frequently. A uniform walked by that I used to know.

'Hiya, Jaws,' he said. For once I didn't mind the nickname.

'Hiya, Joe, how are you? How's the family?'

Joe stopped to talk. He always had. He went through the current state of spotty kids, wife, family. I listened patiently, nodding like a therapy doll. I wanted the new face to realise I was trustworthy and one of the team.

'I'm checking on stolen or abandoned vans,' I said in a gap. 'Dry when stolen, wet when abandoned.'

'There was a Bedford stolen yesterday afternoon. I'll get the details for you.'

'But—' the new body on the desk protested.

'Jaws is all right, she's one of us,' said Joe. I could have kissed his stubbly cheek. He always had a rapid growth.

I took details of the van. It was the tyres

23

I was interested in but there was no record of make or state. The owner ran a greengrocer's shop on the main road out of Latching to Brighton. He sold a lot of cut price fruit and veg, not in A1 condition but still edible if you consumed them quickly. It didn't take me long to cycle to the shop.

The greengrocer was indignant about the theft of his van. It cramped his style. 'Nothing's safe these days. I need that van. I'm hampered.'

'I know,' I said sympathetically. 'No consideration these people.'

He remembered that the right-hand rear tyre was pretty worn. Practically down to the threads.

'On its last legs,' said Fred Hopkins. 'It's a wonder I wasn't stopped by the pigs, begging your pardon, miss. I'll get a new set on the insurance, if I'm covered.'

'You might get your van back.'

'If pigs could fly.' He had little confidence in the police finding his vehicle. 'They're not interested unless it's got a bomb inside it.'

'They don't have the resources,' I trotted out.

'I've got plenty of nice strawberries in. Last of the season. Five punnets for a pound, just for you, miss.'

'I can't resist them,' I said, the remembered taste surging into my mouth. If only all kisses were like strawberries, fresh and sweet and juicy. Men thought that presenting their mouths was enough. Beards were like Brillo pads, smoker's breath like old socks in an ash tray, beer drinkers like a brewery on a hot day. Metallic fillings tasted like metallic fillings. The waves of rotting debris from the mouth of a non-brusher could knock you back with nausea.

Men that cleaned their teeth, rinsed their mouths, drank water, sucked a peppermint, were heaven to kiss. Line up, please, no pushing. I didn't know about DI James. He had never kissed me as yet. It was a dream on hold.

DI James was everything a woman could want in a man, except for sensitivity, romanticism, demonstrative affection. And to cap all that, I don't think he even liked me at times. But occasionally, when he was off guard or in a moment of stress, he might say something that was almost nice. Once he nearly touched me. But he didn't follow through. The mask dropped and the magic fled. But it had been there, a fleeting ray of light and that gave me hope.

There was no hope with the jazz musician. Lots of peppermint kisses and huggy warmth, but then he went home to his long-bedded wife and I didn't see him for months. I often heard him on the radio and that roaring trumpet's liquid notes were singing a song for me. Because he had once told me so.

'I only play for you, Jordan,' he'd said when I first met him. 'The top F is for you alone.'

'A pound's worth, then,' I said, finding a coin in my jeans. I had taught myself to recognise coins from their size and shape. A useful trick in the dark.

The punnets bounced home in a carrier bag, swinging from my handlebars. I would eat them all. Each one would be a kiss. My dreams would be good. A lonely heaven.

It must have taken the thieves several hours to shovel up so many underwater plants in the dark. Then the gang had to heave them over the wall and load them into the van. And who would want to buy so many water lilies? They could hardly be toted round the Sunday morning car boot sales. No one in their right mind would pay more than fifty pence for a plant from a hatch-back.

And ... crisis, crisis ... they had to be kept in water all the time. It did not make sense.

I cycled back to my shop. It had once been an optician's with two small bow windows, perfect for displaying designer specs and contact lenses; also perfect for my special-ised junk. My stock came from Latching's numerous charity shops. They were getting

26

to know my swift swoops and sometimes put goods by for me. I had an eye for the unusual.

The cut-glass flutes were one such find. They had been at the bottom of a box of dingy glasses the hard-working ladies didn't have time to wash or sort. The champagne flutes were wrapped in faded tissue and hidden under some hideous tumblers. I washed them, put my usual £6 price label on the stem of each glass. Having the same price for everything saved a lot of time. They were beautiful, not a chip in sight. An empty champagne bottle – saved from Cleo Carling's house-warming party – dressed the window. A silk rose added the final touch. I almost bought them myself, just in case DI James looked at me with longing in his eyes. Fat chance.

The shop door opened. Daylight was blotted out. I knew that tall, bulky shape by heart, but not by touch. His build was so familiar.

'Is this a new venture, Jordan?' he asked. 'Have you started Latching's first lonely hearts club? Is there a form to fill in?'

'Do you want to join?' I asked. 'I'll make the form simple for you and give you a discount on the fee. I'll even feed you strawberries and coffee.'

'I'll take you up on the coffee,' said DI James, his presence crowding the shop.

When he was around there was no room for anyone else. 'But pass on the strawberries. You might have designs on me.'

'I'm purely interested in your brain. Brawn is obsolete. You are safe in my office but keep your mobile switched off in case I have a relapse.'

His drawn face did not move a muscle. I was talking nonsense. Not a glimmer appeared in his tired blue eyes. They were a colour as dark as the deepest ocean. I could have drowned in their blueness.

'I understand we are overlapping on a case.'

'Yes, the ninety thousand pounds' worth of water lilies case. Mr Lucan was not impressed by your officers. Aren't they expensive? No wonder people grow nasturtiums.'

'One of my officers gave you information that he should not have.' DI James had his schoolmaster expression in place. I would have sat in his class anytime. The hem of his sleeve needed repairing and I mentally reached for thread and needle.

'No, really?' I made my eyes round and innocent. 'Totally by accident, I'm sure. Slip of the tongue. By the way, have you checked the tread marks in the mud? Mr Hopkins, the greengrocer, who had his van stolen on Friday, said his back right tyre was pretty worn.'

'Thank you, Jordan. I will bear that valuable information in mind. Now, where's that first-class coffee?'

So, OK, he rated my coffee more than he rated me. I could live with that. It was a start.

He went through to my back office, straight to the corner sink in the scullery and began to wash up two bone-china mugs. A vision of cosy domesticity swam before my eyes. Him washing up; me drying up in my huggy-bear nightshirt. A surge of hormones tipped me over the scales of respectability.

'I can't believe that this visit is based purely on water lilies,' I said, trying to sound sane and sensible when I was clearly neither.

'No, it isn't,' he said, watching the faintest tremor as I poured fresh coffee. 'You certainly know how to make good coffee. One of your few talents.'

I swallowed the opportunity to list my other talents. I would be so good, so very good in bed with him. But that was fantasy world land. Dream on, Terry Pratchett.

'We have at present a serious missing persons situation,' he began. 'Tarrant Close, number twelve.'

'Lord Lucan?'

'Pack it in.'

'I love it when you talk pompous.'

'He's a bank manager called Leslie Fair-brother, manager of the Sussex United Banking Corporation.'

'Hostage situation?' I could be very quick.

'I'm not at liberty to say,' he said, looking deeply into his mug of coffee as if it held a forecast of the future. Nor am I at liberty to kiss you, I thought, my wanton imagination wrapping warm arms around him. 'But I thought you might keep an eye open for any sightings of him.' He handed me a photograph. Leslie Fairbrother was a forty-ish, overweight, moon-faced man wearing NHS gold-rimmed spectacles. A stereotype bank manager.

'So, what else can you tell me?'

'Not a lot, except that Mr Fairbrother left for work on Thursday morning and hasn't been seen since. And we think he has the vault keys with him.'

'Naughty.'

'Or careless. Mr Fairbrother is a very respected member of his profession. We believe that he may have been taken ill or wandering about with amnesia.'

'And you'd like me to keep an eye open? Can I put that on my ID card? Visual aid to police investigations?'

'I don't care what you put on your ID card. Your card is a joke anyway. You could-n't investigate a crooked game of conkers.'

'Pure jealousy,' I said, not letting him

30

know how much that hurt. 'I won't put it about who solved the missing War Currency mystery.'

DI James looked astonished. A sort of amazement cornered his eyes. 'You didn't solve it. It solved itself.'

'I contributed,' I said staunchly. 'You can't argue with that.'

'I wouldn't argue with you about anything,' he said, finishing his coffee and putting down the mug. He was going. I couldn't stand it. He was always leaving me. I went through that drained-out, gutted feeling a dozen times a week. I knew that as soon as he had gone, I would be dipping calorie-laden shortbread biscuits into pale cream sherry. If I had any.

'I'll watch out for any gold-rimmed yobbos, stoned to the gills and sleeping it off in a beach shelter,' I called after him. 'It's a familiar sight. Perhaps he's got a shopping trolley piled with sleeping bags and gold bullion.'

'I knew I could depend on you.'

He went out, not looking back. He never looked back. The past was nothing to him or perhaps he had too much past. Only the future was of interest and I was not part of it.

Funny how I had men queuing at the door and I didn't want any of them. They varied in intensity, variously lusting after my cooking, my body, my ability to sew on buttons. One even had his eye on my ready cash. As if I had to pay for kisses. A fiver for a smacker, tenner for a grope. Yuck, pass me the mouthwash.

But this time James paused in the doorway. His face was still a mask but he was trying to be human. Had he any idea how he looked, as a man?

'You walk on the beach, don't you?'

'Frequently. I need the air, the solitude, company of the gulls.'

'Be careful. We're getting reports of incendiary bombs being washed up. They're dangerous. They can explode and cause nasty burns.'

It was almost the kindest thing he'd ever said to me. I stored it in my memory for dark days.

'I'll make sure I don't step on them.'

'Some of the fishermen have reported underwater explosions.'

'Interesting.'

I wondered whether to tell him about the Lancaster bomber which ditched into the sea during the Second World War. It was one of the legends of Latching. The pilot was a local hero. Somehow he missed the seafront hotels, skimming rooftops, made it to the sea, caught the tide on its way out and crashed into the wet sand. They say the wreckage is somewhere out there on the seabed, washed beyond the pier end.

Older residents, those that have been around, say they can still hear the sound of the faltering engine phut-phutting in the sky.

I watched James step out of the shop, shift from sight, my temperature dropping by degrees. It was time to pull myself together and get on with the water-lily search. Mr Lucan wasn't paying me for daydreams. Besides, I wanted that ladybird.

I phoned in an ad to the local *Evening Argus*. 'STOCKING A POND? WATER LILIES FOR SALE.' It was a remote chance. And the ad was for free.

# Three

'It was an awful sight. We could hardly believe our eyes. I immediately thought of you, Jordan. I said to everybody, I know exactly the person to help us. She's a brilliant investigator.'

I bathed in a warm glow, pretty much like the sauna only with more clothes. It was Joey's owner, Mrs Edith Drury, Joey being the wandering tortoise that DI James had so conveniently found on the A27 and fed at the station. I hadn't meant to take all the credit but Mrs Drury had assumed the best.

'Come in,' I said, opening the door to my office behind the shop. Business was very slow, practically paralytic. I hadn't sold anything for days, even though I had dressed and redressed the windows half a dozen times with class items of junk. Perhaps it was the weather. The chill of autumn numbing purse fingers. Christmas beckoning. 'It's not Joey again, surely? He of the rampant reptile hormones?'

'Joey's fine. Slowing down for his winter hibernation, bless his leathery legs. But we're not! We're hopping mad. That's why we want you to come right away. My car's outside. I'll tell you everything on the way.'

'Who's we?'

'Latching Women's Institute.'

I shut door and shop immediately. Put up GONE FOR LUNCH again and followed Mrs Drury out to her car. It was a large, ancient Ford, practically Vintage Run to Brighton era, dented in places. I hoped she knew how to drive. I checked her licence disc out of habit. It was up to date.

Mrs Drury threw the car into gear with enthusiasm. I searched for the safety belt and strapped myself in. She drove using one eye and one hand. She kept swivelling round to make sure I was listening, gesticulating with the free hand.

'The Latching WI, that's the Women's Institute. I'm the Federation Chairman. We've got a marquee at the West Sussex Agricultural Show and we've won first prize in the home catering for a wedding section. Absolutely brilliant. Our entry was first class and the wedding cake centrepiece a perfection of icing artistry...'

I let Mrs Drury ramble on, remembering how promptly she had paid me for the two days' work when I had done nothing. I was not into wedding cakes or home catering. If DI James and I ever tied the happy knot – miracles could happen, you only had to find

35

your angel – we'd celebrate with a pub lunch for our mates. A cake with crossed truncheons on top? I wouldn't care.

'Thank goodness they'd done the judging and we'd won,' Mrs Drury went on. 'The cup was on display and we were as proud as punch. We took ten minutes off to look round the other displays and winners, especially the water tent, and when we got back we couldn't believe our eyes. Everything was in chaos, smashed or gone! Flowers broken, plates smashed, napkins torn ... It was a horrible sight.' Her voice was shaking with emotion.

I made sympathetic noises but I doubt if Mrs Drury heard.

'Vandals, thieves, desecrators. But worst of all, every crumb of our superb food has gone. Pâté, profiteroles, quiches, even the wedding cake has been carted off. Three tiers, lattice work, filigree gold piping, sugar-paste roses, gold ribbon, the lot. They'd have needed a wheelbarrow.'

'Heavens, even the cake. Perhaps the thieves are getting married.' Why am I always flippant about weddings? It shows a deeply flawed character.

'It's so disappointing especially when we could do with the publicity. Our numbers are falling. It's a sign of the times. We expected lots of visitors to look at our entry and some of us have lost really nice plates.

Mine was the last of a Crown Derby set. One of my mother's plates. I'd made a watercress and feta cheese quiche with fennel garnish. Delicious. I must make you one.'

'Lovely,' I said, my mouth watering. Gourmet food did not play any part in my lifestyle. 'What a mean crime, Mrs Drury. Despicable. After all that hard work. Was it a silver cup?'

Mrs Drury took her eyes off the road to nod vigorously. 'Absolutely. First class cup. Very ornate. But they didn't take the cup. You couldn't sell it. Presented by our MP's wife, Mrs What's-her-name. You know the woman I mean.'

I did indeed. I had been on WPC duty the night of the last General Election, guarding the count, in case some intrepid terrorist from East Sussex took off with a box of ballot papers. The wife had been much in evidence, making tea, exchanging small talk, already acting the part. It was a fairly safe seat.

Stolen pâté, profiteroles, cheese straws ... Still, my casebook was nearing empty and I needed the work. The water lilies would be half dead by now. I couldn't turn down a gift horse, or a gift crumb.

'I told them not to touch anything,' said Mrs Drury triumphantly. 'Clues etc. Here we are.' She parked like a Formula One driver doing a pit stop. 'You can't miss our marquee. Decorated with yards of gold ribbon. Got a cheap batch at Shoreham Green Market. Absolute bargain.'

The Latching WI prize-winning display was a mess. Bits of crushed food and pastry trodden everywhere. The table looked as if it had been trampled on by a herd of elephants on a boozy day out. I doubted if I would find anything of use in this shambles. I wandered about making notes, nodding and tut-tutting. The shocked ladies of the WI gathered round, full of suggestions, mostly gleaned from TV whodunnits.

'Find the motive and you'll find the man.'

'I'm sure it's a woman. It's a typical, female revenge thing.'

'They must have been hungry,' said Mrs Drury who was now getting over the shock and indignation and beginning to enjoy the drama. 'Do you think it could be a rival WI? The competition is quite intense. I wouldn't put it past them. One or two of the other branches are quite envious of our cooking.'

'But you had already won the cup. What would be the point?'

'Anger, disappointment? Or perhaps the wedding cake! It's valuable. People pay hundreds of pounds for a wedding cake these days. Funds are always low in WIs. They could sell it.'

'I'd like to speak to the member who made

it. She may have taken a photo. Then we could circulate local wedding photographers. Get a match on the cake.' It was very unlikely but I had to give it a shot.

'There, I knew you'd be wonderful. I'll phone her straightaway. It's Mrs Hilary Fenwick. She's the wife of Councillor Fenwick.'

I knew the councillor vaguely. He'd reached Latching Council via the Rotary Club route. He owned a string of estate agent shops along the coast and had been a moving figure in the formation of the local Crimestoppers. Pity they hadn't been able to stop the theft of his wife's culinary masterpiece.

'Hilary's out shopping,' Mrs Drury beamed back minutes later. 'But I did catch her on her mobile. She says she'll meet you in the multi-storey car park on the front at four p.m. Blue BMW, third floor.'

A clandestine meeting. How weird. Maybe it was not good PR for a councillor's wife to be seen talking to a PI. Keen on keeping the public image pure for the voters.

'I'll get in touch with you,' I said, closing my notebook of meaningless notes. I collected a few fag ends in a plastic specimen bag to show I was taking the case seriously.

'Same daily fee?' Mrs Drury asked. I nodded. 'Worth every penny.'

★ ★ ★

39

The multi-storey car park had been built on the site of Highdown House, an elegantly pillared Georgian house which was demolished in the late seventies when the council thought the power of the car more important than conserving an architectural gem that no one could afford to live in. I'd have turned it into flats or a residential home where the elderly could have snoozed out their last days in a garden within sight and sound of the murmuring sea.

So I had a built-in dislike of the concrete mausoleum. Even less when I had traipsed up several flights of dingy spiral stairs, walls defaced with repetitive graffiti. Blue BMW. Third floor. Did she have a reserved place?

Mrs Fenwick appeared out of the shadows. She had obviously been watching and waiting for me. A good sign. She would be polite, helpful and considerate. The kind of woman who made pretty wedding cakes.

'I haven't got a photograph,' she said straightaway. 'And I couldn't care less whether they get the cake back or not. I never want to see the damned thing again.'

Ah. She was about thirty-two, younger than I expected. Mark II model maybe. She was pencil slim, short hair polished bronze, the kind of off-white trouser suit you could only wear once between dry cleaning. Her long manicured nails said she did little in

40

the kitchen beyond status cake-making.

'Why not?'

'Oh no, you're not getting anything out of me. I know how you lot work.'

'Then why agree to see me in the first place? This is a waste of time for both of us.'

I almost turned to go, but I was curious. There was something more to this.

Mrs Fenwick opened her cream leather handbag and took out a lace handkerchief. 'I had to meet you somewhere. You see, I want to employ you,' she said, dabbing her eyes and nose, but careful not to disturb her make-up. 'It's all very embarrassing. I want you to follow my husband, Councillor Adrian Fenwick. Discreetly, of course. I want to know what he's up to. Damn and blast him.'

A whole load of wants. And another errant husband. It must be the sea air. 'You suspect he's seeing another woman?'

'I don't suspect,' she snapped. 'I know there's another woman. I want positive proof so I can divorce him quick and get my fair share of the business. He's pretty well off and I helped to build up his niche in the property market.'

'Right,' I said, equally businesslike. 'Please give me some details. Any favourite haunts, as far as you know. I'll need a photograph of your husband and you'll have to sign a client contract. The forms are in my office.

You can either drop round or I'll post one to you.'

'No need for a contract. Time's far more important. Better still, give me your bank account number and I'll arrange for a standing order. Would a weekly standing order suit you? How much?'

Standing order? The words were music, Elgar, Dankworth, Kenton. No one had ever paid me by standing order before. Before the shock could wear off, I gave her the number of my bank account. I was so stunned I forgot to insist on a client contract.

'My rates are fifty pounds a day. So weekly that would be three hundred and fifty pounds, if you want me to work Sundays as well.' The ladybirds spots grew brighter and blacker, more in focus. I could almost feel my hands on the wheel. 'But this investigation should only take a week,' I heard myself add. Where do I get this fool honesty from?

'I don't care how long it takes,' she said, shutting her bag. 'I want everything, photos, receipts, times, places. He's very devious. He covers his tracks well.'

'Maybe two weeks then,' I agreed, swallowing. I wasn't going to argue with her. I put 'buy decent camera' on my shopping list. Up to now I'd been using one of these instant throwaway things. They weren't made for poor lighting. 'Do you know who the woman is?'

'That's the first thing you're being paid to find out,' said Mrs Fenwick turning on her spiky heels.

Suddenly I had three cases. Water lilies, WI tent massacre, errant estate agent. Life was outrageous fun. I was doing what I enjoyed doing. I only needed DI James to complete the elation. Where was he? Pounding the streets on some dull break-in, chasing ram-raiders in the High Street? I was missing him. I was getting burn-out, withdrawal symptoms, hang-ups.

I called in at Latching police station late that evening. No messing about. If the mountain wouldn't come. Same depressing concrete walls and dingy desk. 'Where's DI James?' I asked.

'Upstairs.'

'Tell him Jordan Lacey's here. First Class Investigations. FCI. Tell him we're both on the same case.'

The desk sergeant, the same new one who had forgotten me already, looked bewilder-ed but impressed. 'OK. Please wait, Miss Lacey.'

DI James appeared, irritated, face in tram-lines. He looked caffeine-junk-food depriv-ed. When had he last eaten? Those brilliant ocean-blue eyes had murky depths like he was diving and lost off the end of the pier. He rubbed at his lashes. 'I hope this is not some stupid red herring.'

'Do I bring red herrings? Fish I like to eat so when are you going to take me out to a fish supper? But I suggest you go along to the West Sussex Horticultural Show and look at the water tent.'

'Are you serious?'

'It's full of water lilies. Floating in tanks.'

'Just when I wanted to put my head down and sleep.'

'Later. Your pillow can wait.'

I loved him when he was flaked out. My pillow was cold. It needed warming up. It drove me mad, imagining that dark cropped head, turned away, resting on my pillow, bare brown neck and broad shoulders, glistening with sweat. If ever.

'Have you checked the ownership of the water lilies at the show? Mr Lucan is not the only grower in Sussex.'

'No, but he is accepted as an international expert. His water lilies are exported all over the world. Nymphaea. Oil-rich sheikhs buy them for their palace gardens.'

'How do you know?'

I didn't. I'd made it up but it sounded good. 'Everybody knows. That is, everyone who reads gardening profiles.'

'And you do, I suppose. Another of your interests? Gardening, along with the crochet and lace-making.'

He knew I didn't know one end of a trowel from another and the extent of my gardening was overwatering house plants. Still, I had his interest now.

'Mr Lucan and I are going along to identify the water lilies. He would recognise his own plants, I think, being said expert. They took ten different varieties. Mr Lucan told me that as long as the plants were put back in water quickly they should survive.'

'And you'll let me know if they are his,' DI James said heavily.

'Of course,' I said, all smiles. 'My middle name is Cooperation.'

'No doubt at a price. Computer access?'

'What? Me? Never.'

I sailed out of the police station, chalking one up. Although it was getting late, Mr Lucan was waiting outside in a rusty grey Land Rover held together with string and blu-tak. He looked anxious as if his water lilies might die in the water tent, deprived of his TLC.

'Well, what did they say?'

'DI James said to go ahead,' I said. 'And report back. I've sorted it out. They have every confidence in me.'

The show was still open. A few stragglers toured the displays. The WI marquee had been cordoned off by show officials.

They were Mr Lucan's water lilies. Not many, about a dozen plants in exotic bloom, their flowers like cups of waxen pink, but enough to bring a stiff paternal smile to Mr Lucan's face.

'Yes, they're mine. This is American Star, star-shaped, semi-double deep pink. And this canary-yellow, semi-double cup shape is Chromatella. Note the maroon and bronze leaves.'

The exhibitors of the water-lily display were confused and bewildered. They did not realise they had acquired stolen plants. The water tent had been a last-minute idea.

'We were talking about it in a pub and this man came up and said he could get us a few plants. They seemed a reasonable price so we bought them. We already had the tanks as we did fish last year.'

'Fish?'

'Goldfish. Aquariums. It was very popular.'

'Well, I'm sure it was all very innocent but these plants legally belong to Mr Lucan. They were stolen from him in an overnight raid. Supposing you quickly put up a sign saying the water lilies were kindly supplied by his nursery and then Mr Lucan will be happy just to take them home when the show is over.'

Mr Lucan, who was now on his knees examining his plants, nodded vaguely in agreement. I wanted to remind him about the Morris Minor car but he seemed in another world. Although I had not solved his case, he must be impressed by the speed of my detection.

'What pub?' I asked. 'This man that you met in a pub.'

'The Bear and Bait.'

My heart jumped. The Bear and Bait was my favourite pub in Latching, not for the beer or its smoke-laden atmosphere. It was for the jazz. Occasionally my musician played there, just for free. Because he wanted to. Because he was mad, sweet, a brilliant trumpeter, married.

It was quite dark now, tents glistening with a sudden shower. I didn't fancy the long walk home. The streets weren't safe at night.

'Could you give me a lift home?' I asked Terence Lucan. 'I've no time to waste. The rest of your valuable plants could be wilting in some warehouse.'

'I can't bear to think about them,' he moaned.

'Never mind,' I said brightly. 'We've made a good start.'

'You just don't understand,' he said, the engine of his old Land Rover waking up with a reluctant cough and splutter. 'Those water lilies are special. They are my life. I can't live without them.'

I hoisted myself up into the front of the

Land Rover. It was pretty high up and, in his distress, Terence Lucan forgot to pull the doorstep down. It was an ungainly arrival, like getting on a horse without a block. No one saw me. A sprawling female detective, all legs and arms, is not a pretty sight.

'You'll live,' I said. 'Believe me, you'll live.'

# Four

The Bear and Bait is my kind of pub and I'm not known as a pub person. Faded gilt lettering on the overhead timber beams advertise beers long gone and Mrs Docherty's most excellent meat pies have passed their sell-by date. The bar is horseshoe-shaped, all gleaming brass and polished wood. Brown framed photos on the walls are sepia reminders of old Latching.

There were misty pictures of fishing boats drawn up on the shore, the old pier, the original Bear and Bait, with horse-drawn beer delivery vans, its customers standing outside in self-conscious groups wearing cloth caps or Sunday bowlers.

I don't go there for the draught beer or the clientele. I go for the jazz, always hoping that one evening my trumpeter will turn up, blowing his heart out on his own, playing 'Melancholy Baby' just for me.

Tonight it was an Irish band, a toe-tapping, foot-stomping group with a scratchy violin, a thumping guitar and mad-wristed drummer.

I coasted up to the bar and ordered a glass of red Cabernet Sauvignon from Chile or an Australian Shiraz from a dried-up creek. My veins clamoured for the flavonoids, the essential heart-saving stuff.

'Turning cold, Jordan,' said the bulky owner, Eddie Norris.

'Too soon,' I said. 'No seasonal run-in. It hasn't given my chilblains time to adjust. And I hate winter clothes. They always smell damp.'

'There's still time for an Indian summer.' He poured me a generous glass of Cabernet Sauvignon. He wouldn't make much profit out of me.

'Tell that to the weathermen.'

It was difficult to talk over the lively Irish music. There was a touch of Riverdance in the air. I saw a few stiff arms and heel knockings around the bar. Wishful thinking. Not a Michael Flatley in sight.

'Anyone been in here trying to sell water lilies?' I asked casually. I couldn't think of a more subtle approach.

'Got a pond, have you?'

'No, but a friend of mine has.' The friend being the bereft Mr Lucan. I love the way I use the truth.

'Funny you asking about water lilies. That's the third time I've heard them mentioned this week. You can go for years without hearing a word about something,

50

then suddenly it's all the news.'

'What do you mean?'

'Some fella was in here trying to buy tanks. Them lilies live in tanks, don't they? He was desperate. He'd even look at a disused swimming pool, he said. We all thought he was off his rocker.'

I snatched at the word. 'How desperate?'

'He was offering real money.'

'Do you know who he was?'

'Could be one of them stallholders from Shoreham Green Market, I think. Couldn't be too sure. Selling mops one week, window cleaners the next, water tanks the next.'

'Or water lilies?'

'Your guess is as good as mine.'

'And when were the other two occasions?' I asked, sipping. the nectar, letting it slip into my veins and fire them.

'Don't remember, Jordan, sorry. But water lilies were certainly mentioned.'

'Well, if you do remember, will you give me a ring?'

I wrote my phone number down on the back of a cardboard coaster for Stella Artois beer. Shopping list: professional business cards. A beer coaster gives the wrong impression.

'Sure.'

Eddie Norris tucked the coaster into his shirt pocket and turned away. As he did, I knew I was not alone.

51

'You're that lady detective, aren't you?' said a man, sliding up to my side out of the smoke-laden atmosphere, his beer slopping over in a shaking hand. My asthma was already at red alert. I nearly told him to put the beer down. 'I'm in danger. I need help. Are you expensive? I don't have a lot of money.'

He was weedy, gaunt, worry carving his face into grooves. His eyes flickered with fear. His clothes smelled of fear. I cringed without being seen to cringe. He made my flesh creep. Yet there was something genuine about his reed-thin voice that told me that he was really afraid.

'Let's sit down before you spill that beer,' I said, sounding like a mother hen. 'There's a free table in the far corner.'

I squeezed my way passed the foot-tapping, Irish-happy drinkers and took the furthest chair. The man hesitated by the table.

'Do you mind changing places?' he asked. 'I don't want to sit with my back to the room.' He glanced behind him. 'You never know.'

'OK. Swop over.' Stab in the back syndrome here. His eyes darted round the crowded pub like a petrified ferret. 'Tell me what's the matter and I'll tell you if I can help.'

He sipped his beer nervously, foam rimming his upper lip. He looked as if he was wondering how to put it into words.

'If you don't tell me what's bothering you, how can I help?' I prompted. He was spoiling a lovely glass of Chilean. Any minute now I would discover I had an urgent appointment at the other end of Ferring.

'They think I'm Al Lubliganio.'

'Lubliganio who?'

'Al Lubliganio, the Mafia gang leader.'

Hardly my scene but I nodded knowingly as if the Mafia featured daily in my case schedules. 'Who thinks you are this Al Lubliganio, the Mafia gang leader?'

'The Scarlattis.'

'And who are the Scarlattis when they are at home?'

'A rival gang. Deadly rivals. They're old criminal mobsters from the south of Naples. They are always killing each other off. Now they are after me. I'm terrified out of my wits. I can't sleep, eat, daren't go to work. They have already blown up my car. They send me threats. Watch my every movement. They may even be in here, at this very moment.'

The Irish band started up a new wild skirmish, the fiddle screeching almost a tune. It was enough to scare off any Italian Mafia.

'Am I hearing right? This gang from Naples are trying to kill you, here in

Latching, a small sleepy seaside town in West Sussex featured in many holiday brochures?'

He nodded. 'I'm serious. I'm in deadly danger.'

'I don't think I can help you,' I said, mentally sliding off. Nor did I want to. Water lilies and errant husbands were more my style. The Mafia was a totally different cup of cappuccino. I had a basically fearful nature. 'Perhaps you'd better start by telling me your name.'

'Al Lubliganio.'

'No, your real name.'

'That is my real name. Albert Lubliganio. My father was an Italian merchant seaman. That's the trouble. It's a case of mistaken identity. They think I'm this gang leader in hiding when all I am is a mechanic at a local garage. They think it's a … a...'

'A cover?' I suggested.

'Yes, that's it. They think the garage is just a cover. But it isn't. I've been there eleven years. And before that I worked for a metal company in Brighton.'

I let Al ramble on. There was nothing I could do. It was a case for the police. The man needed special protection especially if they had blown up his car.

'Do you have a family?'

'No, I'm single.'

I was not surprised. No woman would

want to take on such a pathetic specimen of manhood. Only a saint. And she would need to be deaf and blind.

'I can't help you,' I said. 'But I know someone who can.' I sounded like that advert for the AA. 'They'll know what to do. I'll put them in touch with you. They'll know the right way to handle this. Give me your home address and the garage address.'

'Thank you,' said Al, staring into his beer. He came to with a jolt and scribbled the addresses on a slip of crumpled paper. 'How much do I owe you?'

'Nothing,' I said. 'I don't charge for advice.'

I had to get out of the Bear and Bait. His fear clung to me like a sticky cobweb. I finished my wine but didn't taste it. I needed to walk the pier, even in the dark. I had to escape from the pub.

The wind met me outside with ferocious gusts, taking my breath away. How the wind could change in Latching. One minute calm and balmy with the lightest breeze, then suddenly some wild tiger tore down from the north-east, whipping along the coast, churning the sea to mud, thrashing the waves on the shore.

It took all my strength to cross the seafront road. The side road had turned into a wind tunnel. Another Force 6 nearly blew me over. I hung on to the railings that curled round a garden patch where an old fishing boat was filled with dying pansies and rotting ferns.

They normally close the pier when the wind reaches gale force. Perhaps they had forgotten to lock the entrance or thought that no one would be that foolish to venture tonight. The gulls had disappeared, taking refuge on shopfronts, affronted and sulky.

Parts of the pier had disappeared too. They had lifted sections of deck planking and a blank, gaping hole was enclosed by a metal fencing. I nearly didn't see it in the dark. The moon was hiding behind scuttering clouds.

Poor old pier. Just had her seventieth birthday and already they were amputating bits. I peered down the hole and saw only wet sand and rusted girders.

The tide was going out fast. Even in the dark I could see it racing over the flat sand in a froth of brown, leaving a carpet of murky seaweed behind. Out at sea, the dan lights from the fishing boats bobbed uncertainly. They had been caught out. The wind had been moderate when they pushed off from the shore. Now it was dangerous and certainly uncomfortable.

I couldn't walk round the end of the pier. The wind was too strong. I could barely stand and was aware that the unprotected area at the fishing end of the pier was dangerous and the gusts would soon bowl me over. I had no wish to be found clinging for life to a railing.

The walls of the closed amusement arcade gave me some protection. My progress was spider-like, sideways flattened against the wall.

But the wind had blown away my fear. Optimism surged through me and life was great again. It had also erased the cigarette smoke from my clothes. I'd been hung out on a washing line and blow-dried. I couldn't remember when I had last eaten. Food had taken a back seat, somewhere next to writing my thesis on suburban culture.

I zigzagged close by the protective shops to my bedsits, out of breath, clutching my keys. Don't ask me why I have two adjoining bedsits but I'm not used to sleeping in the same room that I live in. There was not much food in my kitchen area but I managed to make a gargantuan sandwich with granary bread, tuna, cheese, sliced beef tomatoes, Chinese leaves and a dollop of herb dressing. Fit for a king. I could barely get my mouth round it.

Latching's summer always ended with a carnival and a fireworks display. They held it the same weekend as the Agricultural Show. But summer had long departed and spectators shivered on the pavements as the floats paraded the streets with frozen kids dressed up as anything from South Pacific dancers to Stone Age hunters, their bare legs blue with cold, miming to taped music.

I had rolled out of bed, stretching my brain into action. Time to roam the streets, get my bearings. I was not really watching the carnival, merely a walker who kept pace with the motorised floats. Occasionally I clapped for a brave effort; put money in a rattled pail. I was pretty detached.

A float rumbled by, an open-topped lorry belching fumes. Green-clad fairies gambolled self-consciously at the bottom of the garden among plastic flowers and ferns. And masses of water lilies. I did a double-take.

Shopping list: mobile phone (urgent).

I found a phone box and dialled Latching Water Gardens. Terence Lucan answered. He sounded weary as if he'd been up all night talking to his plants.

'There are some more of your water lilies on a float in the Autumn Carnival. I've just seen them. American Beauty, I think.'

'American Star.'

'That's right, the pink pointed kind. They are on a kids' float going along the seafront at this moment. Guides or Brownies. No, it's a nursery school.'

'I'll be down right away. By the way, do you still want that car?'

58

'Yes, why?'

'I've got someone else interested in it.'

My heart hammered for a few seconds. I thought fast. 'I'll let you have a deposit. That should confirm my serious interest.'

I had no idea how I was going to pay for it, but vaguely thought of going to the bank and getting a personal loan. But I had no security for a loan. A rented shop selling class items of junk was hardly collateral.

The carnival floats were assembled in Summerstead Park by the time Mr Lucan got there in his delapidated Land Rover. He bounded over to the fairy grotto lorry like a man with springs in his boots. The nursery-school owners were bewildered and apologetic. It was the same story. They had bought them off a man in a pub.

'They were going cheap,' said the woman. 'And we'd used these plastic flowers two years running. It was time we had a change.'

'I must have them back. This environment is no good for them. Look at their roots, hardly in any water. Inches! They need a real depth of water to survive. And you've put them in pots. They need tanks, ponds. Not pots!' Mr Lucan spluttered out the last words. His face had gone a serious shade of red.

'Of course you can have them back but would you mind waiting until the judging is over? It won't be more than twenty minutes.

It's such good publicity for the school if we win or get placed.'The woman smiled hopefully but it was wasted on Mr Lucan. He was leaping around the lorry with a watering can, dousing his plants with a generous waterfall. The fairies got in the way. Soon sprayed fairies began to cry and flap bedraggled wings.

'Water fairies! How lovely!' said one of the judges. 'And real water!' I think it was the mayoress again, still in unsuitable shoes for a churned-up grassy park.

The phrase, good publicity, instantly replayed in my mind. Mrs Edith Drury had said the same thing. Winning the wedding stand display would be good publicity for the Latching WI. Was everything done for publicity these days? Had good old-fashioned pride in an achievement been replaced by public imagery?

The wet fairies got second prize, good enough for everyone to be pleased. As the parents hurried round with towels and changes of clothes, Terence Lucan was busy loading the water lilies into the back of his Land Rover.

'Pots, indeed!' he muttered. 'Don't they know anything these days?'

There were about a dozen plants. At this rate it would be months before he got all his water lilies back. If they survived at all, that is. At least I had justified my daily rate, I thought complacently.

Suddenly guilt struck me with the force of a twenty-ton lorry with brake failure. I was charging Mr Lucan the daily rate, also charging Mrs Drury and Mrs Fenwick. All at the same time, for the same day. It was a colossal con. My day rate was meant to encompass services solely expended on one case for a whole day. Not three cases at the same time. I'd have to sort it out. My income plummeted. But I was still going to give Mr Lucan a cheque for a deposit on my car.

My car. It felt like my car already. Spots or no spots. She was going to be mine. I was not sure how I was going to handle being a spot-conspicuous PI but I'd manage. My ladybird might be useful as a decoy. Park her in a different place ... giving out the wrong message.

'Thank you, Miss Lacey,' said Terence Lucan, heaving the last plants into the Land Rover. 'I'm most impressed. But you appreciate this is just the fringe of my stolen plants?'

'I do realise that. But these small hauls may lead us to the big one. Don't give up hope. The thieves must know the plants need water to survive. I've a lead on a man trying to rent a swimming pool.'

'That's it,' exclaimed Terence Lucan, his face lighting up for the first time. 'A swimming pool. That's what they'd need to keep the plants alive. You're on to something. Well done.'

I wished I hadn't mentioned it. My lead was hardly a lead. Still, I might get lucky.

I opened up my shop late next morning. A man was waiting on the doorstep. He tapped his teeth with a chewed biro.

'I wondered when you were going to open up. Thought you'd got the bailiffs in.'

'Busy at auctions,' I lied. 'Lot of good stuff moving. The trouble is that everyone is after it.'

'That clockwork duck in the window. How much do you want for it?'

It was an ugly thing, sulphur-yellow paint chipped and stained. The face of the duck, black-eyed and leering, looked pretty evil.

'There's no key,' I said.

'That's OK,' he said easily. 'I've a box full of keys at home. I bet I've got one that fits.'

He turned the duck over. 'Not exactly Jacques de Vaucanson,' he said. 'He made a clockwork duck that could quack, digest and eliminate.'

'Fascinating,' I said, surfing prices in my mind. In my hurry to re-dress the window, I had forgotten to put my usual £6 label on the duck's bottom. I wondered how much this particular oddity was worth. To the chewing tooth-tapper anyway.

'I have actually got a dealer coming in this

afternoon,' I said. Two lies in a single day. Was this a new trend? I'd have to watch it. 'What would you like to offer me for this unusual clockwork duck?'

'Fifty quid.'

I pretended to hesitate but it was difficult. 'OK,' I said, trying to sound reluctant. 'Just for you.'

I wrapped the duck in tissue paper, took the money. He, in his turn, was trying not to look pleased.

'You don't know how much this is worth, do you?' he gloated.

I didn't care.

'I don't do it for the money,' I said. Lie number three. The trend was getting worse. 'I just want my specials to find good homes.'

He went out humming at his good fortune. Hell. Still I had £50 in a previously empty till and that couldn't be bad. Anyway, the duck was hideous.

# Five

The shop had produced little income in the last few days, apart from the duck. A clutch of books fetched a handful of coins. A pair of tarnished sugar tongs earned a pound. What on earth would they be used for, I thought, as I wrapped them in second-hand tissue paper. Serving pickled onions? I wanted lots of real money, crinkling notes, some fivers and tenners, blues and browns. Mr Lucan was not the kind to pay me in cash. He'd probably expect me to take gift vouchers.

Food was not a problem. I had enough pasta and rice to live on for weeks. Boring but sustaining. A clove of garlic, a few drops of olive oil, throw in some sun-dried tomatoes, pine nuts. I was no culinary expert but own-brand baked beans were not a last resort.

The hole in the wall beckoned me. I punched in my pin number and requested fifty pounds. It did not object. Amazing. The notes slid out, pristine and newly pressed. Next was not something I normally did as I know my account details by heart. But for once I keyed in mini bank statement, please. It was an automatic reflex, stalling time. Momentary euthanasia. A touch of curiosity to see if the works had already registered the withdrawal.

I glanced at the print-out. The total was £2,633.00. Wow! Two thousand? I must need prescription glasses. It was a mistake. I knew I had only £600 plus in my account, yet it was showing over £2,000. I began the procedure once again. Punched in my pin number, asked for a mini statement. £2,633.00. There was no point in celebrating. The two thousand pounds were not mine. A clerical error, or whatever you called a computer cock-up.

The branch was closed for lunch. I'd have to wait until later. For a few hours I'd pretend I was solvent, quite healthily rich in fact. Spend, spend, spend. Two thousand might not be much to the average pay-roll high-flying executive but for this struggling PI, it felt very good. I could even spend it but what if someone came along and demanded it back? No, I couldn't cope with the worry.

I bought myself a modest camera with flash; left tape recorder, mobile phone on the stand-by list although I hate mobiles. People walk about, even school kids, with them glued to their hand or ears like some obscene black growth that attaches them to the world. I could live without a mobile, but perhaps First Class Investigations ought to have instant contact with its clients.

Fenwick Future Homes had about eight branches strung along the coast. The Latching branch was their main office, a newish corner showroom with wall to wall grey carpets and spread-eagled desks, computer terminals and glossy photographs with panoramic views. If you wanted a run-down fisherman's cottage sagging at the seams, they were not interested, barely bothered to take your name. But a villa and pool, garage for three cars, security lighting, and you were their man. Out came coffee served in cups, bourbon biscuits, photo-shot brochures in laminated folders.

I cycled passed the wide window display of imposing properties and planned tomorrow's surveillance. A bag lady was out. My charity clothes box would have to kit out a woman with assets. Tough assignment.

The bank cashier was confused. 'Not your money, Miss Lacey? But it was paid into your account this morning. A cash payment. Surely you paid it in yourself?'

'I did not,' I said. 'I know nothing about it. Could you make some more enquiries? I'd like to know how this sum got put in my account. And, of course, it should be removed.'

'Oh no, I'm not sure how we can do that. It's been properly paid in, Miss Lacey.'

'But that's ridiculous. It's not my money and it should not be in my account. I want it out.'

'I will have to ask the manager, Mr Weaver. If you do not accept this deposit...'

'For heaven's sake, I don't accept it. This is a mistake,' I said. 'How can I convince you? Get it put right, please. I can't see what's holding you up. It's not my money and I don't want it.'

'I'll report the matter to Mr Weaver.'

I was fast losing my temper with the girl and she was trying to remember her training in the face of one very annoyed customer. It was a bad case of bank rage.

I walked with my head down, ears tingling, towards the pier, trying to cool down. The wind was promising an early winter, testing resistance. The decorations for the birthday celebrations had been taken down. I walked the length, my mind spinning about the odd £2,000. My thoughts looped the loop. The anglers were minus luck today. Nothing was biting. They stood hunched by their rods, buckets empty, munching cold burgers. I had no idea how the money got into my account or who put it in. It was their mistake. Let them sort it out.

Meanwhile I had my water lilies, the wedding cake and Cllr Fenwick to sort out. I did not feel confident. I was being stretched in several directions without a foot on any ladder.

Latching's overworked wedding photographers were more than cooperative. Even now, approaching winter, the brides wanted to be photographed on the beach, veils floating, hair tangled by the sea breeze. Small bridesmaids ran about, kicking off their shoes, paddling in the shallow waves, suddenly having fun. The photographers caught the fun in their lenses.

That weekend's nuptials were already in photo print but none of the cakes matched the description.

'Thank you,' I said, closing the last album. 'You've been very helpful. You must have been up all night printing this lot. But I can't spot the stolen cake. Perhaps it's too soon. Shall I come again?'

'Have you tried the British Legion or the Salvation Army? They have lots of impromptu wedding parties. They use the Community Hall.'

'Thanks. I'll pop along.' An impromptu Salvation Army wedding? A shot-gun affair? Perhaps it was the uniform.

By this time I was sick of weddings and went home. I was sinking under showers of confetti and bouffant skirts. The ritual suffocated me. It put me off sugar icing for life. DI James was safe. No close shave imminent. He had been married once, he'd told me. I knew nothing about the aftermath, except that it had left him bitter and withdrawn. It was hard to get a smile out of him. I had my small victories. A few times I had even made him laugh.

'Jordan. Are you in? It's DI James. Let me in. I have to talk to you.' He was calling up to my open window.

I flew downstairs from my bedsits. He was standing on the doorstep, hunched in a navy anorak, growling like a bear in rehab.

'Don't you ever ring a bell? Didn't your mother teach you how to be polite?' I asked.

I drank in the sight of him. Even in bear-mode he was so attractive if you like that craggy, cropped-head look. And I did.

'I haven't time to be polite. I could see you were in.'

'So what's all this about, James?'

'Water lilies. Thousands of pounds' worth. Did you put that damned-fool advert in the paper? "STOCKING A POND? WATER LILIES FOR SALE". I put two good men on to that lead.'

'Well, more fool you, Detective Inspector, for taking the bait. Would a thief really advertise his stolen goods? Fresh off the back of a lorry stuff? I credited you with more sense.'

I steered him upstairs as I spoke, towards my upright moral sofa and sat him down. It only held one person in comfort, but still it was big enough for two in an emergency. At the same time as talking, I was making good coffee as he liked it, opening a packet of shortbread, tipping figs and prunes into a dish. Before he knew what was happening, he had a mug of coffee, my special coffee, in his hand, the aroma relaxing the tenseness of his well-toned muscles.

'Milk, cream, coffee-mate?'

'Black, Jordan.'

Just as well. I only had black. I put two mugs on the saffron tiled coffee table. The coffee table had style and class, right height, right size, all warm colours.

'I want you to leave this case alone,' said James. He looked a few degrees more human with my best mug in his hand. His body sagged against the unrelenting back of my upright sofa. There was room for me too but I did not intrude, sat on the floor, my back against the ribbed radiator, its heat easing any pain.

'But Mr Lucan is employing me so I can't leave it. He doesn't feel CID are taking the case seriously. That is, before you realised how valuable the plants were. And did your O-level sums, etc.'

'We've got some information. You are just holding things up, Jordan. I want you out. Get on with your other cases, whatever they are.'

70

'What do you mean, out? What sort of information?'

'You know I can't tell you but it may be mixed up with something bigger.'

'Forget it. Mr Lucan is paying me good money and I need that money.' A driving vision of red with black spots appeared before my eyes and almost crossed them. 'Remember, I don't get a monthly salary and an index-linked pension nor a stress payment if the going gets hard. I have to work all hours for every penny. What information?'

'What about this community spirit of yours? Has avarice taken hold? You are interfering in normal police procedure. We've leads in Amsterdam outlets already. The flower markets on the canals. It's a big operation and too complicated a set-up for you.'

'Good, I'm pleased. You look after Amsterdam and I'll look after the Latching end.'

'You are an impossible woman. Don't you know your own limits? This may be some international smuggling gang.'

'Oh my, what a big story ... international smuggling in water plants? Has Mr Lucan been growing cannabis on the side? You're right, I may not be able to handle it. On the other hand, perhaps I'd better brush up on my Dutch. *Ja, Herr James. Hoe gaat het?*'

DI James put down the empty mug. The

caffeine had revived him. He had that sharp look again. Those ocean eyes glimmered with intelligence and for once, the merest grain of humour.

'I don't know why I come here, Jordan. You talk complete nonsense. Where did you learn Dutch?'

'We found a young Dutch girl sleeping rough on the front, a runaway, when I was still with the force. I looked after her for a few days, picked up some phrases. You know why you come here, for my coffee, you know that. And my particular variety of scintillating company. It makes you feel men are the superior race for a few isolated moments. No one down at the nick is half as much fun.'

His eyes riveted on mine like a flash of electricity. He'd know me if he saw me again.

'No one down at the nick is any fun.'

Ten seconds later he had gone, shutting the door behind him. I heard the street door close downstairs. His mug stood on the table. I moved over and sat on the sofa on the exact spot where he had sat so that I could feel the residual warmth from his body. I drank it in through my pores, touched the crushed velour, melting with desire for the man.

I needed a head test.

The charity box produced a fox fur. The speckled red fur was in good condition but I hated the sad glass eyes of the fox. Had they hunted him and the trauma stayed fixed? A two-piece beige suit was Jacques Verte but I wore the label inside. A pair of painful court shoes and a black pull-on thirties cloche hat made me look a wealthy eccentric, the kind of woman who had all her money in real estate and not on her back.

'My goodness,' said Doris, coming out of her grocery shop to replenish the newspaper display. 'Off to Ascot, are we?'

'Ascot's over. Besides I always wear Antonio Berardi to Ascot.'

'I should have known. You've such good taste. Your trainers are the talk of Latching.'

I cycled part of the way, ignoring the odd looks, left my bike chained to some railings round the corner and out of sight, and walked into Fenwick Future Homes. No, I couldn't see Mr Fenwick, said the receptionist. No, he wasn't free today. No, he never saw anyone without an appointment. Pity. The haughty young woman had been to elocution classes and said no with elongated vowels, both of them. I did not feel she was the object of Mr Fenwick's menopausal desire.

'Then I'd like to make an appointment for tomorrow if that's not too much trouble,' I

73

said, with all the courtesy of old money. I wanted to talk to him, get the character of the man, wanted him in the office at a certain time so I could snap him arriving, leaving, start tailing him.

'Nine thirty tomorrow morning,' said Miss Tone and Tonsils, fingers twinkling over a keyboard. 'Or is that too early?'

'I don't sleep much,' I said. Too busy counting my money. 'That's fine.'

'And what name shall I say?'

'Mrs Barbara Hutton.' She did not blink a stiff, mascaraed lash. Before her time. I stroked the sad hard head of the fox, took his limp body off my shoulders, and hung him over my arm. He felt better that way, more at home.

I decided to walk back to my shop, cruising the charity shops on the way. I needed more stock. A couple of carrier bags later and I'd a nice selection of memorabilia to dress my windows.

While I was in the shops, I asked if anyone had offered them a wedding cake.

'Heavens no!' The ladies had been much amused. 'Left in the lurch, were they?'

It never worried my conscience that I was two-timing the charities. I paid their asking price. If I could resell an item for more, that was their look-out. It felt like I was keeping stock moving. Most things found their way back to the charity shelves a few years later.

74

Small ads in shop windows also drew a blank. No one was advertising a three-tier cake for sale. Gold ribbons included.

The evening was making notes time. The trademark of a good PI was detailed notes. Never rely on memory. It can play tricks.

It was a cold night, temperature zeroing on minus. I thought twice about putting on a T-shirt but was too lazy to get out of bed, lay there shivering instead, toes frozen. DI James would have kept me warm but that was a pointless fantasy. He might isolate me, even in bed, with his long back turned away. Intelligence and brawn on the law side of the bed, independent female PI falling off the other. To him, Jordan Lacey was an alien creature, her face retreating into the night, scattering clusters of stars as she drifted away. At some point, I fell asleep.

But near dawn I awoke, stiff and cold, bells ringing in my ears. A fire engine was clanging down the road, closely followed by a second appliance. I thought I could smell smoke. Had I left something on? I staggered, stiff-legged, round my two bedsits, checking. Something was burning but it wasn't here or my shop. The engines were heading away in the other direction, thank goodness.

I grabbed some heavy jeans, a brushed sweat shirt and anorak and let myself out. The morning air was sharp and biting. Frost hung on last summer's leaves, turning them brown. Dahlia heads had lost any petal colour. I weaved along the road, half asleep, my breath puffing out in cloud vapours. I couldn't go back to sleep so I might as well find out what was going on.

It was easy to follow the sounds and the smell into the centre of town, taking a short cut through Field Alley. The appliances were screeching to a halt and I could already see flames and smoke rising above the roof-tops. The firefighters flung themselves out, opening hatches, running the hoses along the pavement. It was a scene I knew all too well from my days with the police. We were always called to a fire scene soon after the firefighters had put out the blaze.

I stood on the corner of the street in the early morning mist, suddenly shocked awake by the sight.

Fenwick Future Homes was on fire. The brand new showroom was ablaze. Not much of a future now. A crowd was gathering. They were being kept back for their own safety. I slipped round to the side, out of the way, but partly to see what I could see.

'Anyone live upstairs?' I heard the sub officer ask. He was the one in a white helmet and a first class physique. He looked as if he knew what to do in any circumstance. The impression was of cool intelligence and judgement. A bit like DI James.

Without the height or looks.

'No one upstairs, guv!' someone shouted back. 'It's all offices.'

The fire was spreading rapidly and the extreme heat was forcing the crew to tackle the blaze from the pavement. One firefighter was directing a hose from the top of an aerial appliance. Four fighters crouched on the pavement directing water jets through the door and the broken showroom windows. In their navy and red fire kit and coordinated movements, they looked like a row of line dancers. Huge clouds of steam billowed out. Video cameras on a tripod were recording the scene.

I could not understand why the fire was so intense or what was causing the combustion. Paper, desks, computers, carpeting, copier cartridges, photographic equipment, paint? There had been discreet no-smoking signs on all the desks. Computers generate a lot of heat and nowadays many were left on all night.

Tongues of flame, bright orange and yellow, reflected in what was left of the glass. The fire was reducing the opulent corner showroom to blackened walls and barely recognisable debris. Steam eddied upwards. Glass and plastic melted. Dirty water flooded the road and ran along the gutters. Miss T&T was howling on to someone's shoulder. She looked as if she was wearing an outdoor coat over her nightie.

'I've lost everything,' she gulped. 'All my things.'

There were no police in attendance yet. It was West Sussex Fire Brigade's pigeon. A tangle of dull orange hoses littered the gutter like arteries and veins, cables like capillaries. I heard glass shattering and blowing out as the flames spread upstairs. The noise was horrific like an animal devouring Adrian Fenwick's prize show-room.

No nine-thirty appointment now. I wondered which bystander was Cllr Adrian Fenwick. I had only a hazy idea of what he looked like. One councillor is much like another. But surely he would be here, checking on his insurance. Getting the sympathy vote. The crowd was growing as workers stopped on their way, talking in groups, shocked by the devastation.

They were damping down the premises now. Pockets of fire sometimes existed under debris. I could see the office was a mess, equipment destroyed, a mass of sodden paper and charred furniture. Bits of personal belongings were strewn among the debris, a coffee jar, mugs, burnt sugar bag. Shopping list: get a smoke alarm. Get two smoke alarms.

The fumes were no good for my asthma. I didn't know why I was still there. Plain curiosity and being unable to turn down any new experience. The firefighters would soon be handing over to the police. I didn't want to be around when the plodders arrived.

The fire investigators would also be on the spot. They had to find out how the fire started. Perhaps Miss T&T had left an aromatherapy candle burning on her desk. Or maybe it was arson. Some mindless gang of youths on a spree, leaving one of Latching's nightclubs, worse the wear for a dozen pints of bitter. Latching did have such clubs, hidden away in alleyways. The pounding music shook the night air, cracked pavements, stained glasses left on the roadway.

'It's too awful,' the young woman shuddered, almost relishing her star role. 'I can't believe it. Everything's gone.'

She would have been good in an old black and white movie. Before sound. I could just see her roped to the rails, an express thundering towards her at twenty miles an hour.

'Do we know how this happened?' I asked a dishevelled fireman. Firemen are 90 per cent dishy. It's the bulky uniform and the aura of courage and strength. This one had a jutting jaw.

'No, miss. Probably an electrical fault. It usually is.'

'Which is Mr Adrian Fenwick?' I probed.

'He doesn't seem to have turned up yet.'

'Overslept,' I suggested.

Errant husband would have to go on hold. I doubted if he would have much time for erotic dalliances in the next few days. It was back to plants and wedding cakes house-to-house or Mrs Drury would be losing her faith in me.

'Do you want to go in, officer?' It was the sub officer, the one in the white helmet.

He thought I was still in the force. It was a little unnerving. Hadn't the news got around yet? Or had the Chief Super suppressed my departure for some unique reason of his own? The dodgy CID officer who caused all the trouble was not reprimanded, simply moved on to another area. I was the one who got her knuckles slapped for being right and fair.

'Great,' I said, not complaining. I stepped over the threshold to devastation. Fire was not nice. Everywhere was under water. My feet were getting wet. I was squelching in sodden soles. Trainers are no substitute for the rubberised boots the firefighters were wearing. The scene was depressing, desks, chairs, computers, all twisted, charred and ruined, barely recognisable. Only the safe in the far corner had survived. The door was slightly ajar, debris piled against it. I was about to go when I caught a whiff of something different and it was a horrendous stench. I found a handkerchief and crushed it to my nose.

Suddenly I knew what it was. I had been to a lot of barbecues on the beach in my time and knew the smell of roasted meat. People got missed in fires. It happened all the time; a child could crawl into a three-inch gap under a sofa. Panicking victims hid in wardrobes.

Someone had crawled into the safe, thinking the one-inch thickness of steel would protect him. But something had gone wrong with closing the door. Or his smouldering clothes had set the stored documents and stacked money alight. He had ovened himself.

I caught hold of a firefighter, reeling in a hose. He was sweating heavily, his face grimed.

'Excuse me,' I said, trying to hold my voice steady. 'Have you looked in the safe recently?'

It was beginning to rain, light autumn, coolish. The innocent fall put out the last of the smouldering embers and the crowds scattered to cafes and shops, work premises, unfolding telescopic umbrellas. I did not mind getting top wet and the rain cleared the smell from my nostrils. It saved me from trying to look tidy.

A police car arrived. DI James got out, hunched up in a collared trench coat. I turned away. He was followed by two other CID officers. I inched nearer, but tried to stay invisible. There was a lot of activity. I spotted Sergeant Rawlings, my friend with the tiger face. Unusual to find him out of Custody.

'What's happening?' I asked, artlessly. 'Seems a lot of activity for a shop fire. Do you know anything?'

'Not sure, Jordan. Just a rumour. They've found a body, huddled in the safe. Someone trapped by the fire. Nasty, if that's true. And if it's arson, then that makes it murder. I should leg it if I were you, Jordan. And I shouldn't be seen talking to you.'

'OK,' I said. 'I'd hate to rocket your pension rights.'

I drifted away. I had to talk to someone. I perambulated. Someone must tell me more. The body in the safe couldn't be Mr Fenwick. He'd not been in that afternoon when I'd called. If he was not at work in the afternoon, he'd hardly return in the middle of the night. It wouldn't make sense.

The haughty young receptionist was trying to repair her make-up. The media had lost interest in her. So had the firefighters.

'I'm so sorry,' I said, sidling up, hoping no one would recognise me. 'You must be terribly upset. It was such a lovely showroom and you had everything so nice. What's this about a body being found?'

'I don't know,' she said, clearly shaken. 'There was no one there when I locked up. I always make sure. I was the last to leave.'

'So who do you think it is?'

'I don't know. I've no idea. Perhaps someone broke in. It must be a burglar. Or perhaps I locked someone in by mistake and it's all my fault. Oh God, this is so, so awful.'

Her emotion was genuine. The elocution lessons were swallowed. She was pure Sussex now and I liked her more for it.

'I don't think I know your name,' I said to take her mind off the discovery of the body.

'Leroy Anderson. I'm Mr Fenwick's personal assistant. Oh, where is he ... I don't know what I'm going to do. I must speak to Mr Fenwick. I suppose I'd better phone him at home.'

It was obvious he was not at home or he would have turned up by now. He was needed. There must be all sorts of questions the police would want to ask. Perhaps he had been otherwise engaged in some country hotel while his showroom was burning down and therefore he would not care to answer those questions.

Mrs Fenwick of the blue BMW was paying me well to get those answers. Then I remembered her gimlet eyes and I was suddenly not so sure of her motive.

'He's bound to turn up soon,' I said to Miss Anderson. 'You go home and have a nice cup of tea now. You deserve one after all this. It'll help.'

'Thank you,' she said tremulously. 'You're very kind.'

I wasn't being kind at all. It was called paying the rent.

# Six

It was all the buzz in Latching. It was even more newsworthy that week than the burning down of Fenwick Future Homes. They had found the wreck of the Lancaster bomber only a few hundred yards out from the end of the pier. Helicopters circled over the spot. The national media turned up in speedboats, balancing zoom cameras, trying not to get sprayed. Police divers made a few preliminary dives in the area, more for the cameras.

Everyone knew the Second World War legend of the Lancaster. Some said that most of the crew had got out and staggered up the beach. But no one really knew the truth. It was so long ago. Now they would find out. They were going to send divers down to the wreck.

I went back for my bike. But it had gone from where I'd left it chained to the railings. Who on earth would want my clapped-out wheels? Without thinking, I marched into the police station, red alert.

'My bike's been stolen,' I stormed. 'Is

nothing safe in Latching?'

'Calm down, Jordan. I'll get someone to come and see you.'

After a long wait, DI James appeared, somewhat shambolic. His shirt sleeves were rolled up. His five o'clock shadow was nearing ten o'clock. He treated me as if we had never met.

'What's your full name?' he asked, starting to fill out a form. 'Address?'

'Get wise,' I said, averting my eyes from his bare wrists and the sprinkling of dark silky hair on his forearms. This innocence had many delights. I could go overboard just looking at his wrists. 'You know me. Once we even went to Cleo Carling's party together. Remember, champagne, dancing in the dark? Way back in the Middle Ages. My bike's been stolen and I want it returned. It's essential for my work.'

'Your bike's here. We know it's your bike and it's evidence. It was found close to the scene of an arson attack. A witness confirms that the vehicle was there at the time of the fire. Pretty suspicious. We need it for forensic.'

Joshua, my eccentric inventor friend, had made the metal label for me and screwed it on to the handlebars. Classy, he'd said. It had cost me a meal, a bottle of Shiraz and half a bottle of brandy. I hadn't even wanted it but I had a soft heart. He'd hoped that he'd be screwing more than a label, but years of inaction had made action impossible.

'Oh brother, am I hearing right? My bike has nothing to do with the fireworks at Fenwicks. Arson, you say? OK, I was there, the day before. I was making an appointment with Mr Fenwick. Check with Leroy Anderson, his glamorous PA. I couldn't ride it home and left it chained to some railings in the pedestrian precinct.'

'Ms Jordan Lacey, looking for property along the coast? Won the Lottery, have you? Couple of million. Why couldn't you ride it home?'

'I wasn't dressed for riding a bike.'

'Ah, you need special clothes for riding a bike now?'

I could have torn my hair out except it was plaited tight and it would have hurt. 'No,' I groaned. 'I wasn't there as me. I was undercover. Mrs Barbara Hutton. Moneyed lady investor. You could check.'

'Everything has been destroyed. You could say anything and we've no way of checking.' DI James swung away, none too steady. If it wasn't that I knew he hardly drank, I would have said he was drunk. 'You can't have your bike back. It stays here.'

'Why? You haven't given me sufficient reason for keeping my bike.'

'I think a can of petrol is sufficient reason.

It was in a bag strapped to the back of your bike. And your bike was found in a parking space behind Fenwicks, apparently abandoned, and not chained to anything.'

'Petrol? For heaven's sake, it's not mine. I don't buy petrol. Why should I?'

'You might want to buy a secondhand Morris Minor or give watching fire brigade a busy night.'

'Abandoned? I don't abandon my bike,' I said coldly. 'You're making this up. My bike was obviously stolen.'

'It's your bike. It's got your name labelled on the handlebars. A pointless gimmick, if you ask me.'

'I didn't ask you,' I choked.

'It stays here for the time being.'

'How am I going to get about?'

'Walk. Get a taxi like everyone else.'

I flung out of the station, fuming. How could this have happened to me? It was ridiculous. I'd got to sort it out before DI James got any more silly ideas. Leroy Anderson would confirm my story. I'd got to find her pretty quick.

I looked up Anderson in the phone book. There were a lot of Andersons. Anyway, she might not live at home. She might be shacked up with a Smith or a Jones. She was attractive in a brittle sort of way. She only had to cough and she would break a nail.

Instead I phoned Mrs Fenwick. A woman

answered the phone. She sounded middle-aged, a housekeeper perhaps.

'I'm sorry to be ringing Mr Fenwick's home but Miss Anderson, his assistant, made an appointment for me and in view of the fire, I wondered how I could get in touch with her.' I had my Barbara Hutton voice on.

'Just a minute,' said the housekeeper. 'I think Leroy Anders⌣⌣ lives with her sister. Yes, here's her a⌣dress. Tarrant Close, number twelve.'

'Do you know her sister's name?'

'No, sorry. That's all I know.'

'Thank you, anyway. You've been very helpful.'

Tarrant Close ... it rang a bell. Several abbey-sized clangers. Nothing to do with phoning a friend and becoming a million-aire. It was the address of Leslie Fair-brother, the manager of Sussex United Banking Corporation who had gone mis-sing. Suddenly I put two and two together and came up with a frightening four. The corpse in the safe. It might be him, more than just a missing bank manager now.

Perhaps Leroy had been hiding him in the office. Something odd was going on, even if I couldn't make out what it was at this stage. I had no desire to pass this information on to DI James, not after the way he had com-mandeered my bike. I wondered if I could sue Latching police for loss of wheels.

I was getting nowhere fast. I'd nothing on celluloid for Mrs Fenwick; dead-end for Mrs Drury; a few dozen plants for Mr Lucan. Hardly a sparkling success. I should be concentrating on one project at a time, not juggling three cases in the air.

I wandered into Maeve's Cafe on the sea front. It was one of my regular haunts, mainly because Mavis knew my taste in food and drink. I regarded her as a friend.

'Tea with honey?' she signalled from the counter. I nodded. A hot teacake dripping with butter appeared on my table before I had hardly sat down and taken off my coat.

'Get this down you,' she said. 'You look half starved. You can't live on sandwiches and soup.'

'Who says I do?'

'I know where you shop.'

Doris and Mavis were long-time mates. I bought most of my groceries from Doris whose small, crowded shop was two doors down from mine. They were an observant pair and took a delight in being one up on me.

'OK,' I said. 'What can you tell me about stolen water lilies, vandalism of the WI prize-winning wedding entry at the Agricultural Show and the nocturnal activities of Cllr Adrian Fenwick?'

'That's a tall order,' said Mavis, bringing

over a full mug of honeyed tea. She sat down at the table with me, pushing the tea cake towards me. Melting butter was sliding all over the plate like a golden pool. I broke off a piece of toasted dough and mopped up the glistening liquid. The mixed fruit went straight to my sweet tooth bud and said hello.

'I don't know anything much about any of that stuff, but I do know that Terence Lucan is nearly broke. Comes in here and orders half a portion of chips. He gambles, you know. Puts his money on the horses. And all that WI home-baked wedding catering, home-baked my eye. They bought half the stuff. I saw them in Safeways, buying up quiches and profiteroles and ready-cut salads by the trolley-load. As for Cllr Adrian Fenwick. I wouldn't be surprised if he has got a fancy bit on the side. His wife is so saintly, I bet she makes him say grace before they get into bed.'

I choked on a crumb. The glossy Mrs Fenwick had not seemed particularly saintly to me. 'Gossip,' I said. 'Pure gossip. You're winding me up. I bet you and Doris made it all up over coffee this morning.'

'That's your job, isn't it? To find out what's the truth and what's lies. Well, there, I've given you a few ideas to be getting on with.'

'It's help I need,' I said, nearly burning myself on the hot tea. Mavis's idea of boiling water was several degrees above 100 centi-grade. 'Not half-baked gossip.'

'Never turn down gossip, young lady,' said Mavis, getting up to see to another custo-mer who had just come in, banging the door behind him. 'There may be a gram of truth in it.'

'Grain, you mean.'

I stared at the pattern on the oil-cloth-covered table top. I had eaten at Maeve's cafe a hundred times and never really taken in the intricacy of the pattern. Someone with an Arts degree had designed this cloth. Geraniums and pots and trellises. It was someone's life work.

Life work. It was time to get back to base roots. Not a flora joke. I had to start all over again. I'd missed something or perhaps there was nothing to miss. Latching Water Gardens was several miles inland and the Stagecoach bus service went nowhere near. My flushed finances gave me the solution. Fifteen minutes later I'd signed the rental agreement on one Raleigh Sunrise lady's cycle, wheels with alloy rims and hubs, can-tilever brakes and semi-raised handlebars. It was mine for a week, all 18-speed index gears with gripshaft. Cheap at the price.

'You have to wear a helmet,' said the assistant. 'It's the law.'

'It's the law in Australia, not here,' I said. 'But OK, I'll wear a bone dome.'

It felt like wings after a day of walking everywhere. The bike was in good nick. I only had to change the saddle height. O ladybird, ladybird, come fly home with me. I'd nowhere to park a car but I'd find space for her.

Even the hill did not seem so steep second time around. I did not announce my presence. I put the bike in bushes, cupped-hand a drink from nearby standing tap, unzipped anorak for escape of excess body heat.

Avenues of plants, shrubs and saplings stretched in all directions like a sea of green, tinged with autumnal russet. Winter was on its way. Although water lilies were Mr Lucan's speciality, he obviously grew other things. The route to the ponds looked well trampled as if the Old Bill had held a reunion march.

I wondered if I had come to the right place, blinked, checked landmarks. Everything had changed since my first visit. All the ponds were empty. They had been completely cleared out. The concrete bases and sides were murky and cracked, algae clinging to every crevice. A sea of mud rimmed the edges. It looked and smelled worse than when I'd first inspected the scene.

And where were the rescued plants? At a rough count there'd been a dozen or so from the Agricultural Show and about six from the kiddies' float. Not an American Star in sight. Surely they hadn't died from mis-handling?

Mr Lucan did not seem to employ much in the way of staff. Trees grew by themselves but surely there was mulching and pruning to do, whatever mulching was. I could only see one khaki-clad figure in the distance, rhythmically bending over in a digging movement between lines of bushes. Very rural.

'Miss Jordan. What are you doing here?'

I jumped. I hadn't heard Terence Lucan come along behind me. He looked closed up, withdrawn, not particularly pleased to see me, khaki combat trousers streaked with mud.

'Hi there,' I said cheerfully. 'Thought I'd have another look round. I might have missed something.' Especially when I don't know what I'm looking for, I added to myself. 'I see you've emptied the ponds.'

'It seemed a good opportunity,' he said morosely. 'Routine maintenance. Bacteria, you know. Can't be too careful.' He kicked a nearby hose. 'Soon fill 'em up again when you find the rest of my plants.'

'When did you first start growing water lilies?' I asked.

'About ten years ago. Always liked them, their serene beauty. I wanted to develop a speciality side to the business. Trees get boring,' said Mr Lucan. 'No real skill needed. I wanted to be known for something.'

'I didn't realise you had so much land. Do you employ many people? I'd like to speak to them.'

'Only odd-job men, now and again. I employ students in the summer.' Mr Lucan looked vaguely towards a line of saplings.

'But I saw someone over there.' I waved in the direction of the line of bushes but the figure had gone. A mist was creeping up the hill off the sea. It was going to rain. I was going to get wet. No fun.

'You must have imagined it. There's no one around today. They've all gone home.'

'Perhaps it was someone stealing a bush. What sort of bushes are they, over there?'

'Deciduous, perennial, evergreens mostly.'

Not a lot of help. 'And your car, the red Morris Minor,' I changed the subject swiftly, sensing his discomfort. 'Can I put a deposit on it? Say, three hundred pounds? I can send you a cheque now while I arrange finance for the rest.'

Shorthand for get a loan from the bank, ha ha.

He paused, doing arithmetic in his head. 'I'd rather have cash,' he said. 'I don't want to put it through the books.'

'Understandable. I'll see what I can do. Nice to see you again. Don't worry, we're getting somewhere.'

Freewheeling home downhill was a joy. I'd discovered something but I was not sure what it was. Mr Lucan had not wanted me there. He was not pleased that I had seen the empty ponds. He did not want me to interview anyone who worked for him. As for the car, he'd only agreed to the sale to get rid of me. I was no nearer owning that car than I was to living on the moon.

The promised rain came lashing down. My Raleigh Sunrise held the road well but I soon felt icy fingers creeping down the back of my neck as the rain soaked through my anorak. My hair was a wet rope, eyelashes stuck with glue.

I prayed for a panda car to come and pick me up. They could cook up any charge: riding a bike without insurance; riding a bike without a helmet; freewheeling down-hill with my feet off the pedals. All I wanted was a vehicle roof over my head.

Later I phoned the bank and requested an appointment with Mr Weaver, the manager. I checked whether they had removed the two thousand pounds. They hadn't. The manager came on the line.

'Miss Jordan. This is William Weaver speaking. We simply don't understand your request. A further two thousand pounds was deposited in your account today. Why put it in if you then want us to remove it?'

'But I didn't put it in,' I snapped. 'Don't you understand? It's not my money and I'm not putting it in. I don't care what you do with it, but don't leave it in my account.'

'It's not that easy. It was correctly deposited, both sums, and has to remain there. If you want it out of your account, then you must withdraw it in the normal manner and take it away.'

'But I don't want to take it away. It's not mine. Haven't you got some dead account you can put it in?'

'We are not allowed to remove money correctly deposited unless under police instruction.'

There are red bits in my tawny hair and those bits suddenly heated up, detonating like a mine underfoot. 'I shall make a complaint,' I almost shouted. 'Get rid of it. I want it out before I see you tomorrow about a personal loan to buy a car.'

'I take a very serious view about your complaint,' said the manager, all stiff and official.

'And I take a very serious view of your incompetence. My patience is evaporating fast.' I slammed the phone down. A severe case of detonation. Stress activated. Too late to count to ten.

The retread of Latching Water Nursery had been fruitful but there was no way I could look at the WI marquee again. The

97

Agricultural Show had been dismantled and all that remained were brown patches where the tents had stood. I thought about Mavis and the Safeways mega-buy. Her remarks could have been sour grapes. Maeve's Cafe has a limited menu. Chips with everything. Even chips with chips.

'Mrs Drury,' I said on the phone. 'It's Jordan Lacey of FCI. Could you let me have a complete list of your members and mark which ones contributed to the display and what they cooked. A tall order, I know, but I feel it's necessary to get a complete picture.' I used the same phrase. Too tired to think up new words.

'I can tell you're on to something,' said Mrs Drury. 'I can hear it in your voice. I know! A couple of our members were disappointed because their exhibits were not up to scratch and not accepted. We are very particular and our standard is high. You don't think they deliberately sabotaged the stand, do you?' Her voice went up a scale. 'How absolutely dreadful! But, of course, it could happen...'

'No, I don't think that happened at all,' I said soothingly. 'The Latching WI is far too nice. But it might be someone who was denied membership. Can you think of anyone whose application was turned down?'

Mrs Drury was off. That woman could talk. I held the phone away from my ear and

98

jotted down relevant names, letting the bulk of her meanderings fill the ether. It was an avenue that had not occurred to me before.

'Thank you, Mrs Drury. That's a great help. I'll follow them up.'

'My, my, Jordan, you work so hard. I'm so impressed.'

It was on my bike time again. I had a list of names. As Mavis said, sometimes you get the truth from gossip.

# Seven

They were planning to raise the wreck of the Lancaster bomber. It was the stuff of nightmares, searching for dead bodies in dark water. I knew the female police diver with the Sussex Police Underwater Search Unit from my days on the beat. Her name was Ellen Peach which was a fragrant name for someone who looked tough and had such a murky job. Some days she's looking for a corpse in a river bed or a reservoir, the next searching sewers for drugs or a gun.

I recognised her immediately despite the wet suit and bulky equipment, helmet, mask, respirator. All I could see of Ellen were her eyes, deceptively mild and gentle. She liked Debussy, especially the nocturnes. Her hair was brown, cut short like a boy and she was very fit. She jogged and trained with weights. It showed. I always felt puny and weak beside her but she was nice enough not to comment. I'd once done her a good turn so perhaps that counted. Or rather, a good turn that helped her mother. Still, it counted.

The end of the pier had been taped off, scene of crime tape with no apparent crime. They didn't want gawping sightseers getting in the way, or video enthusiasts and reporters. There were several reporters hanging about in various journalistic stances, most of them glued to their mobiles. There were the plain bored, smoking, major-pollution variety, to those trying to look seriously busy in case an editor caught them on screen. I knew most of them by sight but kept out of their way.

'Zero visibility and freezing,' I heard a police officer say. 'I don't envy them. They don't know yet what they are going to find.'

A police launch was riding the waves, tossing and lurching. The two police divers tipped over backwards into the water, like dolphins, disappearing into the choppy blue depths. The wind was beginning to strengthen. The weathermen had forecast storms and strong winds and I had a feeling they were right for once. I zipped up my anorak and tried to find some small shelter. If the wind went through my ears I'd end up with earache. It was no fun having sensitive drums.

One of the reporters ambled over. He was jumpy, looking for an angle, editor breathing down his polo neck. 'What are you doing here, WPC Lacey?' he asked, another one with information months out of date.

'And in civvies. Or are we plain clothes now?'

'Very plain,' I said, not correcting him. 'I'm interested in the Lancaster, part of Latching's history. A fascinating legend. What do you know about it?'

'Not a lot. They think there's one body still in the wreck, the pilot. Everyone says the rest of the crew struggled ashore and were accounted for. But who knows?'

'What about bombs and incendiaries? Any of them aboard?'

'A full load apparently. Enough to blow up half of Latching. A pretty dangerous wreck. Any of these fishing trawlers could have dragged the debris to the surface and blown themselves sky high. Which makes it even more curious that Councillor Fenwick should have opposed the raising of the wreck.'

'He did what?' I kept the surprise out of my voice. I ought to read council meetings more carefully.

'He opposed it at the last council meeting, vehemently. He maintained that it was a war grave and should be left where it is, undisturbed. Desecration of the dead. Grieving relatives upset, etc. But the vote went through.'

'What relatives?'

'Exactly. Who is there left now to care? I'm only a humble reporter so I can only report,

102

but we're talking over half a century. But there's a dozen letters in today's paper opposing the rising of the wreck. Quite an uproar. Councillor Fenwick is determined to stop this operation. It's a wonder he's not here with a placard, making a fuss, getting in everyone's way as he usually does. It's the kind of headline he likes. Don't Touch Our Heroic Dead.'

'What else do you know about Councillor Fenwick?' I asked casually. 'Has he an eye for the ladies as well as the headlines? Is there an attractive woman councillor who shares his views over a late night drink, non-alcoholic, of course.'

'Now, now, Miss Lacey,' the reporter smirked. 'What kind of question is that? Anyone would think you had an interest in the councillor's private life.'

'Well, I have, in a way,' I smiled. I was not going to give this nosy-parker, twitchy-biro newsgatherer the merest clue. 'I have a close friend who has a crush on him and I wondered if she stood a chance.'

It was a pathetic route, I knew. But it was the best I could do at short notice. The reporter grinned back and was about to say something when his mobile phone rang, an irritating call sign jangling on the air, setting my nerves on edge even when he turned away to answer. My chance had gone. Usual luck.

I wandered off to as near as I could get to the end of the pier. This was only a ten-minute air break from FCI. I had that list of people to see, paperwork to do, a shop to run.

The divers were surfacing, bobbing along on the waves, riding the splashes, waiting to climb back on board the launch. They tipped themselves into the boat. I leaned over the railings of the pier, waved down to Ellen Peach.

'Hi, Ellen,' I called, hoping she would remember me, trying to look memorable. 'Found anything of interest?'

She nodded, pulling off her helmet. Her short hair stuck up like a broom. She un-clipped all the equipment to rid herself of the weight. She looked shocked, thrown, unusual for her. She was used to all sorts of sights.

'Just the pilot?' I yelled again.

She shook her head and held up two fingers. Not a rude sign.

'Two airmen?' I shouted. But she did not answer. She had bent down to say some-thing to her colleague.

The launch was spinning giddily in the rough waves. It washed right up close to the rust-ridden girders of the pier. I could see clearly down into the launch.

'No,' Ellen said, peering up at me, slightly more relaxed. She made up her mind. She was remembering the good turn and that I liked music too. 'One is a woman. Was a woman.'

'How do you know?'

'She's wearing a bracelet on her wrist. There was just bones and a bracelet. Don't ask me any more, Jordan.'

A woman. It was startling news but nothing to do with any of my cases. What was a woman doing on board a Lancaster bomber in the middle of a war? Perhaps she was an agent, ready to be dropped somewhere in France. Did this have anything to do with Cllr Fenwick's wreck-raising objection? But how could it? He must have been a mere baby, a dummy-guzzler, at the time of the heroic run.

I went back to my shop and opened up. I had been neglecting the merchandising of late but still, it was only a front, and not my main source of income. Income? Did I have one? Not a frequent word in my vocabulary.

I thought it was time to run a few thoughts by DI James but I was hesitant. Terence Lucan was my client, he was paying me and I was besotted about buying his beautiful car. Here we go again – conflicting interests. But still I had this stupid morality thing that made me leave a message on DI James' answerphone.

'Hi, James,' I said, all cheery, perky girl

105

informer. 'Just a thought. Have you checked if Terence Lucan has any gambling debts? That invitation for coffee still stands even though you were so rude to me last time. Promise no cut corners with a jar of instant, though you deserve it.'

I didn't say my name. If he couldn't recognise my voice by now then he was an imbecile. A dear, acutely remote, madly attractive, amazingly sexy imbecile. If only he would look at me clearly with those ocean-blue eyes instead of clouding them with distrust.

The dear, acutely remote object of affection rang back within minutes. 'What's this about Terence Lucan?' he said crisply. 'What debts?'

'Er ... not sure,' I said. 'But apparently his financial situation is not exactly healthy. He likes the horses, the running and jumping over hedges kind. And I'm not saying any more. Pure gossip.'

'Then why ring me?'

'Just to hear your resonant tintinnabulary,' I crooned, then slamming down the receiver. Love that word. Never had a chance to use it before. DI James' voice drove me mad. That trace of an accent. Those deep brown tones. It was not fair. No man should be allowed to speak like that. The voice can be the most evocative and attractive thing about a man. Shut your eyes and it doesn't matter what a man looks like, or what he does to your body as long as the voice in your ear is an echo of heaven.

I closed my eyes, pretending I could still hear him. But all I heard was the thrashing of the waves on the shore. It was getting rough again. Something was going wrong with the weather. Global warming was on its way. Latching first hit.

My trumpeter has that kind of voice, caring and enfolding as if you are the only person in the world who exists for him. But he has two voices, for his trumpet is a second voice. His music sings in my ears with a message that is often only for me and I always listen for it. His wife may hear a different message but I know when he plays solely for me. Another gut-ripping scenario. Pass me the Glenn Miller and String of Pearls, no, recap, not the String of Pearls tape. I'd rather hear a little Speak Low, Sweet and Lovely or Mercy, Mercy, Me.

I had not seen my special trumpeter for weeks. I supposed he was off playing dazzling Vegas or New York or doing Bond film credits. I could recognise his trumpet soaring above the theme music. He got paid thousands of dollars for those few notes. I always felt gloriously proud of him and wanted to tell the people sitting next to me in the cinema. I know that man! The man who played those soaring notes.

There was a jumbled message from Mrs Drury. 'I've gone through all our records,' she proclaimed. 'And there is one woman, just one woman who has been turned down three times by the committee. Now isn't that extraordinary?'

'Extraordinary,' I agreed even though she couldn't hear me on the answerphone. I didn't think there was anything more I could do for Mrs Drury and Latching WI. The food had gone; the wedding cake was under wraps in some deep freeze; it was a cold trail. Any moment now I would have to give her back her money and tell her the case was closed.

'It's Mrs Fairbrother, the bank manager's wife. She's tried to join three times. But we won't have her. No, thank you. Weird is her middle name.'

The tape clicked off and I sat back in my chair. Mrs Fairbrother. Leroy Anderson's sister and now blacklisted by the Latching WI. Talk about coincidence and coincidences don't happen. Perhaps I ought to go and see her. Funny how she overlapped three cases ... although the disappearance of Leslie Fairbrother, her husband, was nothing to do with her. Or was it? DI James could keep that one. I didn't want to know.

I looked up the address again. No 12 Tarrant Close. Not far on my Raleigh Sunrise. Two birds with one pebble. I might have a word with Leroy at the same time. Is your boss a nice man, that kind of thing. Does he have affairs?

Tarrant Close was a road of fifties development and a cul-de-sac. The different styled houses looked very settled. Trees had grown and hedges expanded, creeping along perimeters. Everywhere had that weathered look, nothing new or glaring. No nasty extensions or garages turned into extra TV rooms.

Number twelve had a Tudorish timbered porch with ceramic pot for umbrellas, two curtained bay windows, chalet-style gable, a detached garage and a Japanese magnolia in the front garden. Exactly what a bank manager would buy on mortgage, special terms for staff in management, a perk, of course.

I parked my Sunrise and rang the bell. Chimes sounded indoors. A woman opened the door. I knew immediately I had seen her somewhere before but I had no idea where. Her face was out of this world. Plains of beauty.

'Yes?' she said.

I didn't know what a bank manager's wife should look like. Was there a standard model? I suppose I expected the middle-class mould of M&S twinsets and plain court shoes, not the wild-haired vision who opened the door at No 12, all swirling Indian cotton skirts, bare feet and anklets.

'Mrs Fairbrother?' I smiled hopefully. Could be the wrong house. 'My name is Jordan Lacey, a private investigator. I'm making some enquiries on behalf of the Latching WI and I wondered if you could help me.'

'I'm Waz Fairbrother, yes,' she said. She had long black hair, long locks loose, half braided, half beaded as if she had lost interest in the middle of getting dressed. Although not a model-type beauty, her face was arresting with constantly changing expressions. Her hands were beautiful, long and tapered, each nail painted a different colour, some decorated with stars, crescent moons, splatter cuts. Definitely not WI material.

'Ah yes, Waz Fairbrother.' Was there a river called Waz? I was christened after a river. Perhaps her mother also had a river fixation. Or a mountain conception figured. Waziristan was a mountainous region somewhere in North Pakistan. Learned that from a crossword I couldn't do.

'DI James has also brought me into his search for your husband.' That was a close one. Showing me a photograph of the balding Leslie Fairbrother could be construed as professional cooperation. 'Can I speak to you? It won't take long.'

'Come in,' she said. 'Have they found him?'

'I don't think so.'

I followed her through a plain, magnolia-walled, cheerless hallway to the back kitchen. Kitchen. This room hit me like a cyclone. I took a deep breath.

'This is mine,' she explained, waving her arms around. 'No one is allowed in here except with me. If you don't mind, I've some stuff setting now and I can't leave it.'

It was a mega muddle, a mega mess, mega catastrophe. Every surface, including the floor, was covered in objects, boxes, cartons, bits and pieces. The only resemblance to a normal kitchen was a gas cooker on which bubbled various gungy pots, and a sink piled high with plates, mugs, palettes and sable-haired brushes. There was a table lurking somewhere underneath a collection of piled tins and corrugated paper, wire, egg boxes and lengths of garden trellis. My bland bedsits were pure Ideal Home show-rooms in comparison. Latching WI would have binned the lot in the name of hygiene.

'I'm making something,' she added, not explaining. 'Something special.'

'Interesting,' I murmured. 'I wonder if you could go through your husband's disappearance for me?'

'I don't think I was here,' Waz said, stirring

111

some pot like a medieval witch. She brushed her black hair out of her eyes with a flick. 'I think I was away on research.'

Research? Researching a council dump, a recycling plant? Collecting a few choice items of other people's junk. Perhaps I should ask her to keep an eye open for my shop. I was getting low on novelty stock.

'When I got back, he wasn't here. The front door was open, he'd been abducted.'

'How do you know?'

The answer was in her pale eyes, so pale they held no colour. 'Well, it's obvious, isn't it? They drove him to the bank, to get him to open the safe deposit boxes, didn't they? But he didn't have the master key to the vaults.'

'Where was his key?'

'It was here. All his keys are here,' she said with a gleam of triumph, touching a three-foot-high misshapen edifice that stood on the floor. It was a lethal-looking object, green in colour, streaked with rust. 'I've called it "Ruin".'

'Very appropriate,' I said, wondering if I was supposed to understand. 'Can you tell me any more about your husband's disappearance? Supposing he wasn't abducted?'

'He could have done a runner. What's that phrase they all use these days? He wanted some space. Space, my eye! Men today don't want responsibility, nothing marital

112

like it used to be. Marriage once was till death do us part. Now it's just until something else takes your fancy.'

'I'm very sorry about your husband, Mrs Fairbrother, but as I said, it's not my case. I really want to talk to you about the WI.'

She gave a short, sharp laugh. 'Oh, that lot. Leslie wanted me to join. He made me apply three times. To calm me down, he said, to make me more normal. I couldn't have cared less. Anyway, I never cook. We don't need cooked food. Not my style.'

There was no room in that kitchen to cook. Not even to microwave a soup.

'Did you go to the Agricultural Show last weekend?'

'Yes.' She did not hesitate. 'I wanted some hay and straw.'

'Oh, fascinating. Did you see the WI's winning entry?'

'Their what? I don't know ... no, did they have one? Don't ask me.'

'So you never went near it?'

'I wouldn't recognise their entry if I saw it. I'm sorry. I never saw anything. Would you like a drink?' She fished out a crushed sachet from under the assorted debris. 'Camomile and ginger? Very good for the nerves.'

'No, thank you but thank you. By the way, your sister lives with you, doesn't she?'

'Leroy? Yes, she lives here. Somewhere. Upstairs, I think, in one of the rooms. The front room, I guess. I never see her. She has a hectic social life. No purpose or direction except in a straight line towards the male race.'

So this muddy collection of painted clutter had purpose and direction? I suppose it depended on which way you looked at it.

'I'd like to talk to your sister sometime. Can you give her a message saying that and my phone number.' I wrote my number down on an old typed card which she folded and folded until it was a stub which she poked between two tins of rimmed adhesive. Farewell, phone number. It would end up buried in an edifice. Shopping list: professional business cards (again). I made to leave. The glue cooking on the stove was making me feel sick.

'I'm curious about your name. It's most unusual,' I coughed. 'Is Waz short for something?'

'Yes, it's short for I was christened Cordelia Henrietta. Could you live with that mouthful? You look very tired. Have you done anything about increasing your vibrational energy?'

'Er ... do I need to?'

'You could try colour therapy.'

'Sounds fun. I like colours.'

'I'll give you a personalised energy candle to cleanse yourself of bad intentions.'

'How kind. I'll let you know if it works.'

I cycled straight down to the seafront, personalised candle tucked into the saddle bag. It would be useful if the power failed but now I needed to rid my lungs of the fumes from her glue pots. The sea was angry about something, lashing the shingle with beat-up waves. It roared like a beast ready to claw its way up from the depths with slimy, weed-encrusted talons. I could really frighten myself sometimes.

But the ozone in the wind was exhilarating and liberating. It worked like an inhaler, freeing my jumpy airways of impurities, coating them with the fine spray of some faraway sun-drenched Pacific island inhabited by birds and primates.

Ocean. Ocean-eyes. That man again. And I hadn't thought of DI James for at least twenty minutes. Was I getting over him? Was that a record? Perhaps a small hiccup.

'Detective Inspector James,' I shouted to the wind, full of joy. 'I'm getting over you.'

I twirled on the shifting shingle, eyes closed, clothes flapping. It was cold, lip-bitingly bitterly cold. Soon I would have to unpack my winter warmers.

'So, what are you yelling about, Jordan Lacey,' he said, shingle crunching as he slid down the steep bank to my side. He was all coordinated weight and muscle. 'Who are you getting over?'

115

# Eight

I could have stood and devoured his looks for two and a half centuries, but I didn't have time. That ex-wife of his must have hurt him a lot. His eyes were clouded with mistrust.

'Hi there, DI James,' I said pleasantly. 'Come to swop information?'

'You can't possibly have anything I want,' he said, which could have been taken as an insult but I preferred not to think that way.

'How about the keys to the safe deposit boxes at Leslie Fairbrother's bank? And the keys to the vaults.'

'Where are they?'

'In a ruin,' I said, giving him one of my Goldie Hawn smiles. 'That's a clue.'

He was clearly intrigued. 'So this is a game show, eh? I have to guess which castle ... Arundel, Bamber, Bodiam...?'

'Cold.'

'Ruin ... ah, mother's ruin ... pub? Which pub? Any warmer? Do I get to ask the audience?'

'No. Frost settling.'

116

'I haven't time for this,' he snapped, breaking the banter. 'I work for a living.'

'So what are you doing on the beach? Taking statements from the gulls? Have they seen any fishy-looking boats lately, running duty-free tobacco across from France?'

'I came to tell you that you can have your bike back. We've finished with it.'

'And eliminated it from your inquiries?'

'No. We've got all the evidence we need to prove that you were in the vicinity of Fenwick Future Homes early that morning and that you were carrying a can of inflammable liquid.'

'Oh nonsense, I was in bed, trying to get to sleep, damned cold and ... and...' I nearly said 'and thinking of you'. But I grabbed the words back at the last moment. 'And wondering if last year's hot-water bottle would leak.'

'You were seen on your bike. We've a witness.'

'Someone was seen, you mean. It wasn't me. There's no proof it was me. Anyone could wrap up in a BHS anorak and cycle round Latching on my bike. Has everyone gone deaf today? No one seems to hear what I'm saying.'

'They identified your hair.'

'Heavens, am I the only person with reddish hair in Latching? Now there's a front page story: Red hair extinct in Latching.

117

Scientists blame sea pollution. Coastal water to be analysed.'

He was wearing a tie patterned with lines of red London buses. It was flapping outside his jacket. One bus, in the middle, was going in the opposite direction. I'd never seen him wearing a joke tie before. My glance nearly went to his feet. Perhaps he was wearing Mickey Mouse socks too.

'Can you say if the body in the fire has been identified?' I asked offhand. 'I know someone was found in the safe. I half saw it ... him.' I shuddered. 'I mean, I think I saw something in the safe.'

His face hardened instantly. 'What the hell were you doing in the showroom? Checking your handiwork?'

'Checking my what?' I choked on the words. 'For heavens' sake, get real, DI James. Since when have I become a firebug? Why should I want to set fire to Fenwick Future Homes? Remember motives? You've got to find one of those.'

'I have no idea how your mind works, Jordan,' he said, kicking pebbles and staring out to sea. 'It's a complete mystery to me. Logic is not one of its components.'

'You've no evidence, not a shred,' I said. 'It's all circumstantial. The bike, the can of petrol...'

'I didn't say it was petrol. I said inflammable liquid.'

118

'Inflammable liquid is petrol. Why use two words when one will do.'

I was incensed. This was totally unfair. My bike had been stolen from where I left it chained to railings. Someone had been riding it around Latching without my permission. And that same someone had dumped a can of petrol with it. I tried to calm down.

'I'm sure there's a perfectly good explanation for all this,' I said, trying to sound innocent and reasonable. It's not easy to try and sound innocent even when you are. 'I suggest you pursue some other more reliable lines of inquiry. This one has obviously been cooked up.'

Not exactly the right word to apply to a charred body on the scene but it was too late to retract it.

'I'll give you the benefit of the doubt for the time being,' said DI James. 'Only because if you'd set fire to FFH, you would have bungled it. This was an efficient job. They knew what they were doing. Even down to the candle burning in a waste bin. Oldest trick in the book.'

I swallowed the insult. What was one more? Better being insulted than being suspected.

'But if I find any more evidence...' He glowered at me. I love it when he glowers. His dark brows come together making a line across his face. Very visors down. Very King Arthur. Camelot, the Latching version.

'You won't,' I said confidently. 'Because there isn't any. Have you an idea who it was? The body?'

'You haven't explained yet what you were doing there, at the scene of the fire. Only police are authorised to attend when the fire is out.'

'Authorised to attend! Policespeak again. The sub officer thought I was still with the force. He invited me in. A perfectly under-standable mistake.'

'And you didn't think fit to tell them otherwise?'

'I didn't see any harm in having a look round. You know how nosy I am.'

I was getting cold and an easterly wind was getting up, blowing all the way from the North Sea. Any moment now, I might have to hang on to DI James for support. My hair had come loose and was whipping across my face. It was time to go, much as I was almost enjoying his company.

DI James thought the same. He began climbing back up the bank of shingle. It was unstable and slippery. I couldn't even get a proper grip. My feet were sliding all over the place and putting them sideways to gain more purchase wasn't working. Pebbles shifted and scattered beneath our weight.

I felt an iron grip clamp round my elbow.

DI James was heaving me up the bank as if I was a sandbag for sea defences.

'Hold on,' I gasped.

'You hold on,' he said grimly. 'Or I'll leave you down here to spend the night dodging the tide.'

I was hauled up the steep slope. I should have been grateful but I wasn't. It was more the manner of his assistance that I objected to. Not the grip, the closeness, the feel of his brute strength. Add blazing sunshine, the roar of the crowds, give him tattered rags on bulging muscles and, at a distance of a hundred yards, this detective inspector might have been mistaken for a gladiator. On second thoughts, the closest resemblance was the stubble.

'They sell ... disposable razors,' I said, getting my breath back at the top. 'You could keep a supply in your desk.'

'They still sell hairnets. You could keep one in your pocket,' he said, removing a long strand of hair from his mouth. One of mine.

'Men have been known to choke to death on my hair,' I glared.

'And I believe you,' he said, striding away across the promenade. He ignored two illegal motorised scooters who swerved to avoid him. They looked startled.

I had a feeling he was grinning. Had I produced another joke? My score was rising. It was enough for my pulse to leapfrog into near happiness.

Mrs Drury was waiting for me when I went to open up my shop. Her car was parked diagonally with one wheel on the pavement. Heaven help her if a warden came along.

'I've come to pay you,' she said, following me inside. 'I like to keep everything straight.'

'Come on through, Mrs Drury. We ought to have a talk,' I said, going for the coffee pot. I needed caffeine fast. 'Sit down and make yourself at home.'

She sat on my Victorian button-back chair and admired the Persian rug on the floor. My two prize possessions. My reminders of The Beeches, the sad house where the poor nun had once lived. Mrs Drury's house was probably the opposite end of sad. Full of nostalgia and animals and people. A busy house generated by a busy person.

'Now, tell me how much I owe you,' she said, getting out her chequebook. 'We've had lots of publicity in the papers, you know. Quite a lot of interest in the WI. A life-saving injection you might say. Three new ladies want to join already.'

I made the coffee and took it over to Mrs Drury. She admired the bone-china mug and sipped with pleasure.

'You make very good coffee.'

'One of my few talents.'

'I always say there's no excuse for poor coffee. Unless you are poor, of course.' She laughed at her own joke.

'Mrs Drury,' I began, 'I have to be completely honest with you. I can't solve your case. I don't know where to go with it. The trail's gone cold.'

'And the food's gone cold.' She laughed again.

'There weren't any clues. Nothing I could really follow up. No one has handed in a wandering wedding cake at the police station.' This was how I had found Joey, her tortoise. Nothing at all to do with me. A patrol car officer with good eyesight had spotted Joey on the A27.

'But you've made a lot of inquiries, haven't you? All those photographers. And the WI's unsuccessful and unsuitable applicants. Takes time, your time, and I'll pay for that.'

'I did go and see Waz Fairbrother. I don't think she had anything to do with the vandalism although she was at the Agricultural Show, buying hay and straw for some model.'

'I told you she was weird.'

'She didn't really want to join the WI. Her husband was making her apply.'

'Weirder still. We were quite right to turn her down. She wouldn't have fitted in.'

'So I can't really charge you for anything.'

'Nonsense. But it's just like you to be so honest, so we'll come to a compromise and I'll pay you for three full days. That seems fair. One hundred and fifty pounds. There.' She signed her name with a flourish. How could I turn down such a generous gesture? It would improve my zero-based budgeting.

I gave her a receipt. I had proper receipts now. Typed then photocopied on bond-quality paper with the logo of FCI in the top corner.

'On my way in I saw the dearest little teapot in your window. It's shaped like a cat, the tail curled up like a handle. How much is it?'

'Six pounds,' I said without thinking.

'I'll have it. I collect teapots. You can never have too many.'

As I wrapped the pot, careful with the lid, I was in half a mind to give it to Mrs Drury as a present but something held me back. It wasn't meanness. It was the smallest twinge of suspicion at the back of my mind.

We smiled at each other and parted friends. She invited me to pop in any time and I said I would. I watched her drive away, narrowly missing a sleek woman who was crossing the road and talking into a mobile. The woman was Mrs Hilary Fenwick, the wife who preferred to meet people in car parks. I wondered why Mrs Drury didn't wave. Perhaps her eyesight was as erratic as her driving.

Mrs Fenwick didn't acknowledge Mrs Drury either. She was walking fast along the pavement, her sharp-shouldered cream raincoat flapping open. She seemed in a big hurry. She was obviously not coming to see me.

The sale of the cat teapot had left an empty space and I trawled through my box of goodies to find a replacement. There was an old manicure set, implements rusty with age but the satin lining of the case was still a glowing pink. No one used these things nowadays. A couple of emery boards was our lot. Whoever had time to buff their nails with a chamois-leather polisher?

I placed the manicure set in the window with an old bottle of Evening in Paris scent and some bright orange Tangee lipsticks, circa WWII. This was the nostalgia touch. That woman on the Lancaster bomber ... she might have used one of these lipsticks. But a lipstick would have been precious in wartime and she would have taken it with her, not left it behind in Latching.

I wrote up my notes on the WI case and filed it under CLOSED. VERY EFFICIENT.

My coffee was cold by now, but I finished it just the same, leafing through the Terence Lucan file. Another dead end. As dead as his water lilies would be by now. I would follow

125

up his part-time staff, first thing in the morning. They would be early workers, salt of the earth, etc.

Someone pushed the free newspaper through the letterbox. I once put an ad in it which brought me my first client, Mrs Ursula Carling. Cases seemed to come by word of mouth now. Funny that, when I thought I was an invisible asset.

The newspaper was full of local stories, quite a big piece on the WI display being trashed with a photo of Mrs Drury beaming. They were always days behind with their stories as they depended on local people sending in the stuff.

They also depended on pages of small ads for their income. Further on in the newspaper was their own advertisement, giving prices for full-page, half-page and quarter-page ads. They were quite expensive.

The nasty suspicion grew in my mind, not exactly festering because I liked Mrs Drury. She'd paid me £150 but the publicity they had got for the WI was worth far more than that. Add up the cost of several half-page ads ... even the free newspaper had given them a half-page story. And it had been in both Brighton papers and a Sussex coast evening. I even saw it mentioned in a national Sunday, tabloid of course.

I would never know. Unless a slice of matured wedding cake was offered me with tea poured from a cat teapot.

The phone rang. It was Joshua, the amiable sponger, the ambling bearded giant who occasionally did some work and invented something bizarre. His inventions were brilliant but he never made any money from them.

'Hello, cook of my dreams,' he said. 'What's on the menu for supper tonight?'

'Air,' I said. 'You can have it baked, boiled or grilled.'

'Aren't you eating? You know, it isn't good for you, all this dieting. Haven't you read *Barbara Jones' Diary*?'

'*Bridget*,' I corrected. 'Yes, I have, but seriously, I haven't had time to go shopping. Work. Busy. Overtime. You say it, I'm doing it.'

'Safeways stays open late.'

'How wonderful,' I said. 'Why don't you pop in and get some food, then I'll cook it. See you in half an hour?'

I had a leisurely bath in lavender oil and put on a clean track suit, periwinkle blue with a logo of flowers across the front. I knew Joshua would ring again. I had plenty of time. The phone rang as I was watching a news programme.

'Sorry, can't get the car to start,' he mumbled. 'I'll come another time when you are more prepared, got something nicely simmering in the oven.'

Like his head, I nearly said. I knew he wouldn't go shopping. Spend his own money on food? Not his style. The notes were glued to his wallet. I smiled to myself. Poor, lonely Joshua.

'What a pity,' I said. 'I'll just have to curl up in front of the telly with a smoked salmon sandwich, green salad and a bottle of Shiraz.'

I heard the double take. Would his clapped-out car miraculously start by remote control?

He swallowed hastily. I'd cornered him and he couldn't get out of it. 'Glad you aren't going to starve, Jordan. Think of me with my tin of tomato soup.'

'I'm thinking,' I said, putting down the phone.

I had bought a copy of a daily newspaper, just checking on weddings, but had not had time to look at it. I folded it back to the front page and the headlines hit me with a hammer blow. My sandwich stopped mid-air.

CHARRED BODY OF COUNCILLOR FOUND
ADRIAN FENWICK DIES
SHOCK DISCOVERY

Latching firemen's gruesome discovery has today been solved. The body found in the fire at Fenwick Future Homes has been identified as that of Councillor Adrian Fenwick, owner of the showroom.

Dental records prove beyond doubt that it was Cllr Fenwick who lost his life in the fire. Fire Investigation Teams are still working with the police on the theory of arson. 'We have lost a very fine member of the Council,' said the Mayor, Cllr Tom Bedford. 'Our sympathy goes to Hilary, his wife, and their son.'

Mrs Fenwick, a member of Latching Women's Institute, was unavailable for comment.

Miss Leroy Anderson, personal assistant to Cllr Fenwick, said that her employer often worked late at the office. She did not know how the fire started.

The cremation is to be private but details of the Memorial Service will be announced later.

I sat back, shocked. And DI James never told me. He must have known the victim's identity when we met on the beach. That was pretty mean.

There was a blurred photograph of Cllr Fenwick waving to the electorate on the last polling day, his hand raised high in the air as if sensing victory. By his side stood his wife, feather-hatted, smiling hesitantly, bag clutched to her waist.

I took a closer look at the face of the

public wife. She was middle-aged with neatly waved hair and a resigned expression. This woman was not the BMW wife I had met. No way. This woman was someone different.

# Nine

More rain fell in the next twelve hours than Latching normally has in a month. The forecasters measured the downpour in inches. It sounded like a herd of rampaging buffalos on the roof of my bedroom. Another broken night. The roads and gutters were awash, overflowing. I was glad of the step up into my shop. It didn't get flooded, but many shops did and the next morning the assistants were mopping up dirty water and throwing out sodden carpets. Basement workrooms were a foot deep in water.

There were old photographs in Latching Town Museum of the great flood of the thirties when boats were used to navigate the low-lying streets. That was before they built up the shoreline and added groynes along the seafront to slow down the impact of the waves. In the late nineteenth century, a whole pub was washed out to sea. The catastrophe of the year. Drinkers wept.

My wellington boots came in for a good slosh as I waded through patches of deep puddles. Latching's dogs were having a glorious time in the running gutters, spraying passers-by as they shook the wet out of their coats. It's only when there's a downpour of that immensity that one discovers the uneven levels of different roads. The council ought to do something about it instead of pulling down historic houses and turning them into car parks and bowling alleys. My pet pedestal of disgust.

Apart from the wellies, I made an effort to look mournful and decent for my sympathy visit to the recently bereaved Mrs Fenwick. She would not be wanting photos, dates and times of philandering now that her husband was dead. But which Mrs Fenwick was I visiting? The woman in the newspaper photo or the BMW version? Vision of a ladybird car was fast fading. I was doomed to two wheels.

The Fenwicks owned one of the best seafront houses at the Goring end of West Latching. It was white with a green roof, double bay windows with a big sun balcony jutting out along the front of the first floor. A double garage housed their cars, her BMW and his Rover saloon. The garden was spacious and neatly planted with trimmed shrubs and dahlias in rows. It did not seem her style but perhaps he was the gardener. And that seemed unlikely too. Perhaps they paid a gardener and let him do what he liked.

I stood in the glass porch, straightening my black leather jacket and newest indigo jeans. The weather had sent me digging out winter polo-necked jerseys. I had three, one white, one navy and one nearly black. This one was the nearly black, suitably mournful.

A woman answered the door bell. She was middle-aged, her hair a carefully tinted pale brown, figure broadening round the waist, neat blouse and grey skirt, the matt denier of light support stockings on her legs. She must be the housekeeper I had spoken to on the phone. Her face was hollowed and drawn out as if she, too, had not slept.

'I'm Jordan Lacey,' I said. 'I'd like to give my condolences to Mrs Fenwick. May I see her, please? Would it be convenient?'

'I'm Mrs Fenwick,' she said tremulously. 'I'm afraid I don't know you but it's very kind of you to call.'

'You're Mrs Fenwick?' I could not keep the surprise out of my voice. This was no svelte blonde in skin-tight white pants and glossed lip paint, leaning on a BMW like it was a photo-shoot for *Hello* magazine.

Now I saw that this was the woman who had been standing beside Adrian Fenwick in the polling day newspaper photo, the waving photograph. The woman in a feathered hat. And she had been crying recently. Her pale eyes were filling even now. I ought to go. It was the wrong time.

'I'm sorry,' I went on. 'But I'm a little confused. I understood that someone I met recently was Mrs Fenwick, but I must have been mistaken.'

'I daresay it's quite a common name.' She was talking for talking's sake. She took out a hanky that was tucked up her sleeve. It looked crushed and damp.

'I'd better go.'

'No, please don't go. I am Mrs Hilary Fenwick, I assure you,' she said with admirable composure. 'Would you like to come in? I'm just about to make some coffee. Instant, I'm afraid.'

'Thank you. Instant would be fine.'

I followed this different Mrs Fenwick into her immaculate house which was all late fifties and sixties. It had a kind of permanent look, that durable feeling. Homely but with expensive touches that plenty of money bought. The thick mushroom carpeting which continued along the hall and up the stairs; the good Venetian glass on a shelf; the genuine oil paintings of storms and yachts and moonlit liners on the walls.

'My husband loves ... loved sea paintings,' she said, seeing my glance wandering over the seascapes that hung on the walls of the hall.

'I do too,' I said. 'Anything to do with the sea. I'm a sea person.'

'You would have got on well with Adrian.

134

Is your birthday in July?'

'Yes. The fourth.'

She nodded knowingly. 'His was the sixteenth. All Cancer people love the sea. It's part of your genes. He couldn't keep away from the sea. That's why he worked along the coast. He hated being inland. London bored him, made him irritable.'

I suddenly had a different feeling for the charred body in Latching Hospital mortuary. I was always roaming the beach or walking the pier, sitting on my rock. My second home, my pied de mer, left over from a prehistoric crawling out of the sea beginning. I toed off my wellies and left them in the porch.

This older Mrs Fenwick took me into her kitchen. It was purely functional, grey and checked pink, probably quite new. I could just see her making an elaborate wedding cake here, icing the layers on the wide, pink formica work surfaces. The draining board was cluttered with unwashed cups and saucers. She had obviously been drinking a lot of coffee but not eating.

Mrs Fenwick made coffee, enquiring about milk and sugar and carried a tray outside to a big glassed conservatory, very new with a set of bamboo chairs, deeply upholstered and cushioned in a floral material.

'This is nice,' I said, sitting down.

'One of Adrian's ideas,' she said. 'It's

135

brand new. We could be outdoors even in the winter, he said.'

There were more tears in her eyes and I wondered again if this call was a good idea. But I was dead (sorry) curious. It might help Mrs Fenwick to have someone to talk to. She was a million miles away from the other Mrs Fenwick.

'First, I must say how sorry I was to read about your husband's death,' I said, sipping the coffee. It wasn't that bad. 'But I must confess that I thought I was to give my sympathy to another lady.'

'I don't understand.'

'Neither do I. I recently met a lady, who introduced herself as Mrs Fenwick and who asked me to undertake some work for her and who arranged to pay me by standing order.'

'What sort of work?'

This was tricky. Even my good clothes could not take away the tackiness of the case work.

'I'm a private investigator. She wanted me to follow her husband, that is, your husband, Councillor Adrian Fenwick, to see if he was having an affair. She wanted photos, dates ... you know, that kind of thing.'

'How awful. Not my Adrian. Never.' Mrs Fenwick pushed the hanky against her nose. 'It's a ridiculous idea,' she said, blinking. It clearly meant nothing to her. 'My husband?

136

My husband having an affair with a woman? That's not possible, not true, never. Adrian was a wonderful husband. Someone is playing a joke on you. It's a hoax. He was never unfaithful. I can vouch for that, one hundred per cent.'

Oh dear, now I had upset her. Fool. I put down my coffee cup and patted her on the shoulder. I'm not good at sisterly patting. Perhaps I should go to touch classes. They say that touch is often more comforting than words.

'I met this woman in the multi-storeyed car park, this woman who called herself Mrs Fenwick, after the WI wedding display was vandalised,' I said, trying to take her mind off Adrian. 'Mrs Drury asked me to take the case on, then I arranged to meet this lady who had made the wedding cake—'

'But I made the wedding cake,' she protested. 'And someone stole it. I was very upset. It had taken me hours to decorate. Four layers of icing.'

'Could it be that somehow, someone is intercepting your telephone calls? Is that at all possible? Did Mrs Drury call your home or your mobile? Can you remember what you were doing the afternoon of the Agricultural Show?'

'I was there,' she said, straightaway. 'I was at the show.'

'You were there? But Mrs Drury went

away to phone you.'

'I was in a different marquee. I was in Crafts. Yes, I do have a mobile but I lost it the day before somewhere. Adrian's always on at me about losing things.' She stopped. He wouldn't be on at her any more. 'I make dolls. All different nationalities, in national costumes. This year, I entered Greek and Indonesian. Would you like to see them? I've a whole room full of my dolls.' She looked at me hopefully.

My heart sank a degree. I was not into dolls unless I was selling a painted china-faced doll stuffed with sawdust in my shop. 'Perhaps another time? I'd really like to solve the current misunderstanding first. You're saying you didn't get a call from Mrs Drury because you were somewhere else, and had lost your phone anyway?'

'I only found out about the stolen wedding cake hours later. I met some of the WI members in the refreshment tent. They were very upset. So was I. That cake was made for ... for a special wedding. Now I'll have to make another one.'

'So you didn't get the call from Mrs Drury?'

'I never spoke to her. I don't know who got the call.'

Nor did I. Nor would I ever know. Unless there was a way of tracing back a standing order. Big joke. Banks and building societies

138

were tight-mouthed with information.

I put down my cup. I didn't know where I was with this. Perhaps I had imagined the BMW Mrs Fenwick and her standing order. I ought to check with my bank again. Could you get Alzheimer's at twenty-eight?

'Thank you for the lovely coffee, Mrs Fenwick. And I'm so sorry again, about your husband. Do you know what he was doing at the office so late?'

'Oh yes, he often worked late. It was nothing unusual. He liked having the office to himself when it was empty. Liked to catch up on the work. He always took a thermos of coffee with him. He'd rung me earlier to say he would be very late and not to wait up.' She looked away, blinking back tears. It was the last time he had spoken to her.

That's what the BMW Mrs Fenwick had said. He often worked late. Perhaps he did. Somewhere here was a line of truth. But I hadn't found it yet.

'So you made him his usual thermos of coffee that evening?'

Mrs Fenwick burst into tears. 'No, I never made any coffee. I let him down.'

I left the house hurriedly. But I had to ask because there had been a melted lump of silver thermos on the desk nearest the safe.

The floods were draining away, leaving litter and glistening tarmac. Cars drove through the remaining pools, spraying water over pedestrians.

I walked back to town slowly, savouring the fresh air, freshening my airways with ozone. Out at sea some windsurfers were skimming the waves like gaudy butterflies, taking advantage of the wind direction. I could still smell that charred body. Dental records, they'd said. Perhaps a Rolex watch and handmade Italian leather shoes, too. Leather doesn't burn fast. It smoulders.

Two Mrs Fenwicks and each so different. Were they model one and a future Mark II model? It was a fair guess. Perhaps the Mark II model was actually the one on the side, but why had she wanted Adrian followed was a mystery. Or was there a third female, some little flaxen-haired teenager with washboard stomach that had captivated his romantic heart and warmed his ageing bones? He was a Cancerian, after all.

And who had killed him? DI James seemed set on arson, nothing accidental, no falling asleep over a lighted cigarette, no electrical short-circuit. As far as DI James had said, there were traces of petrol and a candle in a waste bin. Very odd. Especially with Adrian Fenwick already in the office. Unless they didn't know he was there. Maybe he was drugged. Already non compos mentis. Only emerging from his drugged state when he could hardly breathe, smoke-clogged, dragging himself to the safe, trying to shut himself inside, away from the inferno.

Why should I think he was drugged? Because he was an efficient businessman, ran a successful chain of estate agents; because it was out of character for him to be caught out.

It was an awful death, especially for a man who loved the sea. I had a rapport with him if you could rapport with a dead man, a cheating dead man. A double-cheating man. It was possible in a funny way.

The bank cashiers changed faces every few weeks. Maybe they wore masks. I never saw the same person twice. William Weaver was now on sick leave. I felt responsible.

'There's a new standing order,' I said. 'Has it been paid into my account this week? I'd like it checked.' I gave the account number.

'Yes, the standing order has been paid in, Miss Lacey,' said the girl, a bright young thing in a patterned bank uniform blouse. She keyed up my account and wrote a sum on a memo notelet. 'Here's your current statement.'

I nearly went up the wall. This was ridiculous. My account showed a total of £6,000 plus. Another £2,000 had been paid in. Correctly deposited as the jargon goes.

'I really must see the deputy manager,' I said with a sinking feeling. 'This is beyond a joke. Something must be done at once.'

141

This was an even younger manager. He looked as if he had just left school or was doing work experience.

'I have checked and see that the sum of two thousand pounds cash was paid into your account yesterday and there was nothing unusual about the payment. You have made a similar payment recently.'

'Not unusual?' I nearly yelled. 'They are all unusual and not mine. I didn't pay them in and the money belongs to someone else. I keep telling you to take it out. Would you please remove it.'

'I have no authority to remove it,' he said pompously, dabbing a speck of sweat off his downy upper lip. He didn't even shave yet.

'I'm giving you the authority,' I snarled. I was feeling really anti every bank and building society that existed. It was back to under the mattress any minute. To hell with the Euro, credit cards, e-mail and technology. I'm a pounds, shillings and pence girl. Correction: pounds and pence. None of those stupid pees, please. I'm not using loo money every time I buy a cauliflower.

I left the building before I lost my temper. They could sort out the muddle. It was not my problem. I washed my hands of it. I fancied some cholesterol-coated fish and chips for a late lunch and stormed into Maeve's Cafe. At least she would give me a welcome and cook fish how I liked it. Fresh from the sea, caught by one of her brown-skinned lovers.

'Hello, Mavis,' I said, shedding my leather jacket as I went into her fried-up heat. I took my usual table by the window where I could people watch through the steamed glass.

'Sorry, we're full,' said Mavis.

'Full? Don't be daft. You're not full.' I didn't understand what she was talking about. The place was half empty.

'I'm expecting a coachload,' she said, not meeting my eyes. 'From Blackpool. Coming down for the lights.'

'Is this a joke?' I asked. 'Latching has lights. Yes, a pretty good display for a small Sussex seaside town but nobody actually comes just to see them, especially not from Blackpool. Fish and chips, please, Mavis, the way I like them. And you know how.'

'I'm sorry, I can't serve you,' she said, her face soldered all stiff and disapproving. She drummed her fingers on the table. 'Would you mind leaving? I'm busy.'

'What? Too busy? Too busy for an old friend? Mavis, please explain in English. I don't understand. What's the matter? What's going on? I've been eating here for years. Why the cold shoulder?'

'I don't serve arsonists,' she said, flouncing off with a twitch of her head.

I froze in my seat. This hurt. The silence drained my mind.

# Ten

Indignation followed immediately. I could have torn DI James apart, limb from limb. Have him mounted for a mantelpiece. I knew he ate at Maeve's Cafe regularly but he had no right to talk about me. I could sue. I would sue the whole West Sussex Police Force, defamation of character, loss of earnings, stress, withdrawal of local eating servery, the lot.

A female Lacey when she is aroused is a fearsome beast. I fled the cafe, stamped the deck of the pier, kicked shingle, trashed seaweed, then opened my neglected shop and dressed both windows in funereal black. Within minutes I had sold a black silk scarf, a black biscuit barrel and a pair of ginettes. Ginettes are thick glasses with little bowls for the gin. I had thought of drowning my sorrows in neat gin. A passing moment of pained, diurnal self-pity. Liver destruction.

I made £18 in as many minutes. It cheered me up no end. Perhaps the clue to selling was colour coordination. A blue window, a pink window, apricot, saffron, indigo,

144

striped, spotted. Give me a colour, I'll make you a window.

I celebrated the easy money by getting some business cards printed at one of those self-service machines in the shopping arcade. The choice of personal logos was bewildering. I was hardly a typewriter or a flowerpot. Nothing suitable for First Class Investigations. I settled for a top and bottom border of question marks. I could always change the design as I only had fifty printed. I practised saying: 'My card,' with a flourish. Then I tried authoritative. Next voice used was more humble. Plain, expressionless won.

What I really needed was a healthy dose of pure jazz. A steady drumbeat, tinkling keyboard, soaring saxes, blazing trumpets bursting my eardrums. Magic. My own trumpeter ... where art thou now? Rehearsing in the studio, taking dearest wife out to a candlelit dinner, driving round the North on nightly gigs? I didn't even know what kind of car he drove.

Work ahead was obvious. I had to get fixes on Terence Lucan, the late Adrian Fenwick and Mrs Drury, bless her grey knitted cardigan. Find out if they had any kind of record that had caught the eye of the police. If I was to clear myself of this arson charge, then I had to find out who had really torched the showroom. Although Terence

Lucan was not linked in any way, the fact that I was investigating the theft of his water lilies might in some way be a threat to someone else. Confusing.

DI James was in Maeve's Cafe, attacking a huge plate of sausage, mushroom, eggs and chips. He was slurping tomato sauce over the succulent heap. I marched in, straight past Mavis and handed him one of my freshly printed cards.

'My card,' I said, plain, expressionless.

He peered at it as if he did not know who I was. 'Most impressive,' he said. 'What do all the question marks mean? That you are not sure what or whom you are investigating?'

'You owe me one,' I said, helping myself to a big, fat chip. It was delicious, taste-bud zapping.

'Quit stealing my chips,' he said.

'You told Mavis I set fire to Fenwick Future Homes.'

'I did not.'

'She knows. I mean, she knows that you suspect me but not that you don't now.'

'Clear as mud. You should take lessons on how to articulate your thoughts.'

'You should take lessons on how to eat properly without getting tomato sauce on your chin,' I retorted.

He wiped his chin with one of Mavis's cheap and scratchy paper napkins. I grinned at the gesture. There wasn't any sauce on his chin, of course.

He sighed deeply. 'You really are immature, Jordan.'

But I noticed that he was almost amused.

'I need a quick decko at the PNC or the CRO. Please? It's all perfectly harmless but I need to know if three people have any record, however trivial.'

'And I suppose one of these people is the late Councillor Adrian Fenwick? Well, I'll save you the trouble. Clean as a whistle. Nothing. Not even a parking ticket.'

'Thank you,' I said, humble-voiced. The practising had come in useful.

'And the second?' The chips were putting him in a good mood.

'Terence Lucan. The stolen water lilies. He's one of your cases, too.'

'I know. I did follow up your chance remark and Lucan does have betting debts. There's a couple of double yellow line fines on the PNC, picked up whilst delivering shrubs to hotels. The bailiffs were called in over an unpaid tax bill. A pretty hefty one.'

Chance remark indeed. It was information. But I let it go. 'The third is a lady you may never have heard of. She's the chairman of Latching Women's Institute. Mrs Edith Drury.'

'Joey's owner.'

'Well done,' I said. 'What a memory.'

147

'How could I forget Joey? One of your more successful cases.'

He was rubbing that in as well but I let the cynic get away with it. I was in a very accommodating frame of mind.

'And what has Mrs Drury done? Been caught selling water lilies at WI meetings?'

'No,' I said carefully. 'She has lost something ... a wedding cake. Nothing of interest to you.'

'Tortoises and wedding cakes. My, my, Jordan. You do lead an exciting life.'

DI James had shaved since our clash. His chin was chiselled, clean and stubborn, jaw set and resolute. Yet the shape and softness of his lips was devastating. I wondered how many of the WPCs at Latching Police Station were losing sleep over him. Or worse, sleeping with him.

A shock wave of jealousy swept through me. It nearly took my breath away. I had never felt anything so sharp, so cutting, so debilitating. It was like being stabbed and took years off my life. I aged and shrivelled, decimated cells dying by their millions. Handfuls of hair might fall out any minute. I touched my thick plait, expecting it to have turned grey.

But it was still a reassuring tawny reddish brown. I gave it a little tug to make sure it was also attached.

James was offering me his last chip which

I took. 'You look a bit peckish,' he said. 'Are you sure you're eating properly?'

'Being a suspected arsonist does dampen the appetite,' I said faintly. 'Especially when you are innocent. And Mavis won't even serve me now. Apparently I'm not welcome here. I might give the cafe a bad name, or worse still, set fire to it.'

His face changed expression, a minute shift. He cleared his throat and signalled to catch her attention. 'Tall tea for Jordan, Mavis,' he called out. 'How she likes it, honey and stuff.'

She disappeared into the kitchen, probably to swear or down a Valium. When she came back, her face was set in thunder but she was carrying a jar of honey. She brought over a mug of tea and dumped it in front of me without saying a word.

'Thank you, Mavis,' said James. 'Put it on my bill.'

I knew now why I loved him.

He was beautiful. The moment I saw him, the sun filled the sky ... the melodic guitar of John Williams calmed my heart and filled my head. I couldn't remember the words but the song played on and on, the strings of his guitar soothing all the wounds.

Mavis was playing a tape of Cavatina, the lyric version. I hoped it was her way of saying sorry.

It was raining again, heavily, but for me

149

the sun was shining.

When DI James went, suddenly busy and professional again, I sat staring at his empty chair, trying to bring back his image. Substance is a strange thing. I could still see him so clearly and yet I couldn't bring back the body with any solidarity.

This is how it must be when someone dies. They are there but not there. My parents dying was that way. What would I do if James died, shot by some dope-crazed hoodlum in street violence? It would shred me. I would only go on half living, mourning him every empty day.

The empty chair filled. A bulky man sat in it, heavy sweater in double-knit wool, blond spiky hair already greying, his face lined but not old.

'Hi,' he said. 'You got me into a helluva lot of trouble. You owe me a coffee.'

'Right,' I agreed. I had no idea who he was. It seemed safer to go along with his suggestion. I nodded at Mavis and pointed to my new companion.

'Cappuccino,' he said loudly. 'Right for dumpy days. Picks you up.'

He had mischievous eyes, lightish brown flecked with green. He did not seem too angry with me. His hair was thinning on top. Tempus fugiting.

'I didn't know you'd left the force. I thought you were one of Her Majesty's valiant women in blue.'

It was the sub officer, the firefighter who had let me wander about the scene of the fire. I recognised the burly figure, now out of uniform and face ungrimed from smoke. He had cleaned up nicely.

'I'm sorry if I got you into trouble. It was too good an opportunity to miss. I'm a private investigator.' I flourished one of my new cards which he looked at, then pocketed. 'The estate agent figures in one of my cases.'

'I've never met a private eye,' he said, spooning the froth off the top of his coffee. 'You look ordinary enough. Aren't you supposed to wear shades?'

I didn't like looking just ordinary but I suppose it was a back-handed compliment. 'I'm off duty, Is the coffee all right?'

'Just the ticket. Investigating the fire for some insurance company, eh? Our people definitely pin arson on this one. Guess you know all about it.'

The sub officer had fallen into my lap, so to speak. A willing gossip in the shop-talk department. I'd buy him a dozen cappuccinos, pint-sized.

'Yes. But I'm out of my depth. I'm no expert on fires. How was it started?'

'Candle in a bin, oldest trick in the world.' Di James had said the same thing. 'Circle of petrol-soaked shredded paper. It left the usual tell-tale ring of ashes with central blow-out. It's the locked door that puzzles us. It was locked on the outside, so the victim didn't have a chance of getting out. He couldn't phone. Wires were cut. Windows all double-glazed and secured. Councillor Fenwick was trapped.'

I tried not to show my shock. My sensitive feelings imagined the panic, the fear.

'But there must have been some other way out. He would have known. After all he owned the place. And he had a mobile.'

'Smoke inhalation acts fast.' The sub officer spooned out the last of the froth from the sides, making pathways. 'It gets very confusing in the dark. He didn't know whether he was coming or going. That's why he crawled into the safe. He thought the steel would save him but he didn't stand a chance. Steel conducts heat.'

'Poor man. What an awful way to die. I want to be in my own bed with a glass of champagne and the Three Tenors.'

'The three whos? You'll be a bit cramped. Adrian Fenwick was out for the count. The smoke gets them first. Course, the PM might come up with something different. These forensic blokes are devilish clever. They might discover he was cracked on the head before being heaved into the safe.'

'Why would anyone do that?'

'To make sure there was enough of him

152

left to identify. If the motive is gain of some sort, then you don't want a charred John Doe in the freezer for months. Sorry, shop talk. Let's change the subject.'

I didn't want to change the subject but I knew when to stop.

'My name's Bud Morrison. Bud's short for Budweiser in case you ask. Budweiser is my favourite beer. You know how firemen get nicknames.'

'Just as well your favourite tipple isn't Stella Artois or Bonnington's,' I said.

'How about a pint along at the B&B tonight? I'll be there about nine.' He was on the make. I could tell it a mile off.

I thought fleetingly of the unobtainable DI James, my distant trumpeter playing to audiences of hundreds nightly, the moody and unstable Derek, the starving Joshua. Did I really want to start dating again? Was it sensible to add a firefighter to the list, even a hunky one?

'Oh ... all right. About nine ... Bud.'

It was sheer desperation. I don't drink beer. And this wasn't dating. I was simply meeting the man for a drink. He was a good contact. I might even put him on expenses. No one in their right mind went out with someone named after a can of beer.

I was sitting on the floor of my sitting room, writing up notes, when I heard a car draw up outside. I peered through a chink in the curtains. It was an unmarked police car. I know them all. DI James got out and looked up. He was accompanied by another officer and a uniformed WPC. Obviously not a social call.

My heart sank. Not my bike again, please. I couldn't stand the hassle. No wonder people got stressed out by police interrogations. It could ruin your sex life if you had one.

'Hello, DI James,' I said politely at the door. 'Is this a deputation? Want a petition signed about pension rights? Do you need any help with an investigation?'

'You could say that. Can we come in, Jordan? This is DC Roberts and WPC Patel. I have to ask you a few questions.' He sounded almost human. I didn't like it one bit. Ominous dark clouds gathered in the hallway. Alarm bells were going off in my head.

'OK. Come in, but either wipe your feet or take off your shoes.'

'Is this a shrine?'

'My mother always made me take off my outdoor shoes. It's a good habit.'

The WPC took off her lace-up black shoes and I could see why. She had dainty feet clad in barely black tights and her toenails were painted crimson. She was making sure DI James saw them wriggling. The two men merely wiped their shoes. Perhaps DI James had a hole in his sock. The detective constable was a young, fresh-faced officer with bad skin. He needed acne medication. I wondered if he'd like to read my book of herbal remedies.

'Can we sit down?'

Heavens. This was so formal. I checked my nails to see if they were clean.

'Of course.' DI James sat on the moral sofa with the WPC beside him. DC Roberts stood stiffly in a corner, dunce-like. I sat on the floor. I know my place.

'Can you give me details of your whereabouts on Tuesday night, early Wednesday morning?'

'The night of the fire?' I was quick.

'That's right, Jordan.'

'Is this still about my bike? It sounds so serious. Shall I put on some music? I've a great John Coltrane tape. Small venue stuff. Walking the bar.'

'Please, Jordan. No music. This is not a social call.'

'I've gathered that. No kettle on, no nuts.'

I was beginning to feel frivolous. My mind was gathering air. I couldn't take this serious stuff. Didn't he know how I felt? My mind was blowing with his closeness. All I could see were his shoes. I wanted to take them off, massage his tired toes.

'What were you doing the night of

Tuesday last?'

'Gee, that was some night,' I said, waggling my fingers shoulder height, head disco-jogging. 'OK. Let's think. I spent an hour at the Reggae Club, then I went on to the Pier Prom, later I called in at the Rose and Seraph. Sometime around midnight I cruised the singles bar in Jarrick Street, sussing the potential, then I went on to the—'

'Jordan! Stop. What a load of nonsense. I want the truth.' He looked distraught, almost paternal.

'I went to bed. I was cold. I couldn't sleep.'

Could I tell him that I had fantasised about him, imagining him lying beside me, keeping me warm, close in his arms. How my heart splintered in the cold. How I wanted him so much that it made a big pain in my stomach.

'Are you telling me that you didn't go out at all?'

'Not until early morning, when I heard the fire engines rushing by, sirens blaring. I thought I might just as well get up, go see what was happening, do a little sleuthing. It was too late for any sleep.'

DI James was covering me with concern, almost a gleam of pity in his eyes. I couldn't understand what was happening. It threw me. I was treading a minefield, blindfold.

'So?'

'Jordan Lacey. I must ask you to accompany me to the station to make a statement. Anything you may say ... et cetera, et cetera. You know the caution. Do you want a coat or something?'

'What caution? Why me? I don't understand.' I was horrified. What was happening? Was this the super massive Black Hole in our Galaxy ... or was I being framed by some criminal network who used innocent citizens? Were they zooming in on me, dragging me down? I couldn't think, my breath sucked away. My airways constricted.

'I am investigating the murder of Adrian Fenwick and I have to take a statement from you.'

'I didn't even know the man,' I protested, taking a deep breath. 'I've never met him.'

'But you know Pippa Shaw ... and you have met her. We have also had an anonymous tip-off that you have been paying in large sums of cash into your bank account. A total of six thousand pounds in the last few days. Maybe this is payment for torching Fenwick Future Homes. Not to be sniffed at.'

'This is completely ridiculous!' I broke in. 'Where did you get this from?'

'You were seen acting suspiciously near the fire and loitering about afterwards. We have several witnesses who have identified you. And Councillor Fenwick was about to demolish Trenchers, your favourite heritage building in Latching, and we all know your excessive feelings about saving the place. You might call it an obsession. That makes quite a strong motive and, knowing the financial straits of your business ... Get your coat, Jordan.'

'I don't know any Pippa Shaw. And that six thousand pounds ... it's a total mystery. Who told you that anyway? I thought banks were supposed to be confidential, like doctors. I've told the bank it's not mine, asked them to remove it but they won't,' I added faintly.

'Do you want a coat or not? It's cold outside.'

'Where are you taking me? Siberia?'

'Close.'

# Eleven

State of shock. I kept repeating and protesting my innocence all the way down the stairs and out the front door and into their waiting police car.

'Got your keys?' asked DI James before slamming the front door shut when I nodded. I'd picked them up automatically.

'Oh, I'm coming back then, am I?' I flared, struggling into my anorak. They had not even given me time to get my arms in the sleeves before bundling me into the panda. 'When this ridiculous charade is over.'

'You're not exactly a threat to the community. Someone will probably stand bail for you,' he said.

Bail. That meant business. I couldn't believe what I was hearing. Who would stand bail for me? None of my friends had any money. Not bail kind of money. I was beginning to wish I had been nicer to Derek. The knuckle-cracking miser probably had thousands stacked away in gilts. He'd charge me interest.

'Social call,' I said airily to Sergeant

Rawlings as they marched me into the station. At least DI James had not used handcuffs. I'd only come to make a statement, hadn't I? This was not an arrest, or had I missed something?

Sergeant Rawlings looked as miserable as a born-again sinner. He obviously did not believe all this nonsense. 'Wanna cuppa of tea, Jaws?' he asked, making like it was a station Open Day. It was a gesture.

I nodded. The Jaws choked me. I never thought I'd be pleased to hear that name. DI James led me into the nicest of the interview rooms. The one with a homely touch. Some WPC had put a pot plant on top of a filing cabinet.

'What, no SO13?' I said. SO13 was the Anti Terrorist Squad at Scotland Yard. 'I'm sure you're going to accuse me of every unsolved crime left on the books.'

DI James slipped a tape into the machine, switched it on, recited date and time. 'Detective Inspector James interviewing Jordan Lacey—'

'Miss Jordan Lacey, please,' I interrupted.

'Miss Jordan Lacey,' he said wearily and continued with the procedural rigmarole. 'Now, Miss Lacey, would you tell me what you were doing last Tuesday night? Speak clearly, please, and don't mumble.'

'I never mumble. My diction is excellent. In school plays...'

'Keep to the subject. Your movements on the night of the fire, please.'

'Movements? You mean which leg did I move first, the left or the right? Was my arm up in the air, that sort of thing?' I could see I had gone too far by the clouds gathering on his face. 'Sorry, just a little light relief on this pretty dismal occasion. OK, what did I do on the night of the fire ... I was damned cold, I remember that. And no, I didn't start the fire to get warm. I didn't start the fire at all. I lay in bed, shivering.'

'Go on.'

'I couldn't sleep. I nearly got up to find a T-shirt but I was too cold to get up.' WPC Patel gave a little cough. She had worked it out that I was sleeping nude. I glanced at DI James. He had not worked it out. Bless his cotton socks, holes and all. The man was an innocent. My face softened.

'Some time I must have gone to sleep. Froze to sleep, I guess. Because I woke up suddenly. Woken up by the sirens and the engines racing by. Of course, I checked everywhere. I thought at first my place was on fire, or my shop, but they were going in a different direction. By the time I'd done all that, I had woken up completely and thought I might as well go out and see what was cooking. Sorry, I mean, what was happening.'

'Are you in the habit of following fire

161

engines at dawn?'

'Of course not. I have odd habits but not that one. It was the first time ... I mean, who in their right mind goes out at dawn to watch a fire?'

'Exactly.'

I'd fallen into my own trap but it was becoming like an aural story-telling group. The picture was growing in my mind and I was warming (oh dear) to the theme.

'I wrapped up warm.' Oh dear again. 'Do you want to know what I was wearing? Right, omit clothes. Well, then, I was not the only sightseer. There was quite a crowd gathering. I hope you are interviewing the dozens of other people standing around on the pavement when they ought to have been safely in bed. It was still a pretty chilly dawn. Clouds of mist and fog rolling up from the sea. Then there was the reception-ist, Miss Leroy Anderson, weeping buckets and moaning the loss of her mascara. I consoled her and gave her a little bit of sisterly advice. Then I spoke to this nice sub officer. Or was it the other way round? Yes, I spoke to the nice firefighter first, then I spoke to Leroy. But he spoke to me before I spoke to him.'

DI James was drawing on his reserves of patience. He threw me a dart of silent scorn.

As I stopped for breath, DI James said evenly: 'I understand you drew the attention

162

of one of the fire crew to the body in the safe.'

'Not exactly drew attention. I didn't know exactly what it was. I was only guessing because of the smell. I mean, I'm no expert. It could have been anything. And there was so much debris piled everywhere. I mean, plastic melts, doesn't it? I've no idea what steel does. Perhaps there were plastic items in the safe. Or somebody's shopping, the weekend joint or pork chops. Perhaps they kept copier toner or primer in the safe which gave off the funny smell.'

Sergeant Rawlings came in with slopping mugs of tea. DI James announced a break and switched off the tape with an abrupt movement.

'You know you've been talking absolute nonsense, don't you, Jordan? I ought to arrest you for wasting police time. I don't know when I last heard such a load of rubbish.'

'That's what this is, James, rubbish. And you know that it's total rubbish,' I said earnestly, my elbows on the table, yawning. Suddenly I was almost too tired to pick up the tea. It was strong, navy-brew, but I drank some just the same, hardly noticing the bitter taste. When I put the mug back down James restarted the tape.

'You know and I know,' I went on, 'that it's all circumstantial evidence because you've nothing better to offer. No leads to go on, nothing. Only the sighting of someone looking vaguely like me on my bike and a can of petrol which anyone could have put there. Anyway, half the population of Latching is carrying around cans since the petrol stations ran out in the VAT tax dispute. Isn't that true?'

'True, but the fire was started with petrol.'

'So, what's new? There are only a limited number of ways of starting a fire. Petrol is an obvious choice.'

'Your choice?'

'Don't be daft. I didn't start the fire. I didn't murder Councillor Fenwick. The money isn't mine. I didn't put it into my account. And I don't know anyone called Pippa Shaw. Can I go home now, please? Anyway, how do you know about the cash in my bank? Who's been talking?'

'I didn't say the body was Councillor Fenwick's.'

'It's in all the newspapers.'

'I didn't say he was murdered.'

'Well, I think he was murdered. If he wasn't murdered then how come the door was locked on the outside?'

Oh dear. Too late. Tongue slip. Bud had told me that. Damage limitation necessary. But DI James knew he had caught me out and it was too late to retrieve what I had said.

164

'Classified?' My smile lied. 'Sorry. Some-one told me. In confidence.'

'I won't ask how you know that. But don't worry, eventually I will.'

He switched off the tape. 'Interview con-cluded at...' He looked at his watch. 'At five forty-five p.m, owing to extreme tiredness of witness.'

'Thank you,' I said, sinking on to the table. 'I like your pot plant. It's a spider plant, *anthericum*. Fully hardy. You have to keep it well watered in the summer.'

They let me go home and I was not quite sure why. I had to walk. They weren't going to waste a car on taking me. I went down to the sea, seeking solace from the waves and the birds. I needed solitude to think. The sea was a cold grey, creamed a dirty white in troughs. The tide was coming in, eating up the shoreline with insidious hunger. It was drizzling lightly and a boisterous wind whipped the rain down my bare neck. Not nice. The moistness crept along my skin with icy fingers.

I walked the length of the pier. Even the noise and heat coming from the amusement arcade did not comfort me. The ice-cream kiosks were closed, deserted, shuttered up for the winter.

My friend Jack, the manager, might cheer me up. But when I looked in, I saw that he was in the middle of an argument with a punter. Someone caught cheating or feeding buttons into a machine. It was not a good time. Jack was one of my fans. I still have the teddy bear he gave me.

I leaned over the rail at the far end. Trawlers and tankers hung on the horizon like items of washing. We were too far away to see the ferries from Newhaven or the cruise liners from Southampton. I drank in the blustery air, hoping the ozone would clear my woolly brain. How was I going to get myself out of this mess? I could hardly hire a PI.

A seagull hopped on to the railing beside me, cocked his head, a beady eye on my pockets.

'Sorry, bird, I've got nothing for you.' I spread out my empty hands and he flew off, wings spread wide, screeching with indignation. Get that, he squawked angrily. She's come on the pier with nothing.

I remembered I had a shop to run and a case to solve. Rerun water lilies. Mrs Drury had paid me off and the real Mrs Hilary Fenwick had not hired me. So who exactly had I met in the car park? Now that was worth finding out, except that no one would be paying me. And, just out of curiosity, where had Mr Fairbrother gone? Now, if the body in the safe had been Mr Fairbrother then DI James would have had a puzzle of mega dimension on his hands.

My shop needed dusting. I did a five-second flit with a J-cloth. I tipped out the old coffee grains and washed the pot. My veins needed coffee. My bones needed heat. My body needed DI James. But I had to be realistic. I made fresh coffee.

A man crept into the shop. I hardly noticed him arriving. He was like a shadow, shallow breathing, tiptoeing on soft soles. He looked behind him as if being followed. His face was gaunt, greenish, unhealthy, hardly customer material.

'Hello,' I said brightly, changing into shop mode. 'Can I help you?'

'I'm still being followed. They think I'm him. One day they'll kill me.'

I scanned through my memory banks. I had met this nutter before. He thought the Sicilian Mafia were after him, or was it the lot from Naples? Did they write operas by the score on crime-off days?

'Are you still being followed? That's a shame. Must blight your social life.'

'What social life? What life have I got at all? They make every minute a misery.'

'Why don't you just change your name? Take on a new identity. If they really think you are this Al person, then make him disappear from sight.'

'But I'd lose my job.'

'You work in a garage, don't you? What's more important? Your job or your life?'

'You mean, just go?' It had not occurred to him before. It sank in like lead.

'Take out what money and savings you have in the bank. Cash everything. Pack your bags. Speak to no one. Get on a train, if there are any running, and go as far away as possible. Change your appearance, grow a beard, dye your hair and start a new life somewhere else. You'll find a job, something different.'

I scanned my classic book shelves. I wished I had time to read them. Retirement fantasy. Reading in bed. I wondered what James would read. 'Here's a nice new name for you.' I juggled authors. 'How about Ernest Dickins? Or William Swift?'

His face lit up with hope. 'Do you think it would really work? I like Ernest Swift. Very nice. I could be Ernest Swift, a real man's name.'

'Then move like one. Get going. Fly! Leave Latching today, tomorrow at the latest. And good luck, Mr Swift.'

Some days later a grubby envelope arrived in the post. The postmark was Newcastle-upon-Tyne, gateway to the world. Inside was a fifty-pound note and a scrawled message on a torn page: 'With swift thanks.'

I hoped he would be all right. My advice had not been considered. More off the top of my head.

★ ★ ★

This had to be almost the worst day of my life. But I was free and determined to clear my name. Someone looking like me had been seen riding on my bike, that's all. It was a slender hope that someone else had seen her/him. There was still time to begin trawling the shops, any traders that opened early, the bakers, the butchers, fishmongers, greengrocers, post office sorting depot.

One of the postmen thought he had seen someone riding my bike. He'd been arriving for work just before dawn.

'Looked like your mountain bike, but I knew it wasn't you,' he said.

'Why? Because it was so early?'

'Nope. They were wearing one of them yellow luminous armbands so they don't get run over in the dark. You'd never bother with one of those.'

I breathed a sigh of relief. 'Do you mind if I pass on that little bit of information? No hassle. Just something that confirms it wasn't me.'

'Sure. You tell 'em. Tell 'em I said so. Mitch Swartz. Anytime. Just ask for me.'

'Thanks a lot, Mitch. I owe you.'

'I'll cash that one day.'

I traced my steps to where I had left my bike chained to railings round the corner from the FFH showroom. I don't know what I expected to find. The chain and pad-lock had been the average Woolworths purchase. Neither the gutter nor the pavement had been swept for days, weeks. The Latching street cleaners had barely glanced at this area.

I got down on my knees and inch by inch sifted the debris with a plastic paddle once used for stirring take-away coffee. It was a disgusting mess of bits and pieces, smelly and sticky brown. I tried to concentrate on identifying the junk, pushing the stink to the back of my mind.

My knees began to hurt from the hard pavement. Two wet stains spread roundly on my jeans. People hurried past, not looking, in case I was an embarrassment.

Then I found what I wanted. A single severed link of cheap chain. It had been cut cleanly with a hacksaw and barely splintered on impact. I put the link carefully in a plastic specimen bag, sealing the top. A sudden rush of hope hit me. Yes! Perhaps the future was not inky black after all. It was possible I could clear myself.

But how to find out who was putting the money into my bank account and how did DI James find out? I would not mind becoming a baggy, bundle of misery, wrapped in a sleeping bag in some shop doorway, doing a spot of surveillance. But my bank had two branches, one at each end of the town. With my luck, I'd choose the wrong one to survey.

I felt a hand on my shoulder and someone crouching down beside me.

'Are you all right, Jordan? What's the matter, baby? Have you lost something?'

That voice. I would know that voice anywhere, in a crowd of a thousand voices. It cut right through to my heart. It was my trumpeter. My music man. He had appeared when I was at my lowest ebb like a guardian angel. The man who had a trumpet and a wife.

He helped me to my feet, his kindly brown eyes filled with concern, wing of silky hair flopping over his eyes. He was my height. We stood facing.

'Yes, I had lost something but I think I have found it.' I waved the plastic bag with the chain link. 'Hopefully this will solve some mysteries.'

'You never got that coffee the last time we met. Would you like it now?'

'Yes, please,' I said like a little girl waiting for a treat.

We sat over coffee in an Italian sea-front cafe that wanted to close up and we talked and talked. I told him about the fire and being accused of being an arsonist. He was appalled, indignant even, talked protests. Then he told me about the gigs he had played round the country and how the band was and repeated the current running jokes.

I laughed, drank in his voice, his kindness,

his casual appearance. Black polo jersey, black leather jacket and black trousers. Very trad jazz looking. Life slowed down and became more civilised.

'Are you playing in Latching?' I asked, suddenly overtired, exhausted with talking, absorbing his energy to stay awake.

'I thought I'd go along to the Bear and Bait this evening, blow a few notes, air a few tunes. Do you want to come along?'

'Yes, please,' I said again, about five years old.

I didn't know where the time went afterwards. The invitation revitalised me. He had things to do. I had two baths, changed my clothes a dozen times, ate yogurt, washed my hair, plaited it, unplaited it. Eventually I arrived at the Bear and Bait, very clean, wearing white jeans and bulky black jersey, my hair braided with beads. It had taken me hours to arrive at such unusual sartorial elegance.

A large glass of red wine was waiting for me at a table. He was waiting too. He kissed my cheek lightly. It was a butterfly's touch. 'Hello, sweetheart,' he said tenderly.

There was a four-piece group playing in a corner of the pub. Drums, sax, guitar and keyboard. The musicians took one look at my trumpeter and they fell apart. Everyone recognised him. They knew him and his magic.

'Mind if I blow a few notes?' he asked, taking his trumpet out of its case.

I forgot everything in the glorious music of the next hour. It was an unstoppable torrent of improvisation that flowed from his heart. He poured out his bittersweet magic, his energy, his fun and one-liners bursting through the smoky bar like rays of sunshine. We were transported. No one wanted it to end. He could have played all night, his muted trumpet swerving through tantalising textures and melodies. I was drained just with living the music. It could have been a moment to die.

'Where's your coat?' he asked, wiping the mouthpiece, then removing it and putting his trumpet away, closing the lid.

'I don't think I brought one.'

'It's cold. It's nearly winter. You need someone to look after you.'

He draped his jacket over my shoulders, waved goodbye to everyone and pushed open the door. It was bitter outside after the stuffy pub. Frost glittered among the stars.

'You'll get cold,' I protested.

'I'm carrying a little more weight.'

He left me at my front door, shoulders stooping. He never came in. There was a wife to consider. A wife he obviously loved. I didn't know where I came in the orbit of his life.

'Goodbye, Jordan. Take care and don't

worry. Everything will work out. They must realise you are innocent.'

'I wish I could be sure.'

He held me in a warm, sweet hug. I felt the heat of his body seeping into mine. 'I wish we were allowed two wives,' he said. Then he turned and left, disappearing into the night.

# Twelve

Trenchers to be pulled down? A small industrial complex to be built on the site? The news item on the radio was brief and depressing. Was this what Councillor Fenwick had in mind when he gave his approval to planning permission?

What would they produce? Cheap clothes, plastic toys, garage tools, garden sheds, gnomes?

I sat on the side of my bed, mug of tea in hand, listening to the news. I had overslept, now I was insensed with rage. That empty shell of a grand old hotel meant so much to me. How could some get-rich-quick developer pull it down? I loved every stone and window and wrought-iron balcony. It was a relic of times gone past, when elegance and quality were paramount. I thought about chaining myself to the palatial front entrance.

Even the name, Trenchers, went deep into Latching's history. It was an old name, probably Saxon. The Trencher family had onced owned a coaching hostelry on a

175

crossroads near the South Downs, then years later bought a tall Georgian terraced property in Latching that grew into a popular boarding house. At the turn of the century they built the most famous hotel along the South Coast. An Edwardian masterpiece. European kings and heads of state had stayed there. It was the first hotel to have a car park.

'Everyone knows how you feel about the old hotel.' I heard DI James's voice accusing me. 'It adds up to a motive.'

But a motive to kill? I didn't think so.

My head was still spinning with last night's music. The trumpeter had saved my sanity and I was not going to let go of the feeling. I took the beads out of my hair, tugging at the tangles. It had not been sensible to sleep in them, but then last night I was past being sensible about anything. I had been floating on a plain where not even DI James existed.

My first call was to the local newspaper office after which I planned an unannounced visit to Latching Water Gardens. I combed through back numbers on the shelves looking for the council meeting which pushed through the demolition of Trenchers. How had I missed it? I usually speedread all the newspapers, pulse on today, etc. This was an item tucked away at the end of a lengthy report. No one had taken much notice of it. The item should have been headlines. Wasn't it a graded building? Then they couldn't demolish it.

'The site will be developed by Culture Conservatories who are hoping to expand business along the South Coast,' I read.

My mind flashed back to a big glass and timber conservatory, gleaming newness and status. 'We could be outdoors even in the winter,' Mrs Fenwick had said. Were we also talking a nice little handout? A conservatory on the cheap. Perhaps a show conservatory very slightly used and no longer in the brochure. Pay later, old chap, no hurry.

I tried not to think bad things of the dead, especially a dead Cancerian. Especially not a Cancerian who died inside a safe. I shuddered. But it was all there, in front of me, highlighted in yellow. Councillor Adrian Fenwick had done a deal.

Had DI James traced the motivation back to me through Mrs Fenwick? He'd discovered that I had visited her, come to a plod-like conclusion about Trenchers and my mental health. Yet he was a good detective, I knew that. But even good policemen get bogged down by the paperwork and administration, sometimes take the quickest way out of a case.

But why me? It hurt. When I think of all the homemade soup and expensive coffee I'd poured down his throat. And that cosy house-warming party, dark paths and even darker landing ... it all counted for nothing, it seemed. I'd stick to jazz tapes and a hot-water bottle in future.

'Jordan! Good to see you, girl. How are you? Long time no see!'

It was Derek. Long time no see because he had got nasty when I halted events and he'd stalked me with intent. Not funny. Whatever had I seen in him? He was small-minded and mean and pompous. Perhaps it was the good teeth. I was a sucker for decent teeth. DI James had perfect teeth, white and strong and even. My trumpeter on the other hand was a dentist's nightmare. It was all that blowing and gripping the mouthpiece. It damaged the front teeth.

'Hi, Derek,' I said, face straight and un-welcoming. 'How are you?'

'I've got a new car. A Honda Club. She's smashing.'

'Great.' All his cars were classed female, some domination thing.

'Want to come out for a spin?'

No, I didn't. The thought of being in such a small space with him was distasteful. But I also thought of that long climb uphill which was attack-inducing even with moun-tain gears. What a creep I could be. I won-dered if I could manage fighting him off in my weakened state.

'I need to go out to Latching Water

178

Gardens at Preston Hill,' I said. Always stick to the truth if possible. 'It's hard work on my bike, uphill most of the way. I should be grateful for a lift. You needn't wait. I'll find my own way home.'

'No problem,' he said, taking my arm as if we had suddenly made up after a row. I immediately regretted my weakness. 'I might go in for a pond myself one day. A few goldfish. We could have a bite to eat afterwards.'

He had a detached house somewhere on the outskirts of Latching, inherited from his mother. I had never been to it. He had preferred my hospitality, my food, my drink. Today I'd buy him a coffee and Danish at a cafe but he wasn't coming back to my bed-sits. Oh no, those days were over. I could see I had let myself in for a sticky exit.

Derek was full of jovial good humour. He obviously thought he was back on the bandwagon, counting the croutons, feet on my sofa while the little woman slaved over a hot microwave. He was in for a shock.

I admired the new car, the radio, the automatic windows. I admired the wheelcaps, the sunroof, the motorway-style gear box. I exhausted myself admiring everything, finally got in, fastened the seat belt and realised I was paying heavily for this lift.

'Just like old times,' he said, patting my knee, cracking his knuckles. 'Fancy coming out with me this weekend?'

'One thing at a time, Derek,' I boxed. 'This is all very new.'

It was too late to get out. I wondered about a quick getaway when the traffic lights were red but timed it badly and Derek anticipated the change of lights. I'd forgotten he was a bad driver, impatient and careless. Serve me right if there was an accident. Perhaps I might be injured, just slightly, nothing too painful. DI James would be sorry then, upset that he had unjustly accused me, dragged me off to the police station. He might bring me flowers, hover by my bedside, consumed with remorse.

By car it was a mercifully short journey. Derek parked in the entrance driveway of Latching Water Gardens, leaned expectantly towards me but I was already out of the car and heading down an avenue. I waved back cheerfully, relishing the feel of freedom and escape, checking that I had my bag and my camera. I walked fast down the path, crunching leaves and gravel. He was looking bemused by my ejection-seat departure.

I knew where I was going, somewhere in the direction of where I had seen those workers. I knew Derek would not follow me. He was too fussy about mud on his shoes.

By hunching down, I hoped he would

soon lose sight of me. These were young trees and saplings, still verdant green, half hiding me from view. Keeping my head down meant looking on the ground. Mr Lucan kept a tidy nursery. There was barely a weed in sight.

Go for a spin. I'd done that, gone for a spin. I'd admired his new car. I'd endured his company for ten minutes. It was not a contract. I'd fulfilled my part. So why was I still frightened of him?

Then I noticed something. The slimmest pointed petal, waxen and palely pink, beginning to curl brown at the edges. There was another petal further along, then another. I put them carefully in a plastic bag. I was not sure quite why at this stage.

In a clearing was an irregular area of newly trodden earth. It was near where I had seen the worker working on my last visit. But there were no workers anywhere today. Perhaps he had paid him off. I walked round the area, leaving footprints. It had rained recently. Come on, I told myself, find something.

I found something. It was a root, about three inches long, soft and smelly. I took a photo of the root where it was lying. It meant nothing to me but I put it in a separate bag. Not a lot for an hour's work. I hoped Derek had given up by now and gone home. Still I would not risk walking back up the avenues, but would find a way out lower down. I might hitch a lift back to Latching or walk.

A long way down I found a broken fence and climbed over it on to the road, tearing my jeans on a scrap of rusty wire. I wondered whether to try for a lift. Just my luck if Derek came along. But the first vehicle down the hill was a white van. Despite all the bad press and Crimewatch warnings about white vans, I stood on the roadside and looked hopeful.

The white van slowed and stopped. 'Hello,' said Fred Hopkins, my greengrocer friend, leaning out of the window. 'See, I got my van back. Thanks to you. Hop in if you want a ride back to Latching.'

Apparently the police had actually done something about looking for his white van thinking it was connected to the water-lily theft. But it was just teenage joyriders and they had found the van the other side of Brighton, full of beer bottles and crisp packets. Mr Hopkins thought it was solely due to my inquiries. I did not argue. I need success.

He dropped me outside my shop and gave me a whole basket of fresh white button mushrooms. I tasted mushrooms on toast, mushroom soup, mushroom pâté. I'd forgotten that I've given up cooking. It's salad, sandwiches and soup only in my kitchen area. Perhaps I could manage the toast.

'Thank you so much,' I said. 'You saved my life with that lift.'

'Any time,' said Mr Hopkins. 'Pop in the shop any time. Strawberries, kiwis, avocados, whatever you want, miss. I'll find you a bargain. They didn't even notice the tyres.'

Time to open the shop, change the windows, make coffee, write notes, sell a few things. I did everything in that order. Chinese theme today. *Crouching Tiger, Hidden Dragon* style. I put out a miniature porcelain pagoda, chopsticks, fan, shawl and ancient martial arts book in one window. In the other I put a warrior, a dragon and a witch. They were good company for each other. Hope they wouldn't cook up spells in the night.

I wrote up my notes. Something was nagging me but I couldn't think what it was. I wanted a clear-cut route. I put the petals and root specimens in a cool place, to be transferred to my home fridge at some point soon. I still did not know why I was doing this.

The phone rang. It was DI James. I knew it was him before he even spoke.

'Jordan?'

'Yes.'

'Are you all right?'

'I have no wish to speak to you. Goodbye.'

'Are you all right?' he repeated.

'Recovering. Though why should you care? Putting me through that ordeal. It was inhuman. I could sue.'

'I had to do it. Everything pointed to you, still does. If I had not brought you in, the Serious Crime Squad would have been on me like a ton of concrete. Don't feel bad, Jordan. I had to go through the motions. It had to be done.'

'Compensation,' I stormed. 'I shall sue for compensation. I couldn't sleep. I was shredded. It has taken years off my life. I feel practically middle-aged.'

'Lunch at Maeve's Cafe in half an hour? My treat.'

'See you.'

I just had time to wash my face, plait my hair, put on a clean navy sweater, wipe the mud off my boots. I went like an eager teenie to the slaughter. He was blissfully straight after the smarmy Derek. I didn't care what I ate. Chips and mushy peas on a paper plate would be a feast from heaven.

He was waiting outside, all huddled and cold, his crewcut almost frozen to his head, hands thrust in pockets. His clear blue eyes lightened a fraction when he saw me, mouth curved into what might almost pass as a smile.

'You've torn your jeans,' he said.

It was a normal eat, drink and talk lunch.

What had I expected? That he'd feed me chips from his mouth? He'd classified and filed me. I wasn't a woman eye to him. More an unreliable witness who might or might not lead him to an answer but was worth keeping a check on.

'Have they finished the PM on Adrian Fenwick yet?' I asked, mouth full of succulent sea bream. Mavis knew how to cook fish.

'I can't tell you that, Jordan, and you know I can't. We have found his mobile phone and are tracing all the calls he made that day. It's a start.'

'And what was the fire investigator's report?'

He looked at me with disbelief. 'You're asking me?'

'Of course. I'd like to know how the fire was started, especially since I've been accused of doing it. I hope you're satisfied now that I had nothing to do with the fire. If not, then this delicious meal is in danger of being spoiled.'

'I had no evidence to hold you,' he sighed. 'But you are my only suspect. You were seen loitering suspiciously near the scene and this is the behavioural pattern of arsonists.'

I digested this. 'Tell me, James, exactly what loitering suspiciously means and I'll remember not to do it in future. Is it a sort of little side-stepping dance, or collar up to

185

your ears and dark glasses at dawn? Does waiting for a bus register as loitering since you never know if one is coming along. Queuing for your pension could be suspicious behaviour if you've a bottle of bleach in your shopping bag. Wow, life is full of pitfalls. I'll remember to be more careful.'

'Living with you must be close to non-stop verbal torture.'

'I also do magic tricks and belly dancing on Saturday nights.'

'Sounds riveting.'

'Do you want to try it?'

His mouthful of cod and chips stopped halfway in mid air. A globule of tomato sauce slid perilously. He looked perplexed. 'Try what?'

'Living with me.' This wasn't me talking at all. It was some utterly wildly demented and abandoned creature who walked around using my body and propositioning police officers in Maeve's Cafe.

He chewed thoughtfully. 'Do you mean that?' he said at last.

I flashed him a big smile. 'Not really. Just testing the water.'

Living with DI James would be a cross between heaven and hell. I could not even imagine it. If I put the idea on hold, would they keep heaven open for me?

It was over cups of tea that I produced the severed chain link and pushed the plastic bag across the table. 'One link from one security chain, found exactly where I left my bike. My bike, my chain, my link.'

'So?'

'And a postman from the sorting centre said he saw someone riding my bike, wearing a luminous armband. I never wear armbands. I don't even possess any. His name is Mitch Swartz. You can check with him.'

'What does that prove?'

'That it wasn't me. Get your people to find prints, debris, oil on the chain, anything that matches my bike and shows that it was stolen. You'll be surprised what they can do these days. They can match a hair to a head and tell you what it had for dinner.'

'OK,' he said wearily. He took a pen out of his pocket. 'Where did you find it?'

I told him the exact spot, to the inch. 'In exchange,' I said, 'I may have some developments for you in the water-lily saga.'

'I don't do exchanges,' he growled.

'You will when I tell you what I've found out,' I bluffed.

'Tell me.'

'Not yet. Too soon. Needs developing. A couple more days and I'll have it all tied up.'

'Sounds riveting,' he said again.

I thanked DI James for my lunch and got out while my dignity was still intact and the service was in my court.

Such was my optimism. First I had to find an expert on water lilies. Not easy when the local expert was Mr Terence Lucan. I'd have to go further away, to distant ponds. I thought of Kew Gardens in London and Wisley Gardens in Sussex and wondered if they had a friendly press officer.

They both had. I learned all I wanted to know and enough to sink Mr Lucan in one of his own ponds. I thanked them and arranged to send the specimen to Kew Gardens for confirmation. Not that he deserved saving from a watery demise. But my ladybird hovered on the surface of my mind, making confrontation awkward. She was so nearly mine and I wanted that dream to come true.

Surveillance in a red car with black spots would be tricky. She would hardly merge into a tired street. How could I turn that to an advantage? Park and ride? I could keep my bike on the back seat, the boot being far too small. It didn't completely defeat the purpose of having a car.

If I brought the water-lilies theft to a conclusion, then I was left almost caseless. Back to pushing junk full time. I'd closed the trashed WI display, no longer needed to pursue the vote-waving Adrian Fenwick's extra-marital pursuits. If he ever had any. Mrs Fenwick did not seem to even consider it while the BMW Mrs Fenwick was pretty sure. Supposing the second Mrs Fenwick was herself the extra flavour of the month, and her motive for the investigation was devious. She might have been exploring whether their affair was foolproof, to make sure that no one could find out. And what better proof than a report from a puppet PI saying there was nothing to report. It might have been a set-up. Would it stand up in court?

People were always using me. Mrs Drury had used me. Mr Lucan had used me. Perhaps I should change my advert. Add: Ideal for Scams, Double-Crosses, False Claims, Anything Devious.

I called Mrs Hilary Fenwick, the one with a brand-new conservatory and a husband who had hidden to death in a safe. She was still tearful.

'I was wondering if you'd call,' she said. 'My beautiful wedding cake. Have you found it yet?'

'Er ... no. Mrs Drury has more or less decided it's not worth going on with the investigation. We aren't going to find out who trashed the display unless they confess or boast about it to friends. Yobbos often boast about their exploits when they've had too much to drink.'

'It's most important that you find that cake,' she said. She seemed more worried about her cake than her husband. 'I'll pay if

189

there's anything to pay.'

I told her my rates. She agreed. It was a lot of money just to find a cake.

'I don't care what it costs but I want my cake back,' she said. I was surprised by the vehemence in her voice. Had she put arsenic in it and half-expected a whole wedding party to be rushed off to A&E with stomach pains? After the carrot-cake episode, I'd got poison on the brain.

'Don't worry,' I soothed. 'I'll find it for you. It's such a distinctive design. Would you mind telling me why it's so special?'

'I made it for my daughter-in-law's wedding. Not my son, you understand, she divorced him a year ago. She's remarrying and I wanted to make a conciliatory gesture. No hard feelings after the divorce, you know...'

'Nice,' I murmured.

'Of course, Pippa doesn't appreciate it. She thinks Adrian and I ruined her marriage to my son but it isn't true.'

Images flashed across my mind. I saw cream and gold and long lacquered nails. Pippa? Pippa Shaw?

'Does your daughter-in-law own a BMW?' I asked.

'Yes, she does. A blue one, I think. She got a generous divorce settlement.'

# Thirteen

There were Force 9 gusts of wind along the seafront and I could barely keep my feet on the promenade. It was exhilarating, blustery, defying the force, low clouds gathering darkly promising more rain and wind. It was blowing hard against my back, propelling me forwards, driving through the padded fabric, chilling my skin, shoulders and spine. I locked my hands behind me to anchor any heat, glad of gloves, regretting the lack of a heavy jersey.

It was not safe. I was nearly blown over. I could end up fish food. They were about to close the pier.

It was still windy but not so ferocious when I later decided to walk back to Latching after a pit stop at the Sea Lane cafe. They make brilliant hot chocolate, frothy with half a Cadbury's flake plunged into the froth. The taste was nectar in my mouth. I went down the shingle and cut across the sand and rocks to as far out as possible.

The beach was in a strange state. The tide had left a lot of water behind, whipped into long lagoons which flurried molten gold from the sun's rays. Streamers of water ribboned across the sand as the wind blasted the water's edge. It was all fluid motion, moving, shifting, uncertain, veering in one direction then skidding off in another.

My boots slipped and splashed through pools of sinking sun reflection; it was a struggle.

Even the seagulls had deserted the beach. The tiny stick-legged pied wagtails didn't stand a chance. The thick churning sea was too inhospitable even for the birds. I spotted an injured bird trapped in the sand, wings fluttering madly, but it was only a strand of seaweed in distress.

No one else was on the beach. The light was fading and the street lamps came on, then twinkling strings of coloured lights, an early Christmas. For a while I owned the entire stretch of sand and rocks and streaming pools and deepening channels. The sea was so far out that its roar was swallowed by the sound of the wind.

I was getting very cold. I turned to face the wind for respite but could barely catch my breath. I'd get pneumonia at this rate, hypothermia at least. But no way would the weather defeat me. I made myself walk the rest of the beach.

The front of me was euphoric over the

vastness and emptiness and rippling saffron pools that skidded across the surface of the sand while my back was being buffeted into chilly misery.

I tried pretending that my back didn't belong to me, that it was a slice of ice that I was carrying around. But my body wasn't fooled. It was my own fault. I wasn't dressed for this walk.

I quickened my feet, ate up the space, knees beginning to stiffen, turned at last into a side street where a tunnel of wind practically blew me over. Then I was round a corner and facing the pedestrian precinct. It was sheltered, still windy but nothing like the open beach. In a few minutes, I was home, inside walls, leaning against the door, absorbing the warmth. My frozen fingers unfastened zips, buttons, shed clothes, boots. I ran a bath, tepid at first, then warmer, added vanilla body oil, stepped in and sank into the healing water.

My muscles came back to life. Hypothermia receded.

It was on to trawling wedding cakes again since I was now being paid by the anxious Mrs Fenwick. I toured the photographers, poring over pictures of endless weekend brides and veils and cute bridesmaids, looking for a stately creation that resembled Mrs Fenwick's masterpiece.

'You're not having much luck with this cake, are you, Miss Lacey?'

I shook my head. 'I'm not even sure it has been stolen now,' I said. I had to go and call on Mrs Drury. Perhaps I ought to warn her in a roundabout way that Mrs Fenwick was determined to get her cake back.

As I expected, Mrs Drury lived in a large old house, back of town, a rambling Portland stone villa with creeper and wisteria and Victorian stained-glass in the front door panel and stairway window. I knew the inside would be a step back in time. She would not have changed a thing.

But she was not in. I rapped the large lion's-head brass knocker, pulled the bell rope, hung on in hope. The garden was a tangle of weeds and overgrown bushes, rhododendrons, azaleas and fading hydrangeas, their heavy heads weighted with raindrops. Any moment I would trip over Joey. Cracking and splintered stones wove a path through the back garden suburban jungle to a summer house in a glade of trees.

I stood in front of it, saddened by the neglect. It was a beautiful small building, like a Grecian temple, tiny but every detail made by a craftsman's hand. I wondered who had built it. Some distant past owner. The building was an edifice to love and taste. Perhaps lovers had met there, hiding from the world.

It was starting to rain. This was not exactly breaking in. I was only taking shelter.

Inside were mouldering deckchairs, a cobwebbed croquet set, stringless tennis rackets, a few cardboard boxes secured with parcel tape, flowerpots and mud-caked garden tools. The rain splattered on the roof, ran down the walls, curtaining me from the outside world. A sudden onslaught of feelings swamped me. I wished I had never met him, that man. DI James, who barely looked at me. I had never felt this overwhelming desolation before. The temple walls closed round me as if it understood; as if it had been there before. Someone else had stood there, living those same feelings.

I froze to the wooden floor. I was not alone. Something was there behind me, enveloping me with arms, yet not touching me. Don't ask me what it was but I was not alone.

The feeling vanished and it was only the pattering of rain that I heard. I found a mint in my pocket and put it in my mouth, fluff and all. The taste revived my senses. What was the matter with me? The traumas of the last few days were taking their toll.

Perhaps Mrs Drury would be home by now. I went back to the house, through the rain, hoping she would not ask me where I had been, but still no one was in. I looked through the windows, desperate not to see a body on the floor. But all I saw was big old-fashioned furniture, heavy and ornamental, and loads of books and ornaments. No wedding cake.

My morals were improving. I hadn't broken in. No using my set of pins to open the door. No breaking of a back window. There was hope for me yet. I turned towards the road.

'Are you coming to see me?' Mrs Drury came to an erratic halt by the kerb and wound down a window. 'Hop in, girl. It's chucking it down.'

I got in, fastened the seat belt even if it was only a few yards. I wondered if she could manage her garage in one go. She parked diagonally. Still, it was her drive. She could park upside-down if she wanted to.

'Come in. Do you mind carrying a few bags? Done my monthly shopping. Hate the supermarkets. So impersonal these days. And the queues. OK, the girls wear name badges and say hello, but they are trained to talk like dogs.'

I obediently ladened myself with carrier bags, brim-filled. I was not quite sure what I was doing. Did I really want to talk to Mrs Drury about the cake?

'I hear Mrs Fenwick wants you to find her wedding cake,' said Mrs Drury, making it easy for me. 'You do that, Jordan. Make yourself a bit more money. After all, I cut short the WI investigation. Not fair really, but I could see that there was nothing to go on.'

'That's very nice of you to understand,' I said, struggling inside with her bags. What did she eat? Had she bought an ox? They weighed a ton.

'I've got something to show you,' she said, huffing and puffing. 'It's going to rain all month, you know, so I've bought in some extra stuff, just in case. We got flooded here once before in 1957. They rowed boats in the road outside.'

'It's raining now,' I said.

'I mean real rain,' she said. 'Inches in hours. Not this drizzly stuff.'

I helped her unload her shopping in her kitchen. She had bought enough for a siege. I knew where to come if I ran out of food. I put on the kettle, guessing she'd need a reviving cup of tea after fighting the shops.

'Now, Jordan, I want you to look at this,' she said, carrying through a tray load of tea and stollen cake. 'I know it isn't Christmas yet, but I like stollen cake, don't you? Sit down. I'll pour.'

She sounded like my mother so I let her pour. She swept me along on a tide of human kindness.

'What do you want me to look at?' I said, taking the tea and sugar-dusted cake, layers of marzipan and thick with sultanas.

'I found this the other day. It's about the Lancaster bomber that is being dragged up from the sea beyond the pier. Shocking, I think. The dead should be left in peace. But just before it crashed that day, there was an appalling theft at Patcham House. It was in all the papers. Masses of stuff taken, classy art pieces, some priceless.'

'Patcham House?'

'Yes, you know, our stately home, not far from Latching. Haven't you been there?'

I shook my head and Mrs Drury tut-tutted at my lack of heritage culture. I had heard of the house, of course, but never had time to visit a stately home.

'So what's the connection?' The stollen cake was delicious, heavy and fat-laden but sweet and satisfying.

'It's a newspaper cutting. I can't think why I kept it. It was in a book, being used as a bookmark. It's about some woman who disappeared at the same time as the break-in. She was a kind of curator, or someone doing a list of the valuables in the house.'

'You mean cataloguing?'

'Yes, that's it, valuing the paintings and silver stuff. Well, apparently, she disappeared. Don't you think that's strange?'

'Yes,' I said weakly. 'But what's it to do with me?'

'Well, you're investigating the death of

Councillor Fenwick, aren't you? And he had vetoed the raising of the wreck, hadn't he? It follows all that, doesn't it? He knew the woman's body would be found on board the aircraft and that's why he was trying to stop it being raised.'

'How do you know a woman's body was found in the wreck?'

'That sweet Peach woman told me. The police diver. I met her at an organ concert, you know, the Wurlitzer. I'd buy an organ if I had room. We are both organ freaks. Elgar in particular. The music sends us.'

Also loosened tongues, it seemed. 'It's a bit far-fetched,' I said.

'I know. That's what's so fascinating.'

'And what do you think is the connection between the dead woman and Councillor Fenwick?' I asked. 'He would have been a toddler during the war. It would hardly be of any interest to a baby.'

'Well, it might be of interest to someone else. That's what you've got to find out, isn't it?' said Mrs Drury, beaming, helping herself to another slice of the solid stollen cake. 'That's your job.'

Not exactly, I thought. I am not being paid to find out anything about Councillor Fenwick's death, nor discover the identity of the mysterious woman found in the bomber wreck. Over to DI James. It was his job.

'By the way,' I asked. 'Was the WI display

insured?'

'Heavens, no! Who would insure a few cakes?'

'More tea?' I got up and took the teapot back to the kitchen for a refill. At the same time, I took a quick look around in case she had stuffed the wedding cake into a cupboard. By the time the kettle boiled I knew what she ate, drank and washed her smalls with. It was not a nice job.

I was walking the front again, full of stollen cake, getting wet, wishing I'd never got involved with the fire at FFH. What was I supposed to do now? I ran through a mental checklist. Time to go back to my shop, dry my hair. At least there I could write my notes and sort out the muddle in my brain.

During the afternoon I sold a tattered book to a woman who wanted to read anything Dorothy Parker had ever written. I only charged her a pound. Later I sold a gilded picture frame to a mean-faced man who wanted the frame for fifty pence. I didn't bargain. I charged him a pound too, but kept the faded picture from inside. I quite liked it, a rural scene, cows and bridges and a haystack. It looked familiar.

I wrote down everything I could think of about the Lucan water lilies, the WI display and the fire at FFH. It all added up to zilch. I was getting nowhere, only myself into trouble. It was time I washed my hands of the lot.

But now Mrs Fenwick was hiring me to find her wedding cake which I was pretty sure was stashed away in Mrs Drury's attic. I shrank from a midnight raid in a balaclava. DI James would be sure to catch me with one leg half out of a window. Or half in.

The stollen cake had left me with a heavy, bloated feeling. I did not usually suffer from indigestion so couldn't think what was the matter with me. I went to my friendly grocer's shop and asked Doris.

'We only sell Rennie's,' she said. 'For indigestion.'

'But is that what I've got?' I asked.

'I dunno,' she said. 'I'm not a doctor. Go ask one but Rennie's won't hurt you.'

'I can't afford to buy medication that I don't need,' I said, humiliated.

'Got any bicarbonate of soda? Take a spoonful of that. It tastes like powdered hell on earth, but it works.'

Eventually I gave up the struggle and curled up on the button-backed chair, clutching a hot-water bottle to my stomach. The heat helped. Perhaps it was time to get out my one and only vest, a pink machine-knitted Damart production, and stop being heroic. Who would see it? Not a soul. I'd put off stripping for men until the summer.

I slept uneasily, chasing weird dreams in

201

the ripples of my mind. But the vest would put body and soul together. A big mug of tea completed the cure, now that I knew the cause. Purely nature. On time, as usual, but I had forgotten. I didn't need a doctor or Rennie's.

Last year's wear had stretched the vest almost to my knees. I'd have to fold it up for a better fit. Latching could produce its bitterest winter but I was ready for it.

The phone rang. It was DI James again. His voice held no warmth. 'I've a few questions to ask you.'

'I'm fresh out of answers,' I said.

'I'm not surprised,' he said. 'One of the calls Councillor Fenwick made just before he died was to you. Can you explain that?'

'No. I've no idea why he should phone me. I don't know him and I never got the call. It's a mystery to me.'

'Did he leave a message on your answer-phone?'

'I don't know.'

'Why don't you know?'

'I forgot to check it when I got in. I'm always forgetting. It's so new. Haven't checked it for days. I promise, James, first thing now, I'll check.'

'You realise that this looks bad, don't you? That he phoned you on the night that he died.'

'Nonsense. It looks good. He might have

wanted to employ me.'

I heard a heavy intake of breath. 'He might have threatened you. He might have said something which made you go and see him. The call was made at twelve forty-five a.m. Your number was logged at that time. Midnight's hardly the time to ring about some work.'

'FCI provides a twenty-four-hour service,' I smoothed.

'Even when you are walking the beach, half-a-mile offshore?'

'Thinking time. Going through checklists. Are you having me followed?'

'You were spotted by a patrolling panda. They thought you were contemplating suicide.'

'Too damned cold,' I said. 'I only drown in warm water.'

'I hear you're thinking of buying a car.'

'How do you know?'

'I'm a detective, remember? Have you driven it yet?'

'No.'

'Checked its MOT?'

'Er ... not yet.'

'Can you even drive?'

'Tut-tut, Inspector. Haven't you checked my duty record? I was taught by the best.'

When DI James rang off, I switched to replay on my answerphone. There was quite a string of calls, mostly operators trying to sell me something. I listened carefully and made a few notes. The call from Councillor Fenwick was uncanny, a voice from the dead.

'Miss Lacey. Miss Jordan Lacey?' The voice sounded slurred. 'This is Adrian Fenwick of Fenwick Future Homes, the estate agents. I need your help badly. I really need to know something ... I'm sorry. This isn't making sense. I'm not feeling too well. But I think I'm in danger.' His voice broke off as if he was listening. 'Could you come round ... I'm at the office...'

I made a copy of the tape and then wiped the original. This was something DI James ought to hear and no one else. If he would listen. If he would believe me.

# Fourteen

The door to the shop opened. Two men came in, both well dressed in dark suits, heavy overcoats, not my usual class of customer at all. I tried to think what I had in my windows that might interest them. At the same time I put the tape in an envelope, addressed it to DI James and sealed it.

'Can I help you?' I asked in my best shop voice.

'We are just browsing,' said the shorter of the two men. 'The books ... maybe you have some first editions?'

Ah, dealers. Well, no luck, buster. My book stock was regularly checked by Mr Frazer, esteemed part-time unpaid book expert. He goes through the boxes of books and anything of value, he sells on for me.

'By all means,' I said, waving around the shelves of hardbacks and paperbacks bought by the yard from car boot sales and junk shops. 'Please browse.'

They browsed and I hovered. It was difficult to look busy when there was nothing to do. I pretended to dust. I caught a few specks. Then I felt my arms being gripped above the elbow, first one, then the other. It was a hard grip, nothing friendly. My arms were jerked behind my back. The two men were standing close to me, wafting eau de garlic.

'Don't make any noise,' said the shorter browser. 'Move through to your back office. We need to have some little talk.'

I could not believe what I was hearing.

'Can't we talk out here? I'll make some coffee.'

'Move,' said the taller one, speaking for the first time. Even with one word, he had an accent. His skin was smoothly olive, eyes very dark. I half recognised the tailoring. It was very ... very Armani. I decided not to argue. The three of us went into my office. I was glad I hadn't tidied up.

'My partner will be here soon,' I said, immediately recruiting DI James, Joshua, Derek, anyone on legs.

'You don't have a partner.'

They pushed me down on to my Victorian button-back. For once the chair gave me no pleasure. The creases in their trousers blurred my eyes with their sharpness.

'Where is Al Lubliganio?'

Ah ... 'Who?'

'Don't play games. Al Lubliganio. We know he spoke to you. Is he employing you?'

The fifty pounds was safely deposited in

my bank account. It had not been employ-
ment. The money was more like a gift.

'No, he doesn't employ me.' There was no
point in saying otherwise. 'He told me about
a case of mistaken identity. His name is
Alfred Lubliganio. He's a mechanic at a
local garage. He's not whoever you think he
is.'

They exchanged glances. It was all very B-
movie.

'A nice touch, lady, but not convincing.
Where is Al Lubligano now?'

'I've no idea.' He could have moved on to
Timbuktu.

'Then perhaps you come with us until you
do have an idea. We are prepared to wait a
time.'

'Well, I'm not prepared.' I glared. 'Who
are you?'

'You do not know us.'

But I did. They were the Scarlatti brothers
or relations of same. Big family. They were
Italian. The looks, the accents, the clothes.
A pair of bullies. I got scary suspicious
thoughts about Al Lubliganio. He could
have been lying to me.

They heaved me up out of the chair like I
was a sack of pasta. Things were getting out
of hand. I started to make a big fuss, noise,
shouts, kicking stuff, hoping Doris might
hear or a passer-by. The shop next door was
still empty.

'Letmego! Take your hands off me! Get out of my shop or I'll call the police. You're making a big mistake.'

One of them clapped a gloved hand over my mouth.

I was dragged out the back way. They knew the layout of the place. A car was waiting, a dark saloon. I tried to read the number plate. I wrenched the gloved hand off my mouth and shouted loudly again.

'What the hell do you think you are doing? This is all a terrible mistake.' Those words, the same words. I seem to have said them a dozen times before. I was bundled into the car. Bundled again. And pushed down into the back well, my wrists roughly tied with twine. Cloth was stuffed into my mouth. The car had smoked-glass windows. It was reeking with cigarette fumes. My asthma gave a double twitch.

The shorter of the two men was a compulsive fidget. He tapped his pockets, checking his dandruff, picked his teeth. Any minute now, he'd fix my hair, do my nails.

'Where the hell are you taking me?' I protested against a mouthful of cloth. It was coarse, revolting, oily stuff. I'd be sick any minute. They couldn't hear what I was saying.

And I couldn't see where we were going. Every time I tried to sit up, Fidget pushed my head down. It gave him something to do.

I was too fighting mad to panic. But panic was on its way. I thought of the poor nun who had been kept hostage in an empty hotel, and the gross orange bedspread they used. I'd demand a duvet. Make a nuisance of myself.

We were leaving Latching. I tried desperately to track roads, traffic lights, roundabouts. We were on the main A27 to Arundel. I didn't like this one bit. When I escaped I could cope in my own area. But somewhere strange, and I'd be as lost as any tourist. That is, if I got away.

When I got away. Positive thinking, girl. Perhaps DI James would turn up at the shop to question me about FFH, or Doris would bring me some bi-carb or Mrs Drury would arrive with a home-made quiche. Hundreds of possibilities. Someone would soon notice my disappearance, the open shop, the chained bike ... surely?

The fumes, the bad driving, the cramped backseat and the stuff in my mouth were all making me feel nauseously car sick. My stomach churned. And it was the wrong time of the month. This was going to be humiliating and unpleasant. Sweat broke out on my skin. I was clammy and getting pins and needles in my feet and fingers. Reynaud's disease was setting in.

I made grunting noises to attract attention. I tried to inject the grunts with pleading rumbles. It seemed to work for Fidget leaned back and took the cloth out of my mouth. Bits were stuck to my lips and tongue.

'Thank you,' I said thickly. 'I'm feeling sick.'

'Don't talk,' he said.

It was getting gloomy. Twilight was tangling the last strands of day. I could see nothing above but street lamps coming on and looming trees, branches waving in dark patterns. We turned off the main road and slowed down in a side street. Fidget leaned over again and this time tied the cloth over my eyes. It immediately made my lids itch. I'd be getting an allergy at this rate.

The driver switched off the engine and the two men got out, then pulled me from the back of the car. My legs wouldn't hold me up. All the feeling had gone. They dragged me across some pavement like a scarecrow, except I didn't leak straw. I could just see cracks below the blindfold. Then we were into some building and I could smell old linoleum.

Everywhere smelled of damp and decay. It felt cracked and peeling. A torch flickered on. Sharp edges kept bumping into the side of my right leg, calf and thigh. The intervals were identical. I was being bumped against rows of something.

Seats! It came to me in a flash. This was an

old cinema. And there was only one old, shut-down cinema in this area. And I knew, because I had been on duty the night of the VIP closure party when protesters stood outside ready to lay down their lives if one brick of the listed building was removed. It was the Picture Palace, Latching's historic old cinema, relic of the days of regular Saturday night picturegoers. The two men had driven in a circle and returned to Latching, to confuse me en route.

I realised exactly where I was. And I knew the inside of the building having searched it prior to the party for bombs etc. It was pure Art Deco, marble pillars and thirties wall paintings. They were taking me up the sweeping stairs, all flaking gilt paint, to the circle. The balcony was the only cinema in England to have double seats, well used by courting couples in the submarine gloom and handy for a snooze if the film was boring.

'Will you kindly tell me what this is all about!' I yelled at them. 'You won't get anything out of me because I know nothing. I've no idea where this man is, or who he is. So let me go!'

They'd given up English and replied in a torrent of Italian. I didn't understand a word.

They were dragging me further and further back towards the projection room.

211

Were they going to show me a film?

But no entertainment. I was pushed down on to a wooden seat and tied to the legs. A splinter scratched my wrist.

'I need a drink,' I croaked.

'You wait. When you want to talk, you get drink.'

I heard the hiss of a match. One of the men was lighting a cigarette. My lungs went into a spasm.

'Would you mind not smoking,' I coughed. 'I've got asthma.'

I got a hearty smack on the back of the shoulders and one of them laughed. Then they left, again talking in Italian. I only knew the names of ice-cream and film stars, gangster movie talk. The gist was food. They were going out for fast food. I heard their footsteps going down the narrow stairs at the back. I tried to control my breathing, slowing down the rate, thinking calming things and of peaceful sunlit places.

When the coughing had slowed and was controllable, I was able to put together where I was and what I was going to do. This Al Lubliganio business was ridiculous. I was not going to be fazed by some vague person with such a ridiculous name. The quicker I got out of here, the better.

For gangsters they were not getting Brownie points for knots. One was a bit loose. They didn't know their left over right or their Italian for it. I jogged the chair over the floor and found a sharp metal edge on the old Simplex projection unit (preserved for posterity) and sawed the knot against it. After a lot of work, it began to fray.

I wriggled it off, rubbed my sore wrists and tore off the blindfold. There was only a glimmer of light from a skylight but I saw I was right; it was the old projection room. It was a cramped soulless cupboard-sized room with two projection units, the preserved one and a newer Phillips unit.

Bending over to untie my legs from the chair made me cough again. I hung on to the chair back for support, leaning over to help my breathing. I did not have my inhaler, of course. I had nothing with me. Only a screwed-up tissue in my pocket. I used the shreds carefully as if it was the last tissue in the world.

I stood up and went over to the door. It didn't move. I had been coughing so hard I had not heard them lock it. I sat on the chair to think things through. I had to get out before the two Italians came back. There was a crooked shelf holding a few dusty reels of film. A coffee-encrusted mug, a broom. A clutter of crushed and empty Coke tins. And on the floor was a dirty box of matches. The smoker had dropped them. There were seven matches left in the box.

I'd never get out of the skylight. It was too

213

small and too high up. No way. I climbed up on to the new projection unit via the chair, balanced myself on the frame, and began throwing coke tins at the glass. My aim was never very good, not even at the seafront fair when I had two feet on the ground and only a couple of yards' projection. The cans clattered down and around, the noise horrendous. I waited, tensely, expecting Italian expletives to come racing up the stairs.

But all was quiet. Except for my breathing.

I tied a can on to the head of the broom using a lace out of my trainers. It reached the skylight and I was soon bashing out a pane of glass. Bits of glass fell around me. I quickly brushed them into a corner. I couldn't risk cut feet.

Then I tied the crusted mug on to the top of the broom. Celluloid burns well, the old stuff almost self-igniting. I was going to burn film in the mug, poke it out of the skylight and hope someone would see the smoke and flames. I had seven matches, so that was seven goes at fire lighting. Not a lot. I needed a small reserve fire going so that I could keep the mug of film alight.

What else could I burn? And in what? The only combustible commodity around was the film. The film canisters looked old, the pre-safety sort. I took a reel down from the shelf and peered at the label. *Casablanca*.

I was stunned. I couldn't burn *Casablanca*.

It would be sacrilege. That film. I'd cried over it more times than I had slept on my own. It was always my jazz trumpeter that I said goodbye to on that foggy, rainswept airfield.

But there was nothing else. It couldn't be the only copy in existence or it would not have been left on a shelf. Perhaps I would just burn the first reel. I was not that keen on the beginning. All period gloss and dresses and funny hats and talking out the side of the mouth. I took the first reel out of the canister.

None of the Coke cans opened further than the ring-pull hole. I made a sort of raft out of the cans, stood my trainer in the centre of a lid and fed film into it. The way to sever the film was on the razor device on the projection unit, the sharp edge used by projectionists to mend broken film. No one had carelessly left a cutting knife around. Tut-tut.

I cut masses of short lengths of film for quick replenishment of the mug. Scene after scene tumbled down, the party, the bar, the restaurant. My fingers were soon cut and bleeding. Piles of black film spiralled round my feet. Indiana Jones would be terrified, thinking they were snakes.

I was sweating like a navvy and I'd only lit two matches. The film ignited in a flash and flared. Flames curled along the edges, burst into a tangle and ignited the pile in my trainer. I lit the bundle of film in the mug from the fire and climbed up on to the projection unit. I felt like the Olympic runner.

My head for heights was going fast. It was not easy. I held the broom aloft, waving it out of the smashed skylight, one hand against the sloping roof eave. I was not at all steady and there was nothing more substantial to hold on to. If I fell, no one would find me. I climbed down and refilled the mug, setting it alight from my burning trainers. My cut fingers were hurting. I climbed up again, trying to stay calm. What if no one saw it? Tears of hopelessness blinded me.

'James, where the hell are you?' I shouted upwards. 'Don't you care about this historic, graded building? Why aren't you out, patrolling the streets of Latching, searching for lost civilians? Get out of Maeve's Cafe and back on the beat.'

My trainers were glowing like Christmas. I would have to sacrifice the second one. And they were almost new. I took the laces out. Laces were always useful. The mug was already slipping on the broomhead. I tied it on more firmly, filled it with film. The fire kept going out in the mug and I couldn't understand why. Where were we in this enduring story? Had she walked into his life yet? Had their eyes met across a crowded gin joint? Was the cafe packed with all my favourite characters?

I lost count of the trips I made. The matches were disappearing. They were not good quality. I had only one left. My trainers were a pile of glowing embers. I had to be careful. I did not want to burn the floorboards or I could be incinerated along with the last reel of *Casablanca*. The acrid fumes were making me cough.

They would be back any minute. Romeo and Juleo. It couldn't take that long to eat a bowl of spaghetti. I was almost exhausted. DI James's ears should be burning. And why not? I was only round the corner from the police station.

My trainers were no more. The embers almost died, flickering out. I went up with the last mug of burning film and stuck it out of the skylight. Too fiercely. It fell off and I heard it clatter down the roof and smash on to the pavement. Goodbye, mug, and thanks.

I climbed down and sat on the chair and cried. I really had done my best. I'd never been trained by Miss Moneypenny or whatever her name was. I was tired, I felt sick and I had a period.

I wound the last of reel one on to the head of the broom, round and round in a bundle, and lit it with the last match. The bristles flared up and burst into flame. It was

217

difficult to hold the broom straight up and climb at the same time. I didn't care if the whole broom caught fire. We would all go out blazing, Humphrey Bogart, Ingrid Bergman and me. The trumpeter would read about the cinema disaster in the papers, DI James might come to my funeral service if there was anything left for a service.

It was my last climb and I was determined to make this one work. I stood holding the blazing broomhead out of the skylight, more than a bit wobbly. Flames and smoke streamed out into the air. Where were those sirens? I was past knowing or caring. It was a pole-axed time. My brain had stopped functioning, entangled communication cells out of action. I never even heard them coming up the stairs or breaking down the door.

'Gotcher, miss,' said a voice.

I felt my legs firmly clasped round the knees in mid air. I thought it was the Italians and started to struggle.

'Give over. I'm here to rescue you, Jordan. Relax and come down. Give me the broom. Bloody idiot. What the hell do you think you are doing?'

My legs collapsed again. I fell against a sturdy male body built like a wall. Strong arms caught me and I saw bulky uniform, white hard hat. Another firefighter snatched the flaming broom.

'Oh, thank goodness,' I gasped. 'I haven't set light to the Picture Palace, have I?'

'Not yet, you imbecile, but nearly. Can you walk?'

'No, I don't think so. I don't think I'll ever walk again.'

Bud hoisted me up over his shoulder. It was a very strange upside-down, folded in half feeling, but I didn't care. I stared at the burnt matches on the floor and the cinders of my trainers. He would carry me out of the building and he wouldn't let any Italians take me away. The other fireman was dowsing the broom and my trainers with an extinguisher.

'Don't let the Italians get me,' I said.

'No Italians.'

'They're after me.'

'Sure. I'm not surprised. You stood me up on our date,' he said, bumping me round a corner. 'I always send the Italians round.'

'Sorry, but I don't remember. Did we have a date? I must have a drink. My throat is so dry. Please, a drink first. Have you got some water?'

Has a fireman got any water? I nearly laughed except I was too dry to laugh.

He put me down outside on the pavement and immediately held a waterbottle to my mouth. I drank and drank. It slid down my throat like rain.

'Hold on,' he said. 'You'll burst.'

'I'm sorry about the date,' I said, my head against his shoulder. It was solid. 'I'd forgotten. Who called the fire services?'

'Some vigilante, on duty outside the cinema in a sleeping bag, in case it was pulled down overnight. He saw the smoke, phoned 999.'

'Thank goodness. It worked then.'

'Jordan, the police are on their way. Sorry about that. And you do need to be checked out by A&E. Your breathing is bad and your hands are bleeding,' said Bud, slipping back the visor to his helmet. He looked down at me, his mouth set.

'I was calling for help, don't you see that, trying to attract attention? Don't you understand? Tell the police that the door was locked, won't you? Explain that I was locked in, that I was a prisoner, won't you?'

'I will,' said Bud.

He went back to his team, stomping about in his big boots. I think he was mad at me. They were packing up their equipment. There was no fire. Just a nutcase who had burnt her trainers on a mound of coke cans.

'Another fire, Jordan?' DI James was crouched on the pavement beside me. His eyes were fathomless. His hair was spiked with rain. I didn't know it had been raining. Perhaps that's why the mug of fire kept going out. 'This is getting to be a habit.'

220

'It was these two Italians,' I said weakly. 'They hijacked me from the shop. Look, I'm bleeding.'

'I understand this injury is self-inflicted,' he said, but he was wrapping clean handkerchiefs round my hands as he spoke.

'Self-inflicted, my foot,' I said. 'I was trying to cut film into bits so I could set fire to the film.'

'So you admit to starting this fire?'

'It's not a fire as we know a fire to be,' I said. 'I was trying to attract attention. I was tied up to a chair first. I got myself free. The bits of rope are up there in the projection room on the floor. Why don't you get them before some idiot sweeps them up?'

'What else shall I find there?'

'My trainers. I had to burn them. Broken glass. Reels of *Casablanca*. Oh my God, I had to burn the first reel. That really hurt but I had no choice.'

'The first reel isn't so good,' said DI James.

'Oh, I'm so glad you agree,' I said. 'I thought I was the only person who didn't ... you know.'

'So this could be called fire number two, Jordan.'

'No, no ... never. Not fire number two. There wasn't even fire number one. How can I convince you?'

'Perhaps you ought to come down to the

221

station and make a statement.'

'I need a lot to drink. Masses and masses. I'm dehydrated, my asthma is bad and they gagged me with this awful rag. You could collect specimens from inside my mouth. Then perhaps you'd believe me. I wouldn't put bits of oily cloth inside my own mouth.'

'I've a bottle of Australian Chardonnay cooling down at the nick,' said DI James. 'It's in the fridge, waiting for a special occasion.'

'And this is a special occasion?' Amazement mingled with disbelief.

'Yes, in a way.'

'Is that why you're carrying *two* clean handkerchiefs? For this special occasion?'

DI James did not answer. He looked surprised. Perhaps he did not know he had two handkerchiefs. Perhaps he couldn't count. A form of numbers dyslexia.

Across the road was a dark saloon car with smoked-glass windows. I clung to his arm, terror rising in my throat. 'That's the car. It's them. The Italians,' I croaked.

'Pack it in, Jordan,' he said. 'You'll be seeing aliens next.'

# Fifteen

Latching police station had never looked more inviting. I turned down the offer of an hour's wait at an A&E. I felt safer in a police station. A fresh-faced WPC of about twelve took me to the washroom so that I could clean up. She even gave me a tampon from her locker. I would remember her cheery smile and kindness. My hands were a mess. I rinsed James's handkerchiefs and squeezed out the pinky water. I'd give them a proper soaking in bleach when I got home. I was totally confident that I would soon be on my way.

Another WPC brought some bandages from the first aid box and soon I had six sausage fingers. The others had escaped mutilation. My hair was a tangled nest. No way could I hold a brush even if I had one.

They took me to the same interview room, the one with the pot plant. Two mugs of tea were waiting.

'Where's the Chardonnay?' I asked.

'Later maybe,' said DI James without looking up from some papers. 'If you start drinking wine now, then I'll have to breath-alyse you and you'd be over the limit. We don't want to make it look worse than it already is.'

'What do you mean, than it already is? You're not seriously considering me?'

'Jordan. It's stacking up against you. You were on the scene of the fire at FFH, and talked your way into the fire spot, possibly to remove incriminating evidence.'

'I didn't remove anything! What rubbish.'

'Please don't interrupt. Councillor Fen-wick phoned you just before the fire broke out. Your bike was found nearby with a can of petrol. We now have confirmation that six thousand pounds in cash has been paid into your bank in the last few days. Six thousand pounds, Jordan, a lot of money. Business is looking up. Hardly your normal fee? Or has it gone up recently?'

'It's planted money. I've been telling the manager, Mr Won't-Listen William Weaver, till I'm blue in the face. It's not my money and I didn't put it in my account.'

'One of the cashiers can identify you, Jordan. She says the cash was deposited by a young woman in jeans with funny-coloured hair in a plait.'

'Funny-coloured!' I splattered.

'Perhaps we should start with the Picture Palace and what you were doing there and why you were trying to set fire to it,' he said, not looking at me.

I drank some tea, wondering when this Alice Down the Plug Hole nightmare would end.

'Coming here is getting to be a habit,' I said, sitting on the chair opposite the pot plant for possible healing vibes. It hadn't grown. 'People will begin to talk.'

'People are already talking. You are in deep trouble, Jordan. Two fires, big payments in cash and a councillor who was clearly murdered.'

'What do you mean, clearly murdered? I thought he died in the fire, shut himself in the safe or something.'

'There's more to it than that, Jordan. Ever heard of Halcion?'

'No. What is it? Sounds like another water lily.'

'It's a short-term sleeping tablet, contains Triazolam. Causes drowsiness, confusion, unsteadiness, changes in vision. Not to be taken with alcohol. May also impair judgement. Traces of Triazolam were found in Adrian Fenwick's blood and in his vacuum flask of coffee.'

'Spiked coffee. Very original. So how am I supposed to have spiked his coffee? With a syringe through the window?'

'He had also consumed quite a quantity of brandy. We found a half empty bottle and dregs in a glass. A lethal combination. He

225

probably didn't know what he was doing by this stage. And the connecting door was locked from the outside. He certainly didn't know that steel conducts heat and would set fire to the contents of the safe, including himself.'

'And how am I supposed to have got the good councillor in this state and why, Detective Inspector James? All crimes have a motive. Find me one good motive.'

'Trenchers, Miss Lacey. That's a good motive. Everyone knows that you are obsessed by that derelict ruin of a hotel. And Councillor Fenwick was in the process of granting planning permission for it to be demolished and a small industrial business built on the site.'

'Conservatories?'

He looked surprised. It took a lot to surprise DI James. Point to me. My service.

'Er ... yes.'

'And the Fenwicks have just had a new conservatory extension built on to their house. Coincidence. Perhaps it was a sample Victorian that fell off the back of a lorry. Have you checked?'

'It's not against the law to have a conservatory built.'

'But it is if it was a handout. I don't wish to speak ill of the recently horrifically departed, but it smells cod-shaped to me.'

'I'd like you to tell me again exactly what

226

you were doing the night of the showroom fire.'

'This is getting so boring. Are you taping this conversation?'

He tapped the recorder box and the attendant WPC smirked. I noticed that she had loosened her shirt collar. Either getting hot or putting on weight. 'Forgotten what they look like? I am taking a statement.'

'You didn't caution me before you started.'

DI James did not move a single lash. I gave him full marks for self-control. But his eyes darkened and they took on that look that I hated. That blank, Titanic, iceberg looming, no survivors look. He wasn't going to throw me a lifebelt.

'Do I have to start again?' he said in a voice that could cut ice. 'I will read you the caution. We will go through this whole ridiculous rigmarole again.'

'You gotta get the procedure right,' I said, then turned brightly to the WPC. 'I wonder if I could have some more tea? I've a throat like dried hemp.'

'No,' he snapped. 'No more tea.'

I turned back to DI James and drew strength from everything that I liked about him. Nothing could change my feelings. I had a kind of rooted certainty that would last a lifetime. I would go to my grave (watery) loving the man. The crisp dark crew-cut, eyes that imprisoned me with invisible tendons, a chin that could repel invaders.

'I might pass out right now or start wheezing. You seem to have forgotten what I have been through. Abducted by two villainous Italians, locked in and tied up in a cinema projection room. Nothing to drink. Asthma attack on its way.'

'How did you know they were Italians?'

'They're part of the Scarlatti gang. Ever heard of them? Not the opera-composing lot. The Naples Mafia lot. Nasty habits. Several giant-sized chips bouncing on those Armani-clad shoulders. They think I know where someone called Al Lubliganio is.'

'And do you?' He was trying hard to see where all this was going.

'He's up north somewhere. I told him to go north. That's all I know. Could we please have a break? I really am feeling quite ill.'

I was feeling bad. It was the truth and no joke. Perhaps I looked a shade of green. My stomach was clutched in cramps, I could still taste that rag in my mouth, my legs were wobbly and weak. Possibly I had caught something off the Italians. Some sort of Mediterranean-based flu.

DI James spoke into the tape. 'Interview ended at six forty-five p.m. as witness taken ill.' He switched off the machine. 'Could you please fetch Miss Lacey another cup of tea and perhaps a sandwich. Cheese and tomato. She doesn't eat meat. God knows when she last ate. The day before yesterday probably.'

I cradled my head on the hard table. Anywhere would do. 'I've forgotten how to eat.'

'What exactly were you burning in the projection room?'

'*Casablanca*,' I sighed. 'I told you. Of all the gin joints, in all the world.'

'Cellulose-coated film, the old-fashioned kind before fireproofing ... you've been inhaling toxic fumes. I'll call the doc.'

'No, please, I don't want any fuss.'

'If you are not attended to by the station doc, you'll probably sue.'

'No, never ... I won't sue,' I murmured, sliding to the floor.

I came to in DI James's arms. He was carrying me, not exactly gently, but nevertheless carrying me like a child. My cheek was rubbing against his shoulder. I could breathe him, feel deep muscles moving. His chin was only inches away. I could see a scar.

'Haven't we anywhere more comfortable? Not in a cell, idiot! Can't you see she's ill. You don't put a sick person in a cell, dammit. Where the hell is there a decent chair?'

I could have told him. My place. Just keep

229

walking, buster. Walk with me to the rainbow's end. We might find a sofa piled with cushions and throws.

They found an armchair from some chief inspector's office upstairs. Reluctantly I let them untwine my arms and lower me into the armchair, put my feet up on a stool. DI James wrapped me in a cellular blanket, pushed a deflated cushion under my head. I felt cherished and loved.

Would he always be like this? Could he be? Was there a layer of loving lurking somewhere neath the steel shield he wore, that he could not allow to be seen? I shut out the station walls, the gawping WPC, the hovering doctor probing my bare chest with a cold sphere.

'A bit of smoke inhalation,' the doc said, putting his stethoscope away. 'Not good with her asthma. But not too bad and no hospitalisation is necessary. A few days' rest at home will do the trick.'

DI James pulled my sweater down for modesty's sake. I could barely believe the tenderness of that quiet action. Thank goodness my bra was clean and white with a wisp of lace in the valley. I could have been wearing a punk-killer pull-on grey sports version.

'James...' I whispered, very *Gone With the Wind*. I was going to relive and remember every second there was of this moment. My

230

one and only cherish time.

'Ssshh,' he said. 'Just rest. Don't worry about anything.'

They took me home in a panda. Someone phoned and offered to bail me out but it was not necessary. It was days before I found out that it was Jack, the man who owns the amusement arcade on the pier. One of my fans. The man who once gave me a teddy bear. Who lusted after me in both a carnal and marital fashion but was a non-starter in the stakes and we both knew it. But he was prepared to stand bail. Put down good money. If only I could fall for him, my days of poverty would be over.

I stayed in bed for several days, living on tinned soup, mushroom and tomato versions alternately. Then pottered around in an old track suit, too weak to do anything except listen to Jazz FM. I barely remembered the cases I was supposed to be working on. They disappeared into a convalescent haze. I slept and dozed. I did not answer the door or the phone. Why me? Why were the police determined to pin it on me? I'd done nothing to deserve this.

I'd have to unsort the tangle myself. If I got the chance before they locked me up again. I found some paper and wrote down all the relevant points that needed investigating. This would be my checklist and I had to prove, without doubt, that each point was flawed in its thinking.

My first furtive somnambulant steps were taken on a cold windy morning. Winter had arrived with a vengeance during my brief absence, stacking clouds in the sky like brooding medieval castles with ramparts and ruined keeps. They were grey and glowering, darkly menacing above the horizon. The sea churned steel-tinged waves that lapped the shore with arthritic stiffness. The gulls tiptoed the wet sand with frozen feet.

I huddled my chin into my collar, pulled a scarf across my mouth and stuck my hands in my pockets. Shopping list: gloves. It was some time before I realised I was walking towards Mrs Fenwick's all-weather villa in the sun. None of the windows were open. The house looked as if it were hibernating.

I set the chimes going. Mrs Fenwick came to the door in lavender twinset and pearls, grey pleated skirt. She had a floral pinny clutched in her hands.

'Sorry,' I said. 'Are you busy?'

'Not too busy to be interrupted,' she said. 'Come in. You look frozen.'

'I am,' I said, stepping into the warmth of the hall. She led the way to the kitchen. Another wave of heat hit me.

'I'm making a wedding cake,' she said. 'Something to do, keeps me occupied. Anything to keep my mind off Adrian's death.

Pippa hasn't been round to see me or written to me. I can't understand that young woman. You'd think she'd come. We were quite friendly, once. She might have telephoned, a few kind words.'

'Pippa? Your son's ex-wife? The one who is remarrying and you made the WI cake for?'

'That's right. Didn't I tell you? Would you like a cup of tea? I don't seem to buy coffee any more. Adrian drank coffee all the time.'

'Tea'll be great,' I said, unwrapping my scarf. 'I know this will be painful for you but I wonder if you'd mind telling me a few things about that evening, the evening your husband worked late.'

'I know so little...'

'Well, for a start, he phoned you, saying he'd be working late?'

'That's right. He phoned in the afternoon to say he would be working late at the office and not to wait up. It wasn't unusual.'

'And he didn't have a thermos of coffee, made by you, with him that evening?'

'No, because he didn't come home for it. But funny that you should ask because I haven't seen the thermos since ... since that day. It seems to have disappeared. He didn't take it with him in the morning because I remember washing it up after he'd left for work.'

'And what else did you do that day?'

'Heavens, I've no idea. It's difficult to

233

remember what one did on any exact day. I went shopping, I suppose. Library ... I don't know.'

'Did you have any visitors?'

She shook her head and poured out the tea. 'No, I don't think so. Oh yes, Pippa called in but only for a few minutes. She wanted some addresses but I couldn't find them. I don't know why she thought I'd have them. Very odd.'

'And did you leave her alone at all while she was here?'

'Alone? Well, I suppose so while I looked in my husband's desk. Then I went upstairs to my son's old room and had a quick look round for an address book but I couldn't find one.'

'So she had some minutes on her own downstairs?'

'Yes, I suppose so, but is it important?'

'Not really,' I said, changing the subject. 'Your mobile phone. Can you remember when you last had it?'

'Oh dear,' she said, starting to look flustered. 'You must think I'm very stupid. But no, I don't remember when I last had it. You see, I use it very rarely. It's just for emergencies. Adrian said I should always have it with me in the car.'

'So it could have been missing for some time, several days in fact? Did you report it?'

'No, are you supposed to?'

'Never mind. So it went missing some time before the agricultural show?'

'Oh yes.' She brightened. 'It might have been stolen or I lost it, any time. Tell me, Miss Lacey, do they know any more about my husband's death? That nice DI James has been round to see me. He's very sympathetic.'

'I'm sure he'll come again if there's any news.'

'I always told Adrian that he'd work himself to death and he did, didn't he?'

It was an odd way to put it but I had to agree. Except that he didn't put sleeping pills in his coffee or lock the door from the outside so that he couldn't get out. I was sure this Mrs Fenwick was not involved. Setting the regulo on her oven was about her limit.

'But have you found my stolen cake yet, Miss Lacey?' Now she was anxious. She knocked over a jug of milk in her haste to wipe the table top clean. 'I do want that wedding cake back. It means a lot to me.'

'But you are making another one now.' Stolen ... stollen cake. Same bell began ringing.

'I know...' She flustered again. 'It's just in case she'd like it. But the first one was special. I'd really prefer to give her that one.'

'Sorry, no sign of it yet. Probably eaten.'

'Oh dear, I do hope not.'

'They enjoyed it, I'm sure, whoever they are. Mrs Drury says you are a very good cook.'

'Er ... yes.' She was all at sixes and sevens again. She could remain calm talking about her husband's recent death, but mention the wedding cake and she was as nervous as a candidate for a *Stars in Your Eyes* audition.

There was nothing more I could do here. I finished my tea and thanked her, wrapping up well for the arctic conditions outside. Mrs Fenwick insisted on lending me some gloves, hand-knitted, WI pattern. It was more than I could bear.

'The tea was lovely, thank you. By the way, can you give me Pippa's address? I'd like to have a word with her.'

'I can't. I don't know where she lives. She wouldn't give it to anyone. Quite strange. I mean, I wouldn't visit her or anything. Perhaps send her a card at Christmas, that sort of thing.'

'Thank you again. I'll keep in touch.'

Head down, I started the long walk back to Latching. I was very tired. Tinned soup is not long-term nourishment. I needed protein. I had to keep going, pushing one leg forward, then the other, face against the wind. My lips were drying out. If I got as far as Maeve's Cafe, I'd have a blow-out fish and chips.

I'd almost forgotten the way. The cafe

236

windows were all steamed up as I opened the door and went inside. Mavis shot me a look across the counter.

'Surprised you got the nerve to come in here,' she sniffed.

'Surprised I've got the strength,' I said.

'After what I've heard.'

'Obviously some walls have ears. Give over, Mavis. Don't start the Cold War again. I haven't done anything wrong.'

'Not what I hear, young madam. Private investigator, my foot. Private arsonist, more like.'

I took a seat by a window and sat down wearily. The cafe was half empty. 'All I want is some decent fish and chips. If it means a moral lecture as well, then I'll take it. But be quick. I'm liable to pass out from under-nourishment and then you'll have to cope with 999 calls and the ambulance service.'

She wasn't talking to me. That suited. But my wan face must have stirred some compassion for she brought me a mug of tea, as I like it, weak with honey. Some minutes later, cod and chips arrived, steaming and golden and succulent. At least it was fresh. Mavis hadn't warmed up some leftovers in the microwave.

'Thank you,' I said.

She sniffed again and plonked down some cutlery, her face set in disapproval. I couldn't understand her sudden antipathy. I had always been her flavour of the month and it hurt. I hoped Doris wouldn't put up the same barriers when I went into her shop for my daily supply of yoghurt and apples.

It took me a long time to eat the plateful. Although it tasted delicious and the chips melted their crispness on my tongue, my jaws had lost their chewing power. Perhaps it was all that soup.

I couldn't even finish the last few chips. I wrapped them up in a paper napkin. The gulls would go for them.

I put a fiver on the counter and Mavis gave me some change without saying a word.

'Let me know when peace is declared,' I said, going out.

Fate must have decided to deal me some good cards for a change for as I was walking across the old Town Hall Square, coming towards me was Leroy Anderson. She looked perky, perched on absurd clumpy high heels, her hair in a smooth chignon, skin flawless with carefully applied make-up.

'Hi, Miss Anderson. How are you? You look well.'

'I'm fine. They've put me in charge of administration since poor Mr Fenwick died. A lot of responsibility but I know what I'm doing. He never really appreciated me.'

'Well done,' I said. 'I'm sure you are the right person to keep things going. People

238

always underestimate the ability of a good secretary.'

She smiled, all raspberry lip gloss and brushed blusher. 'Thank you. Nice of you to say that. Do I know you?'

'Not really.' I wasn't going to remind her of Barbara Hutton. 'But we have spoken several times. I wonder if you could help me. Did a woman called Pippa Shaw ever buy a property from you?'

'No, I don't think so.'

'Did Mr Fenwick have an interest in any properties? I mean, did he rent out places?'

'Oh yes, he owned a block of flats on the front. Very nice, if you like modern red brick and metal balconies. They pulled down several old houses and put up this six-floor apartment block. A sort of investment. It's called Horizon Views.'

'Thank you. Carry on the good work.'

She tripped away on huge heels, quite consoled over the loss of her aromatherapy oils.

I knew Horizon Views, the ugliest block on the seafront. I couldn't imagine Pippa Shaw liking anything but the sea view, but if it had been for free, then you could get used to red brick.

The cod fillet had given me a new spurt of energy. I walked along the front to Horizon Views. The wind was still relentless and biting. The swans on the boating pool were

239

fluffed out like forked meringues as they glided across the rippling surface. I was glad of the WI pattern gloves.

The block of flats loomed like some epitaph to depressed elephants, encased in garish red brick and grey painted steelwork. The architect must have been having an away-day on bad coke.

I scanned the bell labels. There it was: P Shaw. Flat 5. I rang the bell. A female voice answered.

'Delivery from Interflora,' I said pleasantly.

'Please come up.'

The entrance door opened to my touch. I took the lift to the fifth floor and found the door for flat 5. It was painted a uniform white with a gold number 5. I knocked.

Pippa Shaw opened the door, expectantly. Her face fell when she saw me. There was nothing wrong with her memory.

'Hello,' I said. 'Do you still want me to take photographs of your errant husband and his paramour?'

# Sixteen

'So, hello again,' I went on as Pippa Shaw stood in the doorway, clearly lost for words. A nerve twitched at the side of her mouth, disturbing her lip gloss. 'Can I come in? Sorry about no flowers, but we have several things to discuss.'

She was as immaculate as ever in sharp white cords and a white silk jersey. How could she keep so clean? Not a splodge of tomato sauce anywhere. I followed her into a big lounge that spilled out on to a fern-potted balcony. The lounge was all white leather and water-silk drapes. Not a book or magazine in sight. I began to feel androgynous.

'You do remember me?' I asked, not waiting to be asked to sit down. I needed to sit down. It was a deep slippery sofa.

'Yes, you are Jordan Lacey, the PI. We met in the multi-storey car park.'

'I'm glad you remember even though you have trouble remembering who you are married to. That was when you told me a load of nonsense about following your

241

husband, Councillor Adrian Fenwick, and taking photographs et cetera, the councillor who was, in fact, at that time, your father-in-law and possibly your lover. So exactly whose affair were we talking about? You with him? Him with someone else? I'm confused.'

'We obviously need to talk,' she said. This was an understatement but at least she had not thrown me out.

I felt very much in control despite the extended nails. 'Yes,' I said. 'I'm here to get at the truth. Or there's going to be a problem, Ms Shaw or Mrs Fenwick, whichever name you prefer.'

'I took my maiden name after the divorce,' she said.

'Except when it suits you.'

Pippa Shaw had got her breath back. She straightened a cushion, each corner in turn. 'This isn't easy,' she began.

'The truth never is.' I was surprised she even wanted to talk. Something didn't ring true but I was prepared to listen.

'When I married Tony, I found I had made a terrible mistake. We didn't really get along, apart from in bed with the lights out. It was hopeless. Then I found that the man I should have married was his father, Adrian. We were perfect together. We began an affair. I know it wasn't right but we simply couldn't help it.'

'But he was already married. To your mother-in-law. It sounds like one of those confessional stories in women's magazines.'

'I know. And Mrs Fenwick was nice to me, friendly, the kind of mother-in-law one always longs for. It was a difficult situation.'

'And now you've found someone else, is that right? Mrs Fenwick even baked you a wedding cake.'

'I didn't want it. A wedding cake, no way! I wanted to get away from the Fenwicks, even Adrian. They smothered me with kindness. And Adrian started getting possessive. I had to make a new start.'

There was a chink in the glamour. Pippa Shaw actually looked more human. Minute cracks were appearing like on an old oil painting that had been badly varnished. Even her bronzed hair looked duller.

'Why don't you tell me everything, starting from the beginning,' I said, like an agony aunt. 'And don't leave out the mobile phone and the thermos flask.'

She was thrown. Her mind was juggling with what to tell me and what to leave out. Yes, she admitted, she had lifted the mobile phone on an impulse. Yes, she had taken the call from Mrs Drury meant for the other Mrs Fenwick and made the appointment to see me. Yes, she had also taken the thermos flask but simply so that she could make her soon-to-be ex-beloved some coffee. 'It was a sort of gesture,' she added. 'As if I were his wife.'

Nothing made sense. She was still not telling the whole truth. She was feeding me snippets to keep me off the real track.

'So why employ me to take photographs?'

'I wanted to find out if we had been successful at covering our tracks. I was worried, now that I was remarrying. My fiancé is the jealous type. He's in the pop recording business. There's a lot of aggro and stress in the studios.'

'And he's a catch, is he?'

She studied her nails as if calculating his worth in manicures. 'You could say that. A millionaire, several times over.'

I couldn't even imagine so much money. Scrimping and saving was my way of life. Perhaps she'd buy me a poinsettia for Christmas.

'So you didn't see Mr Fenwick the night of the fire at Fenwick Future Homes?'

She hesitated. 'No, I didn't see him.'

'But he got the coffee.'

'I left the flask for him at his office.'

'But you didn't see him at all?'

'I've told you. I never saw him.' Tears spiked her eyes, clogging her lashes and I almost believed her. I think she actually loved Adrian whatever the scenario. He was a father figure. An older man had actually appealed to her, more than his callow son. If

Tony Fenwick had been the callow sort. I'd never met him. Perhaps I ought to find out. Then maybe not. I was spreading the web wide, too wide.

'And the standing order payments into my account?'

'Yes, as I promised. All in order. I made arrangements for the standing order to be paid every week.'

'And nothing else?'

'I don't understand.'

'Someone has been paying large sums of cash into my account. Someone pretending to be me. Is it you?'

She made a little laugh. 'Large sums? Lucky you. I should spend it while you have a chance. But no, I'm not your fairy-god-mother. God forbid, I need every penny. This place ... eats money.'

'But these flats belonged to Adrian Fenwick. Surely he didn't expect you to pay a rent?'

She didn't answer, swallowed. That told me a lot. She shot a glance at a silver drinks tray well supplied with gin, vodka, whisky and mixers. Her eyes reflected a thirst.

'How about the sleeping tablets that you laced Adrian's coffee with?' I threw at her. She went quite white neath the Porcelain Beige foundation. 'Halcion, they're called. Leftovers from your prescription after your divorce perhaps? Divorces are sleepless

245

events, I understand. I only need to check with your doctor.'

Not true. He wouldn't tell me anything. But he might tell DI James.

'How do you know?' she breathed.

'Forensic, Miss Shaw. They can find out anything these days.'

'I didn't mean any harm. I only wanted him to be too sleepy to call on me. You know what I mean. He often called in late. My wedding's not far off and I don't want anything to go wrong. Adrian had been getting very ardent lately, not wanting me to remarry, that sort of thing. I was tired of the hassles. I thought a sleeping pill would ... well, make him sleep instead.'

'It was more than one sleeping pill.'

'I didn't count. I only had a few left over. Perhaps two then...'

'And you took the coffee to his office in the afternoon?'

'Just as they were closing. He wasn't there. I left it on his desk with a little note.'

'Which conveniently got burnt. Did you go back later that night and lock the office door just to make sure?'

Pippa Shaw looked as if she was going to faint. I was sure she had locked the door. She probably had a key to let herself in the back door of the showroom, and the key to his office for little rendezvous. Adrian might already have been half asleep on the cocktail

246

of brandy and Halcion. But she could not admit it. There was that wedding to a several times over stressed millionaire to protect.

I couldn't think of anything more to ask the glamorous, but shaken, former Mrs Fenwick Jnr. I had run out of ideas. I didn't know whether I believed her or not. My legs were miraculously still working so I gathered myself up off her deep sofa and turned towards the door. She was already heading for the drinks tray. Her hand was slightly trembling as she poured herself a generous straight gin into a cut-glass tumbler.

'I won't have anything, thank you,' I said. 'I don't drink when I'm walking.' How I hate meanness. 'By the way, do you ride a bike?'

She flashed me a look of contempt. The 37 per cent alcohol content of the gin had immediately shot into her veins, given her back her self-confidence. 'A bike? I wouldn't be seen dead on one.'

Jack. I went straight to Jack. In his booth, security guarded with devices I've never heard of, in the amusement arcade on the pier, he saw the entire world. He had a boring job, raking in all that money, count-ing it, putting thousands of pounds in the bank, keeping the yobbos out. Long hours, rainswept, windswept, but as cosy as toast in his booth.

'Got a minute?' I said, leaning against the glass.

'For you, darling. Any time.' He grinned.

He coded in some security number and the door opened. He was in his usual greasy T-shirt and jeans. I wondered if they ever saw a washing machine. I knew nothing about his private life. Perhaps there was a Mrs Jack somewhere in a bungalow in Ferring. I didn't think so. He looked a lonely, undomesticated, sex-starved bachelor.

He put on the electric kettle, found two semi-clean mugs. They looked revolting but I had to drink the stuff. I couldn't hurt his feelings. He put in lots of instant, lots of brown sugar, lots of coffee-mate. Stirred not shaken. His ideal brew, thick and sweet.

'Lovely,' I said, finding myself a stool in his crowded booth. It was nice to be surrounded by masses and masses of money, even if none of it was mine. People felt they had to throw it away on his machines and moving shelves. It was an addiction to the lights, the warmth, the feeling of a social activity, the promise of easy money.

He was smiling at me as if he had won the lottery. Dear God, the man actually liked me, fancied me, thought he had a chance, even when he hadn't shaved for days. What could I do or say, except to smile back?

'I want to rack your brains,' I said. 'You know everybody in Latching. Tell me what you know about Councillor Adrian Fenwick, his daughter-in-law, Pippa Shaw, Mrs Edith Drury, Mr Terence Lucan.'

'Blimey. You don't want much.'

'I'm in no hurry.'

'OK. But I still have to work. See to the machines. Dole out money to the punters.'

'You carry on with your work. Do what you have to do. I'm quite happy sitting here with a coffee.' I sat back and relaxed. He might give me another teddy. I had room on my bedside table.

There were erratic interludes when Jack could talk and he rambled on. He was a mine of trivial information. He was also starved of a woman to talk to. A woman who listened. Affection, it's called. A warm feeling. He was a dam bursting with words.

'The dishy councillor ... very good-looking grey-way, pulled the birds. Long marriage to old bird but he was still fond of the duck. Sorry he got burned, but it could have been an accident. I don't believe he knew what was happening. Pippa ... she was one of his birds, but she got wise. Wanted a diamond ring on her finger, security, money-minded. Found some pop geezer, filthy rich, flashy car. Ditched the councillor, not nice, bitch. The WI president, Dopey Drury they call her, mad driver, potty but kind-hearted.

249

Never comes in here, but some of her members do, small-time gamblers, little flutter. They all love the woman. Never a word against her. Salt of the earth.'

Jack stopped for breath and took a long drink of his awful coffee. Heaven knows what it was doing to his stomach. His bad complexion was some answer.

'Yes...' I prompted.

'All that stuff in the papers about kids trashing the wedding show. Don't believe it, na-arh. They'd have eaten the lot, been found on the floor, stuffed to the gills, sick as dogs. And the wedding cake ... who eats wedding cake these days? They'd have taken it on the pier, fed it to the gulls for a laugh. No, ma'am, that's the wrong track. You've got to find some other geezers.'

'Thank you,' I said. 'What about Terence Lucan?'

'The nursery bloke talking to trees. Lost his marbles years ago. Don't know how he survives. Place is a muddle, except for his plants. Can't pay his workers. Up to his ears in debt, serious debt. The racetracks though, can't keep away from 'em. Can't see it myself, horses running about, jumping fences, breaking legs. Who cares? Half of them get shot, anyway.'

'So ... what about the water lilies that got stolen?'

'I should look for a big hole. Who'd steal

something that would die in a couple of days? What else d'you want to know? Ask me. I'll tell you anything.'

'Who set fire to Fenwick Future Homes?'

His face fell. Someone was knocking on the window but he ignored them. 'Can't help you there. I would if I could, believe me. You watch it, me darlin'. Someone's using you.'

I put down the mug. 'You've been a wonderful help, Jack,' I said. He hadn't told me anything that I had not already worked out for myself but it was confirmation.

'Any time,' he said, wondering when he would see me again.

When I got home there was a message on my answerphone. It was from DI James.

'Hello, Jordan? This is DI James. I picked up the tape. You left your shop open. Don't leave the country. If you have a passport, could you please bring it into the station?'

I couldn't believe this was happening to me. Jordan Lacey, the most trustworthy (almost) PI on the south coast. Friend of the homeless, old ladies, lost pets and feeder of swans on boating pool. Giver-away of hideous duck to gloater who made huge profit on same duck. Why me? Clearly I was being set up.

Someone was cycling round Latching on my bike, looking like me. Someone was depositing large amounts of cash in my bank account without my permission. Someone was turning my friends against me. I hoped they'd get saddle sore and bashed shins.

I felt very lonely, Jack was my only friend but he could not really help me. There was Bud, the sub officer at the fire station, firefighter with a bad dose of grievance. He might be sympathetic. But what would it cost me? I had no intention of paying either man in the currency that they wanted.

I rang the fire station. 'Can I speak to sub officer Bud Morrison.'

Voices consulted against a background of activity. 'Is this a personal call?'

'Yes.' I decided not to lie. Odd. I could have said it was in relation to two recent Latching fires and that would also have been the truth.

'Sub officer Bud Morrison,' he said briskly.

'Jordan Lacey,' I said. 'How are you? I wonder if we could meet? I'd like to apologise and buy you a beer.'

I could see the grin. He thought he was going to score. I knew it was a line he'd like.

'Sounds up my street,' he said. 'I approve of women who are prepared to grovel.'

'This grovelling is only in the pursuit of information, for picking brains.'

'Pick away, lady. Be gentle with me. I'll tell you when to move on down lower.'

Save me. I wasn't into this cavorting. Another sex-starved male on the make. Shopping list: chastity belt; spray hair lacquer for use in emergency.

'Shall we meet this evening? After your shift? Say, at the Bear and Bait?'

'Say any time you like. Eight o'clock. See you, kiddo.'

I'm a few years past the kiddo stakes, but I preferred it to sexy and lewd. What made men think it was OK to call you anything that reflected their mental state? I would never dream of letting any man get the merest inkling of what was going on in my head. They might run a mile. Except DI James. It would take him a week before the tenpence dropped and by then I'd be on a surveillance the other side of Sussex.

I was mellowing on my second glass of Cabernet Sauvignon before Bud turned up at the Bear and Bait. He looked scrubbed, hair still wet from the shower. He wore a navy polo-necked jersey, a fawn leather blousson jacket, jeans. Sharp. I got him a pint of Speckled Hen bitter.

After we had bandied a few polite re-marks, exchanged pleasantries and found a corner table, I came straight to the point.

'I'm being set up for the fire at Fenwick Future Homes,' I said. 'It's circumstantial. There was someone, looking like me, riding my bike, seen near FFH before the fire. A can of petrol was planted with my bike. Petrol was used to start the fire, they say. You, mistakenly, letting me wander about said scene did not help.'

'I thought you were still on the force.'

'I know, not your fault. I should have told you but my curiosity got the better of my good nature. And now this Picture House incident. No connection, I assure you. I was only trying to attract attention after being locked in and tied up by two thugs. Foreign thugs.'

'Pre-safety celluloid is very dangerous,' said Bud. 'It can self-ignite.'

'Might have saved me a few matches. I only had seven.'

'Let's get this straight. They think you set fire to FFH because you were seen near there beforehand, your bike carried a can of petrol, and you were seen behaving suspiciously afterwards on the scene of the fire. And I suppose you had a motive?'

It sounded bad. 'It's hardly a strong motive. Councillor Fenwick had given planning permission for Trenchers to be pulled down and a small industrial plant built on the hotel site. I have protective feelings about the old hotel.'

Obviously it didn't sound like much of a motive at all to Bud. He dismissed it immediately. 'Some arsonists don't need a motive. It's the feeling of power they crave.

Got a screw loose. This can of petrol? What size?'

'A gallon, I suppose.'

'How much petrol was left in the can?'

'I don't know.'

'Find out. There was some petrol splashed about the offices and showroom but not necessarily to start the fire. We think a small fire had already started. If the can was full or fullish, then it wasn't used to start the fire. If it was near empty, then maybe it had.' Bud finished his beer. 'I cleared you in my report, sweetheart. Said I invited you in by mistake. Maybe that'll ease the suspicion.'

That was kind. I felt a stirring of gratitude. Not a lot, but enough for me to give him a genuine smile. He was encouraged.

'But what were you doing there, at that ungodly hour, when you should have been tucked up in your little bed?'

'I couldn't sleep. I was so cold.' No bets on how he would respond.

'I'd have kept you warm,' he smirked. But he smirked with genuine admiration. He thought I was a little woman in need of male protection. 'Find out where your bike was found. A true arsonist would have left it close to the blaze, so that the can heated and blew up, destroying the evidence.'

'So if it was left at some distance, it was meant to be found?'

'Something like that.'

'Thanks,' I said, buying him another beer. 'At least I've some ammunition. I can start fighting back.'

A trio was arriving; keyboard, bass and guitar. The jazz evening was about to begin. The pub was crowding up. A couple joined our table and Bud did not look pleased. When the jazz broke into improvised sound, he looked even less pleased.

'Can't stand this racket,' he said, standing up, pulling on his leather jacket. 'Let's go somewhere else.'

He meant my place. Some minds I can read. I ran through a few excuses ... rat infestation, infectious diseases, invasion of aliens ... Instead I stayed with the truth.

For once, I blessed the discomfort, the cramps, the relentless hygiene rigmarole. I hushed my voice modestly. 'Sorry, Bud, wrong time of the month,' I said.

# Seventeen

It was time to wind up these cases. Their convolutions were strangling me. I wanted to be free of them, to get back to missing persons and serving subpoenas. I had to get tough with these people, show them that I meant business.

But who first? I fancied alphabetical order. But before I left my office I got together all my notes, all the bits and pieces I'd gathered from the cases and laid them out on the floor. I stared at the collection then began to swirl them around like a magician, hoping that something would click.

'Come on, baby,' I breathed. 'Come to mama.'

They moved while my back was turned.

I put up the notice saying CLOSED FOR LUNCH even though it was only 11 a.m. Lunch can mean anything in my book. Doris was hurrying past, arms full of shopping bags. She'd obviously been to some discount store to stock up. She winked at me.

'Too busy to eat last night?' she asked.

'Saw you with the hunky fireman.'

'You only saw me with him,' I said. 'Nothing happened.'

'That's what they always say.' She winked again and disappeared into her shop to restock the shelves.

Nothing went unnoticed in this town. I couldn't even breathe without someone noting the time and place. Yet no one had seen a mob of youths trash the WI marquee and carry away a three-tiered cake.

As I cycled to Mrs Drury's solid Edwardian villa the other side of Latching, my knees began to feel round my ears. I got off and inspected my bike. The saddle had been lowered. Whoever had ridden my bike was shorter than me. I nearly punched the air, except I don't let my feelings take over. I unscrewed the bolt and raised the saddle to suit my long legs.

Mrs Drury spotted me from a window and opened the door immediately.

'Come in, Jordan,' she said, beaming like an old friend. 'I was hoping you'd drop by and tell me how you were getting on with your investigations. Have you found the cake? It's all so fascinating. Would you like some tea or coffee? I was just going to make a pot.'

'Coffee would be fine,' I said, any courage rapidly sliding down into my boots. How could I hurt her? She was such a good soul at heart.

I followed her through to the kitchen. It looked as if an Exocet missile had hit it. She must have used every saucepan, mixing bowl, whisk, rolling pin and chopping board that she possessed. They were everywhere, on the table, on the draining board, in the sink, on the floor, liberally doused in flour. I took off my anorak and rolled up my sleeves.

'I wondered why you had done such a lot of shopping,' I said, turning on the hot tap and clearing the sink. 'I thought it was rather a lot of food to buy for one person. Are you throwing a party?'

'I'm past my party-giving days,' said Mrs Drury, trying to find the kettle among the debris. 'I just ... er ... just felt like doing a bit of cooking.'

'Lovely smell of fennel.'

'Oh yes, I've made one of my fennel quiches. I promised you one, didn't I?'

'And all these profiteroles? Cheese straws and vol-au-vents and stuffed mushrooms and latticed sausage plaits ... liver pâtés and salmon mousses. You have been busy. Looks to me like a re-run of the WI wedding display.'

There was a hung silence. The room took on the wrong shape.

I swished in some washing-up liquid. I couldn't look at Mrs Drury. She was having some sort of coughing fit, holding her side and leaning over the table. Not asthmatic coughing, more something gone down the wrong way. My words in fact.

I filled a glass with water and gave it to her. She sipped slowly until her coughing was under control.

'Oh dear me, now what was I doing? Oh yes, making some coffee for us. Here's the kettle. Now, how do you like your coffee, Jordan?'

I nearly said wet. 'Black, please, Mrs Drury.'

'There's no need to be doing all that,' she fussed, trying to stop me washing up. 'I can do it later.'

'Enough washing up here to incite deep depression,' I said, carrying on. 'Let me get on with it.'

It was my peace-offering, my white flag, my twig with white flowers. Any minute now I was going to have to say something about conscience cooking and she would hate me. Perhaps she would hate me less if I left her kitchen neat and pristine.

'So you've had lots of new members applying since all that publicity in the newspapers,' I said casually. She fell in the trap.

'Six definites and two possibles. Very satisfactory,' said Mrs Drury, spooning coffee grains into cups and starting to stir even though she had not boiled any hot water.

She was clearly distracted but managing to hide it quite well.

'Almost like putting an advertisement in the newspapers, wasn't it, Mrs Drury? You know: WANTED: NEW MEMBERS FOR INVIGORATING ORGANISATION. All those press stories. Wonderful publicity and every one for nothing. Quite a bargain when you think what they charge for space.'

'Well, yes, if you put it like that,' said Mrs Drury, filling the kettle. 'Still, it's all over and done with now. History, as they say. We can forget all about it, can't we, dear?'

She was trying to look at me, catch my eye but couldn't quite make it. She bustled around, doing unnecessary things, putting unwashed bowls away. Her guilt was almost visible. She'd organised it like an army manoeuvre, getting rid of everyone in the marquee on some pretext, trashing the display, removing the wedding cake and then running round, shouting for help.

It was difficult to imagine the well-built Mrs Drury throwing food in the air, stamping on meringues, breaking plates. Perhaps the cake had even been in the boot of her car when she had come to collect me from the shop.

I nodded slowly. 'I guess when I find the cake for Mrs Fenwick, we'll be able to forget all about it. Quite possibly, maybe even definitely,' I added, using her words.

'Well, that's splendid, then, isn't it?' she said at last, recovering. 'Come and sit down. You deserve it after doing all that washing-up. What an angel you are.'

She carried the tray through to the front room and we sat down and drank coffee and chatted as if nothing whatsoever had been said in the kitchen. It was hardly real. Any moment I would wake up and find I'd fallen asleep over the counter. Perhaps Bud had slipped me a dream pill last night.

'I hope your friends in the WI enjoy your cooking,' I said, as I got up to leave. 'What a lovely surprise for them.'

'I don't know what you mean,' she said, flustered.

'Aren't you taking all these goodies to your next meeting as a good-will gesture?' It was obvious she was staging a rerun.

Never at a loss for long, Mrs Drury nodded. 'What a lovely idea, Jordan. I'll do just that. They'll be so amused.'

We said goodbye amicably but I noticed that she did not think I was enough of an angel to be given the promised quiche garnished with fennel.

'Whoever borrowed my bike, lowered the saddle,' I said to DI James on the phone later. 'So that makes them shorter than me.'

'Everyone in Latching is shorter than you,' he replied.

This was way unfair to my almost 5 foot 8 inches but I let it pass. I liked being tall, especially in the maddening crowd. It gave me a head start.

'And I should like to know how much petrol was in the can you found attached to my bike,' I went on. 'Was it nearly full or nearly empty?'

'You sound like a politician.'

'And you sound as if you're hedging.'

'We didn't measure it.'

'You didn't measure it?' I put ringing indignation into my voice. 'But you should have. The volume makes a difference. I got this from an expert.'

'You mean sub-officer Morrison.'

'Is nothing of my private life private any more? You'll be taking bets next on what colour pants I'm wearing.'

'White,' he said instantly.

I was glad of the length of the BT cable network between us. At least he couldn't see my cheeks colouring. It was a lucky guess. He had no way of knowing that I never wear pink. My only pink undergarment is the dreaded, passion-killing stretched winter knit vest. My pants and bra drawer is a tumble of white and black with an occasional glimpse of blue. I have been known to mix and match.

'The broken bicycle chain, the fluorescent armband, the lower saddle and the fact that my bike was found intact, all add up to a set-up. If I had been the arsonist, I'd have left the bike and the petrol right outside the showroom where it would have heated up and exploded.'

There was a silence. I hoped DI James was writing it all down.

'You were seen leaving your flat at five forty a.m. by an observant postman on his way to the sorting office. You have a lot of friends at the post office. The brigade was called at five thirty-five from a public phone box. The distance from your flat to the showroom is thirteen minutes fast walking time. I suppose you could have started the fire, got back to your flat, cleaned up, and gone out again by five forty a.m. But it doesn't seem likely. You're not exactly an Olympic runner.'

He'd been doing homework, calculations. My voice disappeared somewhere down my poloneck. Was the man trying to save me?

'But the fire had a delayed start,' I croaked, honest to the point of stupidity. 'A candle in a bin to burn first. A trail of petrol-soaked shredded paper.'

I heard his sigh of frustration. 'I had hoped you would not remind me of that.'

I carried a clipboard and put on gold-rimmed spectacles. I'd long ago discovered that if you carried a clipboard and waved it at receptionists, you could get in anywhere. There was a caretaker at Horizon View flats but it seemed to work just as well on him.

'Number five you say? From the council? I suppose it's all right. Miss Shaw is out but I'm sure she won't mind.'

'Community charge tax, you know. Residential premises can't be used to run a business, so, if you'd just let me in. I shan't be more than five minutes. It won't take long to check. Such a fuss, all these regulations. New ones every day.'

'I don't think Miss Shaw works.'

'Computers, internet, that kind of thing.'

'Oh, I see,' he agreed, knowing all about them, of course. 'The internet. Damned council. Always interfering.'

'Sorry. I don't make the rules.'

The caretaker took me up in the lift and opened the door of No 5 with his pass key. It was a big flat and five minutes was hardly long enough for what I had to do. As everywhere was white, even the carpets, I took off my boots. We didn't want to leave footprints in the snow.

Systematically I went through every cupboard and drawer. Pippa Shaw was so tidy it made me feel inadequate. There was not a scrap of rubbish or litter. No tights on the floor, no screwed-up tissues, not a hair, not a pin out of place.

She was a compulsive tidier. She had

containers for containers, plastic bags for plastic bags. Maybe she employed someone to do it for her. Maybe she was rarely there, preferring the anonymity of country hotels with pools and beauty spas.

There was no imprint of her character. It was like a show home with a few tasteful ornaments on display, the token avocado in a cane basket, wine in a rack, a string of garlic.

It made me feel insecure, a slob, disorganised. But she had the one thing that I had little of – plenty of spare time. She could spend a morning rearranging her cutlery. I just flung everything into a drawer and hoped to find what I wanted later.

If I'd had a toothcomb, I'd have used it. There was not a letter, a bill, a file, a bank statement in sight. She kept nothing. No appointment cards, no diary, no address book. Miss Shaw was a creature from another planet. I bet she didn't even have fingerprints.

My sweep went from room to room; my invisible search did not disturb a mote of dust. I wouldn't find a thing in this immaculate conception. There was nothing out of place. Not a shred of evidence that might be construed as suspicious. It couldn't be so. No one was that impossibly lily-white. There must be something I had missed.

I began again, with meticulous care. Every

jar, every bottle, every carton, every bin, saucepan, dish in the kitchen was closely inspected. Same in her lounge. Even the books were unthumbed. The only sign of normal habitation was the collection of drinks on the tray.

Her bedroom was cool. All her clothes were tidy and stored away. Bed smooth, unruffled. Make-up jars and bottles stood in polite groups on her polished, glass-topped dressing table. I was feeling ill again. One flaw, please, that was all I wanted. A screwed-up Mars wrapper under the bed; an apple core down the loo.

Her shoes were regimented in pairs on special shoe space-saver racks. She had a lot of shoes. Boots stood with long wooden trees inside to keep their shape. One handle emerged two inches taller than its twin. I took the tree out and put my hand deep down inside the boot. Something was stuffed in the foot area, down to the toe. It felt silky yet tangled. Creepy. I drew it out with threads clinging to my fingers.

Bingo.

In a second I had my scissors out, cut off a few inches and put them in a plastic specimen bag. Then I stuffed the rest back in the boot, pushed the shoetree down in place, to the same height as I had found it. Before I left, I took a photograph of her boots, then a long shot with enough of her bedroom to identify the location. A nasty mind might say I had planted the evidence.

I gave up, left No 5, waved my clipboard cheerily at the caretaker. He was relieved to see me go, obviously not laden with loot. He had been having second thoughts, wondering if he would get into trouble.

The specimen bag was tucked in my pocket. Not exactly a wasted journey.

'Lovely flat,' I said.

'You should see the others.'

Water lilies next but I couldn't face the uphill cycle ride. It was splash-out day. I phoned a taxi company and a woman driver called Linda called for me in a serviceable saloon. She was pleasant company, a bit like a friendly hairdresser only she didn't ask me where I was going for my holidays. The ride cost £6, the price of selling something from my shop, plus a £1 tip.

'Beats cycling any day,' I said as she dropped me outside the Latching Water Nursery. 'I can still breathe.'

'Don't buy too many plants,' she said, giving me her card before driving off.

The autumn-tinged slopes were so peaceful, a cool wind barely disturbing the branches, only whispering and rustling like little animals in the undergrowth. I drank in the solitude, the views as dense as a forest from Camelot. And I was just about to bust this idyllic scene. And why? Because Mr

268

Lucan had involved me, innocently perhaps, in a fraud and I didn't like it much. But I did like his car and I wanted it. Terence Lucan was walking towards me, green boots coated in mud. He looked preoccupied, hardly glanced at me, eyes protected. There were no customers about.

'Mr Lucan,' I said. 'I've brought a cheque with me. A cheque for three hundred pounds. The first instalment on the Morris Minor.'

'I said I would prefer cash.'

So he had. Like I'd go all the way back to Latching now to fetch cash.

'Perhaps you could take this cheque and I'll make sure the rest is in cash. It's quite a way to come to Preston Hill and I've already spent on a taxi.'

'Well, I suppose it's OK this once,' he said, recognising real money. 'I'll get the log book, MOT, insurance, et cetera. They're in the office.'

'And a receipt please.'

'You got it.'

'All right to drive the car home? I take it the insurance will cover me?'

'Third party. There's probably enough petrol to get you to Latching, but then you'll need to fill up.'

I could see his mind calculating the cost of the petrol and weighing up whether he could charge me.

His office was the usual chaos but his filing system worked and he knew where to find the papers. The keys were hanging on a hook on the wall with a brown label attached. I made sure I had everything, including the receipt, before I dropped my explosive device.

'By the way, Mr Lucan. You'll be pleased to know that I've found all your water lilies. At least, I know where they are. I'll be sending you a report and we can deduct my fee from the amount I still owe you for the car. I'm sure you will be relieved that it's all over and there won't be any nasty court case to attend, that is if you drop your insurance claim for the theft of your plants.'

Mr Lucan had an outdoor face. Years of Sussex sunshine and coastal wind had weathered it to a fine shade of brown. But at this moment, the colour drained away and he was left with skin a strange dirty grey.

'You've found them?' he croaked. 'My goodness ... you are efficient.'

'A little too efficient for you, I'm afraid, Mr Lucan. I guess you hoped that little ol' me would flounder in one of your ponds and come up with zilch. And zilch it very nearly was until I went on walkabout among your lovely shrubs and saplings.'

'Er ... I'm not sure what you mean...'

'Knowing the state of your finances, I doubt if your insurance policy is comprehensive. It probably covers theft, but not deadly diseases like crown rot. As the experts at Kew Gardens kindly told me: crown rot is when the water-lily rootstocks become soft, gelatinous and with a strong smell. There's no known cure and the only thing to do is destroy them, disinfect the ponds and start all over again.'

'My water lilies haven't got crown rot,' he said indignantly. 'Those plants you saw were perfect.'

'I only saw some blooms, not the roots. Perhaps they were the best of a rotting lot, which a helpful mate hawked around the pubs to add credence to your story. The last of your beautiful collection. I can understand you being upset, Mr Lucan. It must have broken your heart to see all your hard work rotting away. And the putrid smell is just awful, I do agree.'

'You can't prove this,' he blustered.

'I think I can,' I said. 'I sent Kew Gardens a piece of mouldy root found on your property. I have camera proof. They identified water-lily crown rot. And you should remember that it is an offence to waste police time. Latching police have spent a considerable number of man hours trying to trace a van with certain tyre tracks. Probably your own Land Rover backed over the mud. They might not take too kindly to being told it was all a scam, a swindle, a trick to defraud the insurance company.'

Poor man. He looked broken, sucking in air between his teeth.

'Are you going to tell them?' he asked as I turned to leave.

'I don't think so,' I said. 'What good would it do? It wouldn't bring back your plants. You are not likely to do it again. No one got hurt. And you have got to restock your ponds somehow. Perhaps a nice horse will come in first. Your luck deserves to change.'

Two expressions crossed his face at the same time. It was confusing. I didn't know if he was grateful or about to hit me over the head with a shovel.

I put the key in the door lock of the nearly mine red and black ladybird. I wasn't going to let him spoil this moment. The door opened. It was a mess inside, just like his office. But I wasn't dismayed by the rubbish. Ten minutes with a spray can and she would smell as sweet as a field of lavender.

I slipped into the driving seat. It was made for me. We fitted like suede gloves. The key turned in the ignition and the engine started, first time. It was an omen. She knew me. She liked me. It was love at first sight, all over again. The gear slid into reverse and I took her slowly out of her lonely incarceration on the top of the hill. The open road beckoned. She was free again, at last.

Mr Lucan was waving his arms at me. I

wasn't sure whether he was trying to stop me leaving or politely showing me out of the drive and out on to the road. I wound down the window. Old-fashioned wind-downs. I love 'em.

'I guess you don't remember saying that you would give me this car if I solved your case, but I won't hold you to it,' I said sweetly.

'How do you know? Tell me? Howdaya know?' he was barking, clearly incensed, knuckles white as he gripped the top of the window. Teetering on the edge of insanity. Time to get out quick before he did us both an injury.

'Go dig up a big hole that's barely settled at the bottom end of the southern slope,' I said. 'That's how I know. Make sure you put plenty of the right chemicals in it. You don't want the rot to spread.'

# Eighteen

Ladybird and I drove back to Latching in complete harmony. It was the beginning of a long affair. We were compatible in every way. I wouldn't be able to use her for surveillance but it did not matter. She was mine for every other journey. No more drenched cycle rides. I would arrive in style. We might even share leisure when I go walking on the South Downs, Chantonbury Hill, Devil's Dyke. I know all the chalky parking areas. Wonderful views for her.

So that was the end of the water lilies and the WI. Was anyone else actually paying me for my services? The pure white Ms Shaw with suspicious boot would have cancelled her standing order. There was nothing else I could do there – or was there?

But I was still standing in the stocks for the FFH fire. And the death of Councillor Adrian Fenwick. Ripe tomatoes in the face were not pleasant. The juice would drip down my shirt. What could I do to prove my innocence? Wake myself up and climb out of the quicksand?

I'd need a resident's parking permit. Another £20. Worth every penny. I filled in the required form. The clerk gave me a map showing where I could park, but not on double yellow lines. Was I still solvent? Could I eat this week?

Two down and one to go. Not bad. But the one left was so complicated I did not know where to begin. Cast: the late Adrian Fenwick, Mrs Fenwick, Pippa Shaw, ex-daughter-in-law, girlfriend and once Mrs Fenwick Jnr, Leroy Anderson, secretary and receptionist, her wacky sister Waz Fairbrother maybe, she of the Indian skirts and modelling glue, and the so far invisible bank manager, Leslie Fairbrother. I don't know why I linked the unseen bank manager with the fire at FFH but instinctively I did. The councillor had wanted money; Leslie Fairbrother had money, not his but at his disposal. That made a kind of sense.

And who was putting excessive sums of cash in my bank account? Someone with money to throw away for sure. All that un-invited money going to waste, idling in some Jane Doe account, and I wouldn't touch a penny of it. I knew what it was meant to look like, that I was paid to torch the FFH.

Who would want to burn down the show-room? Mrs Fenwick was only into lighting ovens; Pippa said she loved the man; Leroy liked her job and status perks. A rival estate agents? Hardly a good business move especially if they were charged. The Fairbrothers? No motive at all.

That left the deranged, the demented and the deluded. Only my ex-boyfriend Derek fitted those categories and he wasn't even in the picture.

It was as if thinking about him materialised him to my front door. I opened it confidently, hoping an unexpected visitor would brighten the evening. But it was said Derek, clean-shaven, well-groomed in a navy blazer, grey flannels, shifty-eyed, holding a bunch of garage forecourt flowers, on the make.

'Oh, hello,' I said, offhand. 'I'm just on my way out.'

I can be so ruthless.

'That's a pity,' he said. 'I was hoping we could have a little chat.'

Derek's little chats were never innocent exchanges of current topic variety. I always ended up fencing, trying to get his hands out of my clothes, or a tricky manoeuvre on my moral chair when I'm as concerned for the safety of my bone china as I am for my body. The flowers looked forlorn, unwanted, packed by some tired immigrant woman who accepted low pay because she didn't know any better.

'Are they for me? Thank you. You can

276

come in while I put them in water,' I said, shooting myself in the foot.

It would have been churlish not to make some coffee, but I didn't use my best, my Colombian beans. It had been a long time since I had entertained Derek in my sitting room but he made himself at home as if he belonged.

'Where do you keep your biscuits?' he asked, poking into my cupboards. 'Have you got any shortbread?'

As I cut the stems and arranged the rusty chrysanthemums and baby's breath in a vase, I planned a strategy. He might as well earn his coffee. 'Do you know anything about the fire at Fenwicks?' I asked. 'It's a funny business.'

'You're right there, babe. I heard the councillor was drugged or drunk. I know he was up to no good on the council, accepting handouts, that kind of thing. But that doesn't add up to murdering the man. It means getting in on the game, dividing the spoils, sharing the goodies. Know what I mean?'

I didn't. 'Go on, that's interesting.'

Having caught my attention, Derek expanded, took off his blazer, hung it neatly on the back of the door. He had found a packet of Scotch shortbread and was eating them out of the paper, spilling crumbs everywhere. Some men are such dirty eaters. Although DI James's daily diet was fish and chips and tomato sauce on everything, he ate tidily and without haste. Derek was devouring the buttery shortbread as if he'd just been released from solitary.

Derek sensed that for the time being he was not being banished to the pavement, and warmed to the subject.

'It wasn't just handouts. There was a rumoured scam about planning permission for posh residential houses ... y'know, pools and patios. He was tied up with some local builder. Fenwick got the planning permission through for any spare bit of land, the builder built the houses, FFH handled the sales. There's a demand for substantial houses along the coast. You could sell some houses several times over. Nice little earner.'

I could have kissed Derek but I wasn't going to. 'So the fire might have been to destroy some incriminating evidence? Someone getting suspicious? But surely it was a bit drastic for a few files that could have been put through a shredder?'

'Perhaps it got out of hand. Fires do. Someone starts an itsy-bitsy fire to burn a few papers and suddenly – whoosh – the place is an inferno. I remember several camp fires that nearly incinerated the Downs.'

'Excuse me,' I said. 'I have to make a phone call.'

All the lines to DI James were busy. I left a message for him to call me. I got out a dustpan and brush and swept up the crumbs.

'I like it when you're on your knees to me,' he said, crunching the last shortbread. 'Makes me feel important.'

'Don't bank on it. I can see the fluff in your turn-ups.'

'Any more coffee?'

'What do you know about the Fairbrothers?'

'Oh, he's my bank manager,' said Derek, spreading more crumbs as he balled the packet. 'Cool, detached sort of chap. Everything by the book. Hard man to get on with, not particularly helpful. Honey out of a stone would be easier. Obsessed with cleanliness, always washing his hands.'

A chill touched my spine. That kind of obsession was never cosy. Perhaps Waz Fairbrother was making a living statement with her chaos of litter. No wonder he had disappeared, or had he?

I got rid of Derek in the most direct way I could think of. I put on my anorak and boots, slotted a scarf round my neck.

'I have to go out,' I said. 'Take the last of the biscuits with you. Oh, but you've finished them, haven't you? That's all right then, you won't starve till you get home.'

He looked crestfallen, eyes slippery. 'I

279

thought we were going to spend some time together.'

'We have,' I said, rattling my keys. 'Now I have to go out and get on with earning my living.'

'I'll come with you,' he offered. 'I've got a car.'

'I've got a car.'

It was a great exit line. I swept out, ushering the obnoxious creep before me. He was outside on the pavement before he could finish his next sentence.

He was still chuntering on about this was no way to treat an old friend. The words were lost on the wind. Let him go eat someone else's biscuits.

Next morning I backed the ladybird out of the yard behind the shop and drove towards the Fairbrothers' house on the outskirts of Latching, collecting petrol on the way. The cost rocked me. Perhaps I could put mileage on my expenses. I left the car in a car park near the local shops, tucked out of sight between two ugly people-carriers, got a ticket from the machine, and legged it the rest of the way. If there was no one at home, I might have to break in.

The house had a gone-away look. Curtains were still drawn, milk on the doorstep, paper halfway through the letterbox. All giveaways. People will never learn. I knocked and set the chimes chiming. There was no answer. I tried again, stepped back, looking upwards, expecting to see an overslept face peering between the curtains.

It was still shrouded in silence. Leroy would have gone to work hours ago. Waz must be out shopping for more glue or paint or moulding clay.

The back was equally desolate, except for a small black cat sitting gloomily by the door. He miaowed that he'd missed out on breakfast, twisting himself round my ankles for sympathy.

'OK, OK,' I whispered. 'I'll soon have you in.'

He watched with interest as I opened the door a different way. No key. A neat arrangement of pins that I had acquired from a tame housebreaker on my beat days, don't ask me how. We slid into the kitchen like conspirators. Cat went straight to the cupboard where his breakfast was kept. He trod daintily, avoiding the mess.

I stood in the middle of the debris on the floor, wondering where to step, wondering what was priceless art and what was dis-gorged junk. The smell of cooked glue hit me like a bone factory. Cat miaowed piti-fully, shrinking its stomach into starvation mode. I found a tin of catfood with a ring-pull top, tipped half the contents, turkey and chicken bits in brown jelly, on to the only clean saucer in the kitchen.

The cat had good manners. It purred a few thanks before it vacuumed the lot.

In a corner stood 'ruin', the masterpiece that Waz seemed so proud of. Only it was a ruin now. Someone had taken a hammer to the edifice and it was smashed to smithereens, shattered fragments spread all over the rest of the mountain tip. I carefully moved some pieces, searching for whatever might have been concealed inside, but there were no clues.

The structure was mainly crunched chicken wire, old video boxes, empty plastic bottles and egg cartons. I saw no artistic connection. What had Waz said? Something about the key to the safe at the bank ... I had thought she was joking. But apparently not. Someone had wanted the key back.

Unless Waz had destroyed 'Ruin' herself. Not up to her usual standard. I poked around the kitchen, hoping to find something crucial. But it was useless. The fingerprint team would have to take a month's sick leave if dealing with this lot. I moved into the hall, silent as a shadow. Cat followed me, like a ghost host, showing me around politely.

I slipped on some thin latex gloves out of habit. The cat viewed me with suspicion. Perhaps he had recently been taken to the vet's and submitted to having his temperature taken in an unspeakable manner.

The front sitting room was depressingly dismal. No one ever sat there. The room wasn't used. Plastic tulips graced a graceless vase. Peter Scott reproductions merged with the wallpaper. A brown and orange pattern-ed carpet argued with a burgundy uncut moquette three-piece suite. The chairs looked so uncomfortable, I bet the cat wouldn't even sit on them. I was right. He stalked past, tail high.

I searched everywhere, down the back of seat cushions, behind and through un-touched books, under edges of the carpet. There was nothing. No safe behind a picture, no letters inside books, no safe keys sellotaped to the underside of shelves.

The dining room showed a few signs of life. A television set sat in a corner with a current TV programme magazine. Two up-right fireside chairs flanked an imitation gas fire; their worn arms showed plenty of use yet I was having a hard time imagining either the wacky Waz or the immaculate Leroy sitting there.

I began to feel I was on a stage set. The house was not natural. It did not relate to the people who supposedly lived there. It was as if a different cast inhabited the rooms.

Leroy Anderson occupied the front bed-room, that was obvious from the load of trendy clothes and make-up. Talk about an outfit for every day of the week. She was a walking calender. A flowered duvet with pink cushions sitting like strawberry marshmallows covered her bed. Fashion magazines littered the floor. She had an expensive taste in undies and plenty of boyfriends. One drawer was full of postcards and letters, gift tags and show programmes. I scanned them quickly but nothing was signed Love Adrian or Forever A.

I was beginning to get bored. There was nothing here, apart from the chaotic kitchen which I dreaded searching. I would not know where to start. How could I tell which junk was rubbish and which junk was art?

Then came my first surprise. Bedroom number three was a narrow, single room with a 2 foot 6 inch bed and worn candlewick cover, a chest of drawers and a row of hanging hooks behind the door. It was occupied by a man. Striped pyjamas were folded on the pillow and a couple of dark suits and boring shirts hung behind the door. On the chest of drawers were a brush and comb, a bottle of hair restorer and some brilliantine. Leslie Fairbrother, senior manager of the Sussex United Banking Corporation, it seemed, had been banished to the spare room.

Waz's eccentric artistic talent was not their only problem. Perhaps Leslie's lovemaking was limited to cheerless three-minute thrills while Waz yearned for romantic passion and tenderness that time did not measure. I shut the door on Leslie's celibate nights, remembering the obsessive hand-washing.

The bathroom was marginally interesting. Slimy soap, wet flannels, damp towels, par for the course. The last occupant had not wiped round the bath. Someone had recently dyed their hair Raisin Brown. The wall cabinet held no medication, not even an aspirin. The house was all contradictions.

The back bedroom had to be the one occupied by Waz, if she lived there at all. Maybe she slept downstairs in the kitchen guarding her masterpieces. I pushed the door open slowly, wondering what to expect, a replay of the clutter downstairs, feminine chaos or nunnish austerity. Like someone whose personality departed on the way upstairs.

I did not expect to see a shape in the bed. I froze. I thought the house was empty. No one had answered my knocking.

The flowing hair extensions on the pillow told me that the occupant of the bed was Waz. I crept forward, alerted by the stillness.

Waz was no longer Waz. She had reverted to being Mrs Cordelia Henrietta Fairbrother, even though she was daubed from head to foot in gaudy sloshes of paint. Thick paint covered her legs, arms, fingers, face,

285

neck. The cavities of her face were filled with fast-setting moulding clay. Her lashes were spiked with glue, her eyes pools of milky blindness, her mouth a setting well of PVA glue under which her teeth looked like submerged pearls.

She was deceased. Very deceased. No pulse. Suffocated by a mixture of paint and plaster and glue. She had become her own tribute to modern art. She might have approved of that. The bedclothes and walls were splashed with paint. I touched a splodge tentatively. It was still glutinous.

A strong smell of acetone hit me. Paint thinner. I should report this. I should look for clues. I should act like a responsible citizen, except this responsible citizen had been snooping in their house. Instead I went into the bathroom and was horribly sick. Violently but briefly since I hadn't eaten. My stomach heaved. I leaned on the basin and slapped cold water over my face, cleaned up, wiped round with a towel, threw it on the floor.

Somehow I got myself downstairs. I took the phone off the hook and dialled three nines. It began ringing. As I left the room I could hear a female voice asking which service did I require? Fire, police, ambulance? I let her talk to the air.

It didn't matter which service they sent. They would soon discover poor Waz in

Ruin, connect her to the vanished bank manager and the official wheels would start rolling.

The cat looked at me with trust. Without thinking I picked him up and tucked him inside my anorak. I couldn't leave him in this house with the mummified Waz upstairs. The air outside was as chilling as a walk-in freezer. Half of my brain remembered to check that I had left nothing behind and relocked the door. The other half couldn't think of anything.

The cat sat composed on the passenger seat, no roaming or peering out of the window. It was as if he knew this was not the time for attractive feline behaviour. I drove back to my shop, parked in the back yard, went inside, washed again in hot water, changed my clothes. By the time I had made a pint of scalding coffee, the cat was fast asleep, curled up in a filing tray, tail hanging over the end like a black exclamation mark.

'You can't stay,' I said. 'You're evidence.'

But he wasn't listening.

I sat down on my chair and put my head in my hands. I was in for real trouble if the police discovered that I had been anywhere near No 12.

# Nineteen

Doris didn't sell varieties of catfood, nor was I sure I could buy it from her if she had any. No one must know I had the Fairbrothers' cat. I could say it was a stray. A cat lie. Meanwhile I bought three tins of sardines.

'Extra Omega 3,' I explained.

'For what?' she asked.

'Builds bones.'

'Haven't you got enough?'

Surely DI James knew about the body by now. The three nines call might have gone anywhere but I couldn't let poor Waz liquefy beneath the weight of paint, glue and quick-setting plaster. Even though I could think up a legitimate reason for calling on the Fairbrothers, it did not explain how I got in. I needed a tank of air.

The sea had disappeared. Low cloud gathered on the shore having forgotten that it was supposed to be attached to the sky. It felt like wet net. In minutes my hair was hanging in tendrils like a heroine from a Jane Austen novel, my anorak was glistening and my gloves dampened. Lowry people appeared on the edge of my vision and vanished.

It wasn't exactly raining. I was walking through cloud that hid both the sea and the shore in a swirling haze. Dim lights flickered yellowy rays from the road above, occasionally shot with the luminous beam of headlights. The sea was reduced to a distant roar, halfway to France for duty free. Seagulls fluttered like sodden paper, flapping their wings, searching for thermal lifts, scanning the sand for scraps of washed-up fish heads.

The sand was forced into ridges, dark fissures, deeper than they looked. I fell down gullies where water nearly topped my boots. This beach changed character every time the tide went out. New lagoons materialised, new stretches of rocks and pools tricked the unwary, new streams wandered and cleaved the sand. I only knew where I was by the roof line of the houses and flats beyond the promenade. The pier straggled out of sight.

More cloud lowered itself on to the beach, wearied with weight, drifting like a lost being in an alien atmosphere.

I stopped walking. I couldn't see a thing. The hotel shapes and blocks of flats had gone, absorbed into the fog. I barely knew which way to turn. It was frightening. If I fell and broke my ankle, no one would find me. Even the police air service helicopter would fail. Its thermal camera was useless in these weather conditions. The tide would sweep in and cover me with seaweed as thoroughly as someone had painted Waz with glue. Yes, I ought to carry a mobile. Shopping list: think about it.

I stood still, trying to orientate myself. But which way was the right way to go? I might walk in circles and get nowhere fast. Nothing was recognisable. I decided to stride in a straightish line. It must take me somewhere.

It did. Straight out to sea. In a few frightening minutes, cold hungry waves were washing round my feet, lapping my ankles. I did a complete turn in a hurry. I know how fast the tide could come in over the sandy wastes. Now I was in a race, stumbling and half falling, as the sea chased me shorewards.

It was flight time. Ever tried running on sand in waterlogged boots? The sea was gaining on me. I tripped on a slippery rock and fell flat on my face. When I struggled to my feet, half winded, my front was wet with patches down to my knees, legs, chest, forearms, face. The salt water didn't do my cut fingers any good. It stung.

But as I got up, I could see the steep rise of the shingle ahead. It would take the sea a long time to climb that slope. By the time it reached high tide, crashing over the tops of the groynes, I would have been home and dry for hours.

When I got back to my shop, carrying a bag of litter from the pet store, I found DI James about to leave my doorstep. His glance swept over me, taking in my bedraggled state. My clothes had semi-dried on me. I made an attempt to brush off some of the sand.

'Your shop is never open,' he said. 'You'll go bankrupt.'

'Correction. I am bankrupt.'

'What about those substantial cash payments into your bank account?'

'Oh, not that again. Kindly give my brain a rest.'

'I am trying to help you,' he said in a menacingly cold voice, 'and against all my professional instincts. I am using valuable resources to unpin your name from the circumstances of Councillor Fenwick's death.'

Was I supposed to feel humble? I could only look into those eyes and remember the coldness of the sea washing round my ankles. He acted as if he didn't even like me.

'Thank you for nothing, Detective Inspector. We both know that his flask of coffee had been laced with strong sleeping tablets and he'd been drinking brandy. You can't pin that on me,' I said sweetly.

'Halcion was found in his bloodstream and the alcohol content was high. And then

291

I suppose he locked the door on the outside himself, before climbing back in through a window to set fire to the place?'

'No, I think Pippa Shaw locked the door. She didn't want an amorous caller late at night.'

'Have you proof?'

'I've a strong hunch Adrian Fenwick was there destroying incriminating papers which linked him to dodgy house sales with a dodgy builder who had got dodgy planning permission with the councillor's assistance.'

For a second, DI James looked interested but he dumped the look immediately before it could take hold. He wasn't going to give me any points.

'Oh yes?' he drawled.

'He put the evidence through the shredder, then thought he'd burn the lot to make doubly sure, in case some poor WPC was ordered to stick all the bits back together.'

'She'd need dexterity.'

'And patience beyond human endeavour. But when your brain is befuddled with sleeping pills, brandy and a stress-aroused burst of adrenalin and noradrenaline, it's not easy to make rational decisions.'

'I do know about the fight/flight syndrome. It doesn't explain the planting of a can of petrol with your bike. He could have just burned the shredded documents in a bin.'

'Maybe he wanted to make it look like arson, in case his name was ever linked with the builder. Don't you see? He hadn't planned on being locked inside. Snow White did that.'

'Now you've lost me. Snow White? Are we into fairy tales now?'

'Pippa Shaw. His immaculate daughter-in-law, at one time girlfriend, she of the pure white clothes and pristine flat. Not all as innocent as it looks, a very complicated relationship. Not incest, but close. Women often find older men more to their liking.'

'Money,' he said.

'No, manners,' I whipped back. 'By all accounts, Adrian Fenwick was a nice man, even if occasionally weak for a pretty face or accepting a handout. All I've ever got in the way of a handout is a basket of mushrooms.'

'I'm getting confused,' said DI James, with a shiver. 'Could we go inside and at least I'll be warmer while I'm being confused.'

He did look cold. No extra layer of waistcoat or pullover despite the drop in temperature. His shirt was regulation white, the third button missing. Hadn't he got any winter clothes?

'No, I don't,' he said, reading my mind. 'When I walked out, I left everything behind. I need to go shopping.'

'Don't ask me to come with you,' I said. 'I don't choose men's clothes.' When he walked out ... that told me something I hadn't known before. The circumstances of his divorce were a mystery to me; he had not volunteered any information. Left everything behind ... it was a bleak scenario. A middle-of-the-night act of desperation? I thought only women did that. Men planned everything.

I was mesmerised by the blinding smallness of details: that missing button, the frosted fringe of lashes, the downcast of his mouth. The way he stood squarely like a raging bull containing its wrath, feet not pawing the ground, but his weight shifting as the energy swelled to bursting point.

'You'd probably pick black, black, and then black,' he suggested.

'How do you know that?' I was surprised. My trumpeter always wore black. A jazzman's gear. Bones melted as I thought of him, desire surged. It wasn't fair to dehydrate my skin. I'd be getting spots.

'It's in your eyes,' said DI James enigmatically. 'Your eyes are in mourning. What have you lost, Jordan?'

I had to think. What had I lost?

'I've lost how it feels to act like a normal woman.'

'It's your damned profession,' he said, following me into my office.

I sidled ahead but the cat had disappeared the way cats do. The bag of litter had also disappeared, hidden behind the loo door. I switched on the electric fire, hoping there were enough pound coins in the meter for some heat. The fire ate money.

'Much as I appreciate your frankness, Jordan, you haven't told me anything I don't already know,' he went on. 'I need a fresh lead.'

'And I need to know whether the can of petrol was full or empty. I'm presuming, of course, that the contents have been measured now? Also I'd like to know exactly where my bike was found. Its location could be crucial.'

'I will get that information to you.' He wrote something in his notebook.

I pulled out the specimen envelope that contained the lock of false red hair I had chopped off the wig hidden in Pippa Shaw's boot. I sniffed it.

'Hardly fresh,' I murmured. 'But maybe a lead ... hidden in a boot in Snow White's flat. What do you think of the shade?' I held it up to my hair.

'Amateur dramatics.'

'I admit she is a good actress but I doubt if the smell of greasepaint lures her. Too fastidious. Forensic could establish who last wore the wig. Blond hair particles, dandruff, etc. ... She wore this while riding my bike around Latching.'

He hadn't asked me what I'd been doing

in Pippa Shaw's flat. I decided not to tell him. Nor could I tell him about finding Waz Fairbrother. My brain stirred random avenues, trying to discover a way of finding out if he knew.

Also I was starting to think I had talked too much. DI James was firstly a professional policeman. He did not do favours for struggling independent private eyes. It might look as if he was trying to help me out of this mess, but who could tell what was going on in that cropped head? He might have a hot warrant for my arrest in his pocket.

But his mobile rang. No irritating call sign. A plain ring. His face did not change expression. He nodded. 'I'll be over right away. Who's there? What's the address? And get someone to dig out all we've got on the missing husband.'

He switched off the machine. 'I have to go, Jordan. Trouble at mill.' He put a pound coin on my desk. 'In case the meter runs out. And get some dry clothes on. You'll catch your death.'

'Been nice talking to you.'

He left abruptly, a record departure, due now at the scene of the artistic Waz Fairbrother's last exhibited still life.

Mrs Drury had given me a newspaper cutting about Patcham House. I got it out and smoothed the creases. It was browned and fragile, like a dried leaf. The missing woman was described as a 32-year-old Linda Keates, an Oriental art expert from a London museum, cataloguing the art collection of the house. She apparently went out to buy some materials and never returned.

That same day, the Lancaster crashed into the sand when the tide was out. The two stories were linked curiously. A bystander had witnessed both events. The editor of the paper at that time thought it made a story.

Various valuable artefacts also disappeared from Patcham House, including a Tokyo School ivory group by Yoshida Homei, circa 1910. Last sold for £12,000 just before the war. Its value now was incalculable.

The old newspaper report quoted the witness:

'I saw Miss Keates walking along the road towards the station,' said 58-year-old Fred Pierce. 'She had a case with her. In the afternoon, I saw the bomber overhead. The engine was making a funny noise. Then I saw it crash into the sand. It was a dreadful shock.'

Linda Keates ... was she the unknown woman found on the wreck? Who was she? And what was her connection to the dead councillor? Perhaps it was a red herring. For some reason Mrs Drury had fed me a pickled herring.

I found the Fenwick file and took out the newspaper photograph of the councillor and wife waving from the council offices after the last election. I had learned such a lot about the man since that photo was taken. His face was beaming with a political smile, eyes frank and voter-honest, wave presidential, his high forehead only faintly glistening with sweat. He looked happy and pleased with himself. He had no premonition how close he was to waving goodbye to life.

My body shivered to remind me to dress dry. It would have to be the charity box. None of my clothes lurked in the shop. I stripped off, showering sand on the floor, noted a bloodied rock scratch on the mound of my right thumb, had a quick wash down in a bowl of hot water. It felt good.

The cat used the litter tray which was a sign he felt at home. I opened a tin of sardines which he appreciated with small rapt rumbles in his throat.

'I suppose you've got a name but I don't know what it is,' I said, stroking his soft head.

The charity box was short of stock. Mrs Barbara Hutton lay crumpled at the bottom, all creases, no style, flattened. It would

have to be a bag lady again. A good surveillance outfit. The decay of these garments
was authentic. They smelt of cheap gin and
cider and sleeping in the beachfront
shelters.

No way could I rinse the world clean.

I kept on my own undies and trainers.
There was a limit to my search for validity. I
tucked my hair under a tea-cosy beret and
tightened the string belt of the dirty
raincoat, smeared my face and hands with
coffee grains. Yuck.

I shut the shop.

'Still starving, ducks?' said Doris as I
passed her doorway. 'Want a stale bun?'

'Yes, I do, but how do you know it's me?
It's a brilliant disguise. My mother wouldn't
recognise me.'

My mother would have known me anywhere. She would have recognised the baby
smell, the soft baby touch. A woman born to
mother. I missed her.

'Details,' said Doris, surveying me from all
angles like an haute couture designer.
'You're wearing your own trainers, first give-
away; you're wearing your own teeth and
your nose is clean.'

'It's the teeth,' I groaned.

'Boot polish, that's the answer. I've a tin of
dried-up Natural Tan. You can have it for
half price.'

'I've no money on me.'

'I'll add it to your next bill.'

I smeared a bit of dried-up polish over my teeth. It felt and tasted revolting. But effective, as I checked the look in her shop window. A gruesome sight. I felt like a corpse. Shopping list: dental floss, mouthwash, hygienist appointment.

I trudged along the road, picking up a few smelly bags of rubbish for props. The whole scene soon depressed me. Give me some Prozac quick, someone. I took up station at the beach shelter opposite Horizon Views and waited.

'Hello, ducks,' a wino said, reeling by.

The shelter was occupied by a group of homeless men and women, already high on cheap booze, cider, methylated spirits, glue, anything with an alcohol content, noses rosy with veins, their belongings bundled into supermarket trolleys. They were falling about, chortling and pissing themselves. The smell was revolting. I sat nearby on a bench, but not too near. My £50 a day fee was not enough. No one could pay me enough for doing this.

'Wanna drink, darling?'

I moved away pretending not to understand, trying to keep my boot-polish smile in place. Yet I had to feel sorry for them. Where had we gone wrong? These were people. Not aliens. They had once been sweet-faced children. Somebody's baby.

I moved off and huddled down beside a black litter bin. It reeked bad too but it was the smell of rotting takeaways and oily chip paper. But it was better than the boozy party going on in the shelter. It seemed like hours that I waited. It was hours.

Snow White came out. Immaculate as ever, skin-tight white jeans, cream leather boots, white suede jacket, fox-fur collar. Straight from a car wash. She got into her BMW. Had the fried councillor paid for that too? I waited a while until she had driven out of sight, then paddled over to Horizon Views. I had no idea how to get into her flat again but I took off the beret and tousled my hair to near normality.

'Come in,' said the caretaker. 'Having a bad day?'

'Fell into the sea this morning and got soaked. Had to borrow a few things from an old friend. Sorry if I smell.'

'No problem, miss. I know you, don't I? From the council, aren't you? Miss Shaw is out for ten minutes. I'm a bit busy at the moment. Washing machine leaking at Number One.'

'That's a pity. I need a quick look again. Two seconds is all I need. My fault. Forgot to write it down.'

He took a key off a ring. The man deserved the sack. I wouldn't employ him. 'Here's the key. I haven't time to show you in. Damned washing machine, too mean to buy a new one.'

I nodded, clucked in sympathy. 'Washing machines can be the devil.'

I went up to the fifth floor in the lift, hoping I wasn't leaving a trail of dirt. The key opened the front door easily. She really ought to get a security system installed. Anyone could walk in.

Someone had. Someone had been there before me. The flat had been turned over. I heard a minuscule noise, the faintest click. The intruder was still there.

# Twenty

It took less than two seconds to grab the item I had spotted among the piles of strewn belongings littering the floor. A turnover is no fun. I'd seen enough burgled homes on my beat days and I knew the trauma and pain it caused.

The intruder was still in the flat. Somewhere. I had to get out before I was caught. An intruder detaining an intruder? Not in my book. More like a sharp head impact.

Backing out without a sound was a feat of muscle control. Both feet, in fact. They behaved in unison. My breathing went into reverse. It was like slow motion through water.

Out on the pavement I remembered I still had the key to No 5. They would think I had ransacked Pippa's flat if I didn't go back and return the key.

'Sorry, haven't time today after all,' I said, finding the caretaker at No 1, on his knees, spanner in hand. 'Urgent call on my mobile.'

Not exactly a lie. Not exactly the truth. Don't have a mobile, as yet. Spontaneous fabrication.

'Know what it's like,' he grumbled.

'See you some other day. 'Bye.'

I crammed my hair under the knitted beret and waited at a distance, slouched against pedestrian crossing lights, faking a colour-blind walker waiting for the green man to appear. It was easy, slipping into the body language of a bag lady. No one came out of the flat who didn't look as if they lived there. I was almost on the point of heading for a bath when a woman appeared from the entrance to the flats, her heels tap-tapping on the pavement. They were tapping out her name in morse.

Leroy Anderson. Perhaps she'd called for the rent.

I ambled across the road, veering between cars, not looking back. Leroy Anderson. What the devil was she doing there? How could she possibly be involved? Seeing her had thrown me. I couldn't think straight. It must be the hat. I tossed it into a bin.

Latching police station was some distance from Horizon Views but I kept walking despite the curious stares. Sergeant Rawlings was on duty behind the desk. He looked up and shook his head in disbelief.

'Jaws. Have you sunk so low? Business must be bad. I think we could manage fifty pence out of the poor box. It would buy you a cup of tea at the Sally Ann.'

'I've been on surveillance. There's not a lot of career guidance around,' I said through gritted teeth, remembering same teeth smeared with Natural Tan shoe polish. 'Can I see DI James? I've some new evidence.'

'But will DI James want to see you, Jordan? I doubt it. He has a keen nose.'

'I'm not asking to be sniffed at. DI James can keep his distance. This evidence is important.'

Someone was coming down the stairs. Those footsteps had to be his. Funny how I could recognise the rhythm of his walk, the way he placed his weight, the even tread of noise. He took one look at me and shuddered.

'Heaven preserve us. Do you have to come in here looking like that? It gives the station a bad name.'

'I didn't know this was now a four-star station. Do we have to pass a dress code before being allowed in? If so, what about your socks?'

This floored him. 'What have my socks got to do with anything?' He'd found a heavy black sweater to wear, washed without being pressed, creased into his body shape.

'That's for me to know and you to decide,' I said enigmatically. Let him work that one out. I took a bright yellow armband out of my disgusting pocket. 'One luminous armband as worn by unknown person pretending to be me, riding my bicycle. Said armband found in flat belonging to one Ms Pippa Shaw, ex-daughter-in-law of Councillor Adrian Fenwick, recently perished in the alleged arson attack at Fenwick Future Homes.'

'You're talking like a policeman,' said DI James, picking up the armband and turning it over. 'I believe these armbands are on sale in numerous Latching shops, including the one where you hired your Raleigh Sunrise.'

The discovery of the armband in Pippa Shaw's flat, plus the red hairpiece, was decisive evidence as far as I was concerned, but to DI James it proved nothing. My heart rate fell in relation to the disappointment. I didn't show my feelings. It was necessary to maintain some control.

'But,' DI James went on, twirling the band round with his forefinger, 'a certain CCTV positioned on the wall outside a Latching bank, and directly opposite the estate agents' showroom, shows footage of a woman riding a bicycle, looking not unlike you, with a bulky object, possibly a can of petrol, in a bag tied to the handlebars. Although the picture is indistinct, as CCTVs often are, there are a great many similarities between you and the person riding the bike.'

'How many times do I have to tell you that

it wasn't me?' I was tired of saying it.

He ignored me. 'The footage was timed five forty a.m. At the very time you were seen leaving your flat by an observant postman. It seems you know how to be in two places at the same time. We also verified the postman's check-in time at work. It all ties up.'

My mouth nearly fell open. I kept having to remember the Natural Tan. It took some time sinking in. Did this mean he nearly believed me?

'I'm not going to apologise,' he said, handing back the armband. 'I was only doing my duty but I don't think even your versatility could have managed riding a bike, leaving your flat and setting the showroom on fire, in three different places and all within minutes. So I suppose you are no longer our main suspect.'

He was on my side. I would have hugged him if it had not been for the smelly raincoat. I flashed him a Natural-Tan-hued smile and he cringed. 'Thank you, Detective Inspector,' I grinned. 'I owe you one.'

'Not immediately,' he said, backing off. 'I'll wait till you've cleaned up.'

Sergeant Rawlings handed me a miniature tablet of soap as I left the station, the kind the Travelodge give away free. 'Go celebrate,' he said.

At home I stuffed the bag lady outfit into

a bin liner and scrubbed myself clean. I used my own soap. I am very particular about good soap. The Natural Tan was difficult to remove. I might have to swallow it as new teeth enamel is hard to come by.

I couldn't quite get myself to throw Marlene away (Latching's newest recruit bag lady) as she had her uses. A salad with torn Chinese leaves, green peppers, goat's cheese and garlic croutons cleansed the inside of my mouth.

It was a luxury to be sitting on my moral sofa, the black and white switched to a muddy programme on digging up fields for bits of Roman floors. I was soaking up the comfort of my home and glad I was not going to spend the night in a sea-swept beach shelter with drunks for company. The phone rang. It was Mrs Edith Drury. She sounded awful.

'Jordan, my dear, I wouldn't ask you,' she croaked, 'but I don't know who else I can ask and I know how resourceful you are. And at least I can pay for your time ... so it's not like asking a favour.'

She was wasting valuable energy in talking so much. I interrupted her. 'What's the matter?' I said quickly. 'You sound as if you need a doctor.'

'No, no, I don't want to see a doctor,' she said faintly. 'Hate doctors. They ask too many questions. But I do need some of those holiday pills, you know, the kind people buy in case they get an upset tummy. Can you find some sort of all-night chemist that sells them and bring some round to me? I do feel very ill indeed or I wouldn't ask you.'

'Ah, the runs? A stomach bug?'

'Er ... yes, I am doing a lot of running. Oh dear, I'd better go. Can't stop. 'Bye, Jordan.'

Poor Mrs Drury. I put the phone down, heaved myself from the sofa and switched off the television. Now I would never know who ran away with whom in the particularly riveting soap about to follow. How could I survive life without knowing?

I wrapped up warmly and cycled to the nearest Safeways supermarket. I couldn't get used to having a car. It was still open, the last shoppers pushing round laden trolleys like zombies. The assistant in the pharmacy was very helpful, thinking I was the sufferer and hoping I wouldn't stay around for long and become a problem. I bought a packet of Diocalm tablets and some apricot-flavoured oral rehydration sachets. She'd need them to replace the fluid she had lost.

As I cycled against the wind to Mrs Drury's villa, I wished I'd used the car. The ladybird was parked in the yard behind my shop. There was nowhere to park it near my flat even though I had bought a resident's parking permit. Too many double yellow lines. Owning a car was already a headache. All possessions were a burden. I was glad I didn't have many.

The front door was on the latch. Hello, burglar, come on in. I went in and peered into the front room and the kitchen. Empty, though the lights were on. She was obviously upstairs. I filled two glasses with cold water and put them on a tray with the medication and took them upstairs.

'Hello, it's only me. Jordan,' I called out.

It was a solid and spacious house with a wide landing and six doors leading off – bathroom, loo and four bedrooms. One door was ajar, a dim light coming from it. I went in. The room reeked of illness. Mrs Drury was huddled under a plump rose-strewn eiderdown on a sturdy double bed with carved mahogany headboard. Heavy Edwardian pieces of furniture overpowered the room like sentries guarding the walls. I wondered if she had inherited the suite from her parents or Mr Drury's family. It had been in service a long time.

'Jordan ... you're an angel,' she croaked. 'I knew I could count on you.'

She looked awful, her skin a bad colour. The sooner she got some morphine hydro-chloride down her the better. I checked the dosage under the light and broke the seal.

'You've obviously eaten something that

was off,' I said. 'Been out for a curry recently? They are often suspect.'

'No, no … nothing like that,' she moaned. 'I just had a boiled egg for my tea and then I got these awful griping pains, was doubled up. It's ghastly. I'm so sorry, my dear, you having to see me in this state.'

'Don't worry. I've seen ill people before. Chew these two tablets, Mrs Drury. They'll help. Take another two in a couple of hours' time. Now don't forget. But if this goes on longer than forty-eight hours then you must see a doctor.'

I emptied two glucose sachets into a glass of water and stirred. 'And this is even more important. You must drink this. It'll help you replace all the fluid you've lost. And here's some more water for another lot later on. You'll soon start feeling better.'

I helped her wash her face and hands. I'm not nurse material but I tried. Then I tidied the room a bit. It seemed safe to leave her. I didn't want to stay the night. She was less agitated and might sleep for a bit now.

'You go home, Jordan dear. I'm feeling better and I've got all this medicine to take. I'll be all right.'

'I'll come by tomorrow morning, just the same,' I said, relieved. Coward … I felt ashamed.

I went downstairs and threw the empty sachets away in the bin. I caught hold of the lid before it snapped shut. Something gold shone in its depths, catching the light. I peered closer. There was a wedge of scalloped white icing tipped with gold. Several other pieces of broken icing. At least three slices had been cut and the fruity part eaten. I took them out carefully using a big spoon, shaking off the broken eggshell.

Mrs Drury had omitted telling me all that she had had for her tea. The slices were only partially eaten, too sweet perhaps. I wrapped the fragments in some cling film, not sure what I was going to do with them. Take the specimens to Mrs Fenwick and get her to identify the artwork? It would hardly do either lady any good.

I went back upstairs. Mrs Drury was sleeping, her face aged and sunken. Her secret was safe with me. I'd call again early next morning.

The Public Health department at the council office were intrigued by my request for tests on a half-eaten slice of wedding cake.

'Mouse-droppings? Gonna sue the baker?' they asked.

'Something like that,' I said. 'Mickey Mouse land.'

'You'd be surprised how many rats there are in Latching.'

'No, I wouldn't be surprised. I know several of them.'

The month was fading fast into winter, chilled into brisk settlement. A bite was in the air, nipping every uncovered nose. My pockets filled with water in daily downpours. The fields were sodden. Rivers overflowed the towpaths, lapping against garden steps. Sandbags appeared like boils in front of low-lying cottages.

I was not surprised when I got the report back from the Public Health. The cake had been heavily spiked with a strong, proprietary brand of chocolate laxative. Mrs Fenwick's conciliatory gesture towards her daughter-in-law's remarriage had been phenolphthalein. She had planned to make that wedding one to remember.

It seemed right to put Mrs Fenwick out of her misery, even though she would not have to pay me any fee. I could only charge her if I was returning the cake. No cake, no bill. I phoned her, knowing it would be a difficult conversation face to face.

'Mrs Fenwick. It's Jordan Lacey. I've some news for you,' I said.

'Oh my goodness. My cake ... have you found it?'

'Not exactly. But I know where it is.'

'Tell me, tell me, quick. I must go and fetch it.' She sounded agitated. No wonder.

'I'm afraid I can't tell you that, Mrs Fenwick. A few slices have been eaten and you can imagine how that person is now feeling.'

313

There was a silence. 'Oh dear ... I don't think I understand. I don't know what you mean...'

'I think you do, Mrs Fenwick. However, when this person recovers, as I'm sure they will, I think I can assure you that the rest of the cake will be destroyed and nothing will be done to take the matter further. It's best, for both of you, that the whole episode is forgotten.'

'Yes. I do agree, if you say so, Miss Lacey. I should be very grateful. Can you arrange for the cake to be ... er ... be destroyed?'

'I will make the necessary arrangements. But you must promise me that you will never, never do anything like this again. If you do, then I will produce the report from the Public Heath Department who have analysed a slice of your cake.'

She could barely speak. The shock waves came over the wire. I hoped she wasn't going to have a heart attack. Breaking bad news gently is an art they teach by rote at the cop shop.

Both Mrs Drury and Mrs Fenwick recovered but were shaken by the experience. Mrs Fenwick paid a modest bill for expenses only promptly, and added a generous bonus for 'extra services' as she quaintly described getting rid of the evidence. It took time for their confidence to return. Mrs Drury even started driving her car with some consideration for road rules.

Strangely enough, they remained friends. I never said a word and they never asked. Neither ever knew what had really happened.

# Twenty-One

The slate was looking cleaner round the edges but the centre was still a muddy blur. Unresolved: who locked Councillor Fenwick in the safe and thus accelerated his death; who was putting wads of cash in my account causing me immense embarrassment; who murdered Waz Fairbrother? She was hardly a piece of artwork gone wrong.

'Nothing to do with me,' I told Waz's cat who had decided to live with me. He came to work in a cat basket, chewing the corners to while away the tedium of the journey, inspected the premises for rodent infiltration, then went to sleep in the warmest spot. Once he went to sleep in the shop window and a woman offered me £5 for him. I was annoyed. You can't put a price on a cat.

I'm not being paid for any of these cases, I thought. DI James is the man in charge. I can forget them. I'll go back to serving subpoenas and customers.

A firm of solicitors in Chichester kept me supplied with routine bread and butter work. Serving documents was boring but occasionally required ingenuity. The recipients were often reluctant to accept legal papers, especially any writs issued by a court of justice requiring said person to appear in court at said time.

The response ranged from refusing to open the door, slamming the door shut in your face, setting the Rottweiler on you. Pass me a dog-proof vest quick. But after the Scarlatti brothers episode, I fancied a quiet life for a few days. Call it an overdue holiday in sunny Latching. I practised being a shop owner, selling first class junk.

Sunny Latching was pouring with rain, a curtain of water streaming down the windows of my shop. Umbrellas down, no one stopped to look at my classy displays. Today's theme was musicals. One window reflected The Merry Widow with a black lace fan, a silk rose and a champagne glass with a coffee-stained musical score; the other depicted Oliver with an old wooden bowl, a battered spoon that had been used for a century and a threadbare black undertaker's top hat. Gruesome. I thought briefly of high-stepping black horses with plumes and a creaking carriage. Give me a linen shroud, please, and a heap of wild flowers from the Downs. Was I getting depressed?

While I waited for customers, I wrote up my notes and closed a few files. I sorted the photographs which I'd taken and labelled them. Part of the success of any PI was meticulous notes. It was often something tucked away in the memory which opened a new door of enquiry.

The shop door opened. Leroy Anderson, smartly dressed in a belted navy raincoat and red waterproof hat, swept in, her make-up unsmudged by the rain. How did she manage it? She shook out her umbrella and folded it. Then she looked at me dubiously.

'Don't I know you?' she asked.

'I'm not sure what you mean,' I said. 'You may have seen me somewhere...' I did not care to remind her of Mrs Barbara Hutton or the morning of the fire.

'I thought we'd met somewhere before.'

'We may have. After all Latching is not such a big place and we may go to the same events. Can I help you?'

'I'd like to speak to the private investigator, please, the lady detective.'

'Jordan Lacey?' I liked the lady bit. Tried to look like one.

'Yes, please. Her office is here, isn't it?'

'Come this way.' I ushered Leroy into the back room. 'This is my office,' I said. 'I'm Jordan Lacey. Please sit down. Would you like some coffee? It's coffee time.'

She looked surprised. 'De-caff?'

'Of course,' I said smoothly, hoping she couldn't read the label on my jar of plain-jane instant. 'How did you hear about FCI?'

'You left a card with my sister, Waz Fairbrother,' she choked. Suddenly it was all too much. The sophistication cracked. She did her best to control her feelings; first her boss, now her sister. 'Did you know that my sister is dead? She died a dreadful death.'

'I know, I heard,' I said, wishing I did have some de-caff for her. 'I'm really sorry. It's awful for you. Were you very close?'

I made some coffee for both of us while she blew her nose and repaired her make-up. Her wet raincoat was making my velvet chair damp but how could I complain when her sister had been suffocated with plaster and glue.

'She was twelve years older than me so she's always seemed a a bit distant. And then she got married, of course. But she started getting very weird once she discovered she had some sort of artistic talent.'

'So she wasn't always ... so artistic?'

'Oh no. She was perfectly ordinary and normal once, just like you and me. She was a typist at the bank.'

I'd hardly describe Leroy as ordinary or me as normal, but I knew what she meant. I handed her a bone-china mug of coffee and offered survivors biscuits. She smiled her thanks, admiring the cornflowers painted on the mug. She was obviously bursting to talk to someone, anyone. She had been on her own ever since her sister's death.

'Tell me about her,' I said. 'Your sister was such an interesting person.'

Leroy took a deep breath. 'She was always a bit vague, about me anyway, used to forget I was there. Sometimes she was left to baby-sit while our parents went out and suddenly she'd go out too, completely forgetting that I was upstairs, asleep. But she didn't mean any harm. Then she married Leslie and became the usual sort of housewife, shopping and ironing. She didn't have to go out to work after they got married.'

'What happened to make her change?'

'I'm not sure. I wasn't living with them then. It was when I got a job with Fenwicks that I came to Latching and needed somewhere to live. It was something pretty traumatic, I think. She never really said. But she changed all right. She didn't cook any more; didn't clean the house or wash or iron. She shopped in an erratic, tin of sardines sort of way.'

'Tin of sardines?'

'Once she went out to do the weekend shopping and all she came back with was one tin of sardines. Life was devoted to creating her pieces, messing about in the kitchen till all hours.'

'Did she sell her artwork?'

'Sometimes. There was a gallery in Brighton, some avant-garde sort of place, that used to take things to exhibit. She never had

320

much money so I doubt if she sold many items. Just enough to cover the cost of the paint, I expect. She bought all her clothes at charity shops, never ate anything beyond a few raw vegetables. Strange sort of life. And again, she forgot all about me being there, hardly knew I was in the house.'

'And they never had any children?'

'I'm not sure. I think they lost a baby years ago. No one really said.'

'What about the day your brother-in-law, Leslie Fairbrother, disappeared? What can you tell me about that?'

Leroy still hadn't said why she had come to see me but I was too fascinated to stop her talking. Closed doors, drawn curtains. No one knows the secrets behind the most ordinary of houses.

'I don't really know much. Leslie was leaving for work at eight a.m. as usual. I was in the bathroom. They had some kind of row. I heard shouting and a door slam. And he never came back that evening. It was weird. Waz didn't seem to notice at first. It was me who eventually reported him missing to the police. I think she was quite glad that he had gone.'

'Did he take anything with him?'

'I've no idea, sorry. I rang the bank and he hadn't turned up for work that day. They thought he had early appointments in London. Apparently he often went to London for the bank. It was nothing unusual. But, of course, he never returned. Perhaps he's dead, too.'

She sniffed and took out her handkerchief. Fate was certainly dealing her underhanded blows. She was not all that grown-up underneath the make-up. Her lashes wore navy mascara. Probably a young twenty-five. I felt ancient by her side, zimmerframe about to be delivered.

'So, Miss Anderson, why have you come to see me? How can I help you?'

'I want you to find out who killed my sister,' she said, looking anywhere but at me. 'I don't want the police digging into her strangeness, making fun of her, thinking she didn't count as a person because she was unusual. I know you won't do that because she liked you and trusted you. She told me so. She said she wanted to use your face.'

'But this is a police investigation,' I said gently. Use my face? Barbed wire and sellotape? 'Your sister was murdered. They have to find the person who did it.'

'But not if you find him first!' She seemed galvanised out of her grief. 'Please, Miss Lacey. I want you to find the murderer and then just hand him over to the police. I don't want the police involved. You wouldn't be like them. You'd understand...' she searched for the right word '... her strangeness.'

I knew what she meant. The police would sweep through the kitchen and pile Waz's life work into bin liners. If they had not done it already. Waz may not have been a good sister but Leroy wanted desperately to preserve her dignity.

'I don't care what it costs,' Leroy went on. 'I've savings. Mr Fenwick paid me well. I can afford you.'

What a dilemma. How could I work on a murder case which was already in the hands of the police? Besides ... murder! I was barely experienced enough to find a stolen wedding cake. Yet I had found it, sort of. Small beginnings.

'I will try to help you,' I said, much against all common sense. It was flattering to be asked. 'But please understand that I cannot hamper the police investigation in any way. Yes, I might be able to do things which the police cannot. And, of course, having met your sister, I am most sympathetic to all aspects of this case.'

The navy mascara was running now and there was nothing I could do about it. I must go on a counselling course.

'Thank you, Miss Lacey.'

'Jordan.'

'Thank you, Jordan. Here's a key to the house. You will no doubt want to have a good look around. I haven't done any cleaning up. Clues, you know. Anyway,

I'm staying with friends now. I can't go back there.'

'Leave me a contact number and address,' I said, straight-faced. Hypocrite. The floor wouldn't swallow me. It had too much self-respect. 'I'll do everything I can to find out who killed your sister. You really have had a terrible time. We could meet some evening if you like, have a meal or a drink. You do need to take it easy.'

'And you can go into my bedroom, too, if that's any help. Waz might have put something there before it happened.'

'OK,' I said, hiding a guilty face. I got her to sign a client contract. It was business after all, but in the circumstances I wasn't having DI James hauling me off to the station for trespassing on the scene of a crime.

I did a rapid mental run of the initial crime procedure. Artist sketches of the crime scene – too late for the Monet touch. Bag and tag evidence – possible the cops might have missed something. Check previous twenty-four hours of victim's life.

'Can you remember what your sister did during the previous twenty-four hours?' I asked, producing a notebook.

'Not easy. She always shut herself away in the kitchen, working all hours. I heard her make a few phone calls, that's all. We spoke briefly about who would do the shopping.

324

She said she would, but I don't think she did. I don't think she went out at all.'

'Are you aware if anything is missing from the house? Anything valuable?'

'No, nothing.'

'Anything special or nostalgic?'

'No.'

'How about works of art?'

'You mean her things?' Leroy did not know what word to use. 'I haven't a clue. I did notice when I went with the police that the big piece she called "Ruin" had been smashed. But she could have done it herself. If she was dissatisfied with some work, she would destroy it.'

'What about forced entry? Had anyone broken into the house?'

Leroy shook her head. 'There were no signs of that.'

'Then your sister must have let the intruder in. Maybe she knew the person.' I sounded like a WPC. It was all policespeak. 'Or they had a key.'

'I don't know.' She was getting distressed again. I made her some more coffee and talked about something else for a few minutes. The cold weather. It's easy to talk about the weather in Latching. It changed every five minutes.

I couldn't dust for prints or estimate the time of death. I could only get that information from DI James. If he'd tell me. I'd more chance of getting the information out of a whale.

'I'm sorry I have to ask all these questions, but it's crucial that I have a clear idea of where I'm going. Now, Leroy, can you suggest any suspects? Did your sister have any enemies? Rivals? What about at the bank?'

'No enemies, I'm sure. Rivals ... in the art business you mean? Maybe ... she might have had competition but then her work was so unusual...'

'No one could produce anything similar or in the same class,' I suggested.

'Yes, that's what I mean. She was a complete individual.'

'Did you have to identify your sister?' It was an awful question. I remembered the figure on the bed covered in glue and paint and plaster.

Her face glazed over, stunned again. 'It was awful. I couldn't believe it. To do such an awful thing to her. It was the work of a maniac.'

I'd asked her because I wanted to see the reaction. It was genuine.

'I wonder why she didn't struggle,' I said, not thinking. 'After all, one would resist, strongly, to having paint and glue poured over one.'

Leroy looked at me peculiarly, wondering how I knew these details. Big mouth. I'd forgotten that only the police knew.

'I heard about it,' I added hurriedly. 'Down at the cop shop.'

'I thought they were not going to make it public. Copycat crime and all that. But I suppose they might tell you. In a way it helps that you know. She was tied down, you see, with twine. She couldn't struggle. It was horrible.'

I didn't ask the next question. It would hardly help to know if anything else had happened to the poor woman. By now they would have issued an APB, an all points bulletin, on the victim; questioned witnesses (what witnesses?), taken photos and a video, and the first officer on the scene would have made his report. I could find out who he was. Not DI James, because I was with him when the phone call came through.

'So I have to search for a motive. Find the motive and that often leads you to the killer,' I said with more hope than conviction. And I'd heard that before somewhere. One of the WI members. 'Thank you for being so patient with all my questions.'

'Thank you for taking such a professional approach. I know that you'll do your best,' she said, standing up. My Victorian chair was rain-smudged. Still, I guessed it would recover. It could not have been the first time anyone sat in it, all wet. 'It has been an awful time, but I feel much better now that you are going to help with the investigation. Waz was so taken by you. Perhaps it was a premonition ... anyway, I trust her judgement. She knew people.'

It was me who was speechless now. I couldn't remember saying anything significant to Waz. There was nothing remarkable about my face. Maybe ... the eyes. My trumpeter was always saying things about my eyes but then he saw stars everywhere.

'It has been terrible.' She was still going on, tightening her belt, looking around vaguely for her umbrella. For a second she looked like her sister. 'And to cap it all, I've lost my cat, Blackie. He's just disappeared. I'm so worried. Something must have frightened him, perhaps the person who killed Waz. I miss him so much. I've had him since he was a kitten.'

Time stood waiting in the wings. I put my hand on her arm to stop her leaving. It wasn't easy because Blackie had become a part of my life already.

'Come and see,' I said. 'Call it coincidence, call it what you like, but see what I found recently.'

I opened the door that leads to the scullery where I'd put the litter tray under the sink. The black cat was perched on the draining board, grooming himself as if in readiness for the reconciliation.

'Look who's here,' I said to him.

I heard her small gasp. So did he.

His ears perked. He took one surprised look at Leroy then made a flying leap into her arms with a throaty purr of pure adoration. I couldn't compete with that.

I drove the ladybird to Tarrant Close and parked two doors down outside No 18. This was legitimate, no yellow lines. I could arrive openly. There was still crime tape surrounding the house and garden but I ducked under it. If anybody asked any questions, I would wave my licence.

The SOCOs had already dusted the house for trace elements. A film of white powder lay over everything, even the kitchen. They had given up on searching the kitchen. It seemed pretty much the same as when I'd last been there. I took off my trainers and put on a couple of thick plastic overshoes borrowed from some hospital. I didn't want to leave traces.

I did not know where to start or what I was looking for. It was worse than a needle in a haystack, more like a pin in a vast land tip. More chance of winning the lottery. Wow! Champagne by the crate. No spraying it about like a rally driver, I'm going to drink the lot. Or rather, we are going to drink the lot. DI James and some retired female detective.

The body had been removed and so had the bedclothes. The bare mattress, worn in the middle, was a depressing sight. I peered into the wardrobe and chest of drawers. She did not have many clothes or possessions being in the throes of reinventing herself from scratch. Her standard housewife gear had been decanted to the charity shops long ago. I was probably buying the items for surveillance.

At the top of the wardrobe I found a large hatbox, securely tied. It did not look as if it had been opened for years. The police had not touched it. A few hats were of no interest to them, but women don't tie up hat boxes unless there's a good reason.

There was a good reason. It was full of baby clothes. All brand new, price tags still in place, hand-knitted matinee coats folded in tissue paper. Leroy had got that right.

Leroy's bedroom held no surprises except that I found a few black hairs on her duvet. Blackie had been a nocturnal visitor. Her wardrobe was a rainbow of clothes. I held up one of her dresses, a floaty blue chiffon thing, clasped it close to my waist and looked in the mirror. We were near enough the same size except I never wore dresses. The dress made me look different. Softened the shape, gave me a waist. Made my hair look almost normal.

'For heaven's sake,' I said aloud. 'Put it back. This isn't a fashion show.'

I went into the third bedroom, the

smallest room. It looked the same, characterless, cramped, cold. Then I noticed something which made my heart jolt. On the floor were some crumpled striped pyjamas. I could have sworn I last saw them folded on the pillow.

A chill touched the back of my neck as if a door had opened downstairs. I froze. The house was very still. A stairboard creaked. It was the tiniest noise. I hoped it was my imagination.

Slowly I put out my hand to find something solid on the chest of drawers. My fingers closed over the bottle of brilliantine. It would have to do.

'Fancy fixing your hair, Miss Lacey? It's got a nice scent,' said a cool voice. 'Sandalwood.'

'Who are you?' I said, equally cool. It was an effort to keep my voice steady.

'I don't think we've met,' said the man.

# Twenty-Two

'You scared me, creeping up like that,' I said, swinging round, the bottle held high in my hand. 'What are you doing here?'

'I could ask you the same,' said the man. 'And mind that brilliantine. It's expensive.'

'Come one step closer and you'll get an expensive clout in the face,' I warned.

'Little firebrand, aren't we? Do put that bottle down before you do yourself an injury.'

'You haven't answered my question. What are you doing in this house?' It was an effort to keep my voice steady. He could hardly call me little. The man was only an inch taller than me, carrying his weight well.

'My house actually,' he answered mildly. 'This is my house and I live here.'

He didn't look in the least like Leslie Fairbrother. He had a short-trimmed beard flecked with grey, tanned skin, prominent nose above a fleshy top lip. He was wearing well-cut fawn trousers and a blue cashmere sweater. He was nothing like the old-fashioned tubby figure wearing gold-rimmed specs that DI James had shown me in a photograph.

'Are you sure?'

He laughed, showing the even white teeth of status dentistry. 'I don't need to prove anything to you, young woman. Maybe I have changed my wardrobe, got contact lenses, grown a beard.'

'You're the manager of Sussex United Banking Corporation? You don't look like Leslie Fairbrother and I've seen a photograph. He's a bit overweight and wears gold-rimmed spectacles.'

'I wouldn't put it past Cordelia to give the police an old photograph. She didn't exactly want them to find me. She much preferred me out of the way so she could have the house to herself and build her monstrosities in the kitchen. All I wanted was that damned key. How was I to know she'd put it inside one of her talentless monuments.'

'Cordelia?'

'My wife. She called herself Waz for some insane reason. How could a bank manager, a corporate bank manager at that, have a wife with such a ridiculous name?'

I took in what I was hearing. So this was Leslie Fairbrother, the missing bank manager, and I didn't like him one bit. I felt a chill of apprehension. Called herself ... past tense. And I remembered the hand-washing. Although he was smiling at me, his eyes

333

were hard and without feeling.

'Ah, the key to the bank vaults,' I said lightly, wondering how I was going to get out of this one.

'No, wrong. The key to Fenwick Future Homes. The one I used to lock Councillor Fenwick into his smouldering pathway to incineration. Foolish man. He was panicking. Love does that, you know, especially when it's an older man infatuated with a young woman. Not that Pippa's young any more. She'll be going for the collagen implants any year now.'

'You know ... Pippa?'

'She of the uncertain bike-riding ability. I really had to put on the pressure to get her to do that. Of course, she's dead worried about her forthcoming marriage to the pop impresario. Money talks and she wants to hear every word.'

Any moment now I was going to have to sit down. I couldn't take it all in. My legs had no moral courage. This man had just told me he had locked the councillor into the burning showroom; that he had made Pippa ride my bike near the fire, pretending to be me.

'And I suppose you also got her to pay several lots of two thousand pounds into my bank account.' It was a shot in the murk.

'Clever girl. No wonder you are a detective. Not SUBC funds, I hasten to add. Too simple to trace. My own money, but worth every penny if it nails you to the arson and murder.'

'But it hasn't worked, has it?' I said bravely though I was not feeling at all brave. How was I going to get out of this? 'I'm not a suspect any more. Too much circumstantial evidence. And there's a witness who came up placing me elsewhere at the time of the fire.' I didn't mention the CCTV footage.

'Don't be too sure. I can soon fix a postman. Get him to say you paid him. Besides, you're going to leave a confession. All nice and tidy. Then I can disappear for good. Somewhere warm and sunny. I've got my eye on a villa in the Pyrenees. Wonderful views. Can't wait to get there. What do you think?'

'I think you are mad,' I said, pushing past him.

But he caught a handful of my hair and jerked me back. It caught me off guard. My roots screamed in pain. He pulled my face close to his mouth. 'You're not going anywhere, Miss Lacey,' he said slowly.

'Let ... me ... go,' I said, matching the determination in his voice. 'This is getting us nowhere. Supposing we sit down and talk. We could work something out.'

'What a good idea,' he said, relaxing his grip on my hair but not letting go. 'Let's take a little ride and work something out.

This house is so stuffy and it smells ... of paint and that damned glue. Not nice.'

'Not nice to kill your wife,' I said.

'It was not something on my agenda,' he said, pushing me downstairs. 'She just wouldn't cooperate.'

He picked up a sharp knife in the kitchen on the way out, one of Waz's tools. He shot a glance at the kitchen taps and the sink full of saucepans. Somehow he managed to turn on a tap and put a hand under the water while poking the point of the knife into my side.

'Hey, mind the fabric, buster,' I said, twisting sideways.

'I'll use it if I have to,' he said, changing hands.

As he turned to dry his hands, I leaned against the counter top. My hand was out of sight, behind me, trawling the debris like the claws of a lucky dip in an amusement arcade. I thought of Jack with affection. He wouldn't stick a knife into my side, even when he'd been drinking.

As we drove away in a new red Ford Fiesta, I glimpsed my own Morris Minor parked forlornly outside No 18. Some kids were peering in the windows. I hoped they wouldn't vandalise the spots. Kids have little sense of ownership these days.

I had no idea where we were going or why but I was sure that he had murdered his

336

wife, Waz. The man had no conscience at all. He would simply remove anyone who got in his way. It seemed I was next on the list. I needed a less stressful job. Airline pilot perhaps.

'Let's drive around a little,' he said, fastening his seat belt. 'I haven't quite worked out the exact circumstances of your confession. Your arrival at my house was fortuitous but unexpected.'

'You won't get me to confess to anything,' I said stonily, staring ahead. I was hardly prepared for any escape plan. No shoes. Only hospital issue plastics.

'Oh yes, I think I will. You see, I can be quite persuasive. Pippa found me difficult to refuse. We had quite a little talk.'

'So why did you lock the good councillor into his burning showroom?' I asked. Shopping list (if I ever go shopping again): tape recorder.

'He was getting panicky. We had a great scheme going. He provided smooth planning permission, never a hitch. I provided the money. The builder built the houses and FFH sold them. You'd be surprised at the rake-off between us. I raised loans and mortgages through the bank, legitimate but using different names. It was over a million in loans. But head office was getting suspicious. So much business through one small branch. I was having to juggle sums.'

'And Adrian didn't like the juggling?'

'If he was going to blow the lid off, then he had to go. He was getting nervous. He had his reputation on the council to think of. He wanted to be mayor. There were enough properties in the pipeline to get me off the hook. I just needed time.'

'So you locked Adrian Fenwick into his blazing office because he was going to back out of the property deal?'

'Had to splash a bit of petrol around, make it look good. He was only burning stuff in a bin. It was too easy.'

'And your wife ... why kill her? She had nothing to do with the property rake-off.'

'I'm not sure how she found out but she did. She was quite a clever woman despite being an artistic nutcase. She found the showroom key, put two and two together, then refused to tell me where it was. A few dollops of glue and she was gasping to tell me. It was in the "Ruin". But it was already too late. I didn't know the moulding clay stuff was quick-setting. A technical error. Not exactly murder, more ignorance. So I covered her with spray paint just to make it look pretty.'

'Why are you telling me all this?'

'It's nice to communicate.'

Leslie Fairbrother was driving the car and using baby wipes on his hands. Modern infant hygiene to the rescue.

I was nauseated. Was I getting an ulcer? Perhaps I ought to see a doctor. They can catch these things in time nowadays.

'So you have the key back.' I took a deep breath. 'Adrian is dead, your wife is dead. Why bother with me? Why not let me go and you can disappear to your villa in Spain wearing a beard? No one will know.'

'I don't trust you,' said Leslie Fairbrother, leaving the A27 and heading down a rustic side lane. Low-lying branches missed the windscreen by inches. I wondered if I could manufacture an accident, grab the steering wheel and plunge the car into a ditch. Guess I'd be the one to get a broken leg. 'You know too much now.'

'I could conveniently forget,' I offered, coward of the first order. 'I could develop amnesia.'

'You are going to develop amnesia. The permanent kind.'

This was worse than the Scarlatti brothers. They would not have killed me for information. They only wanted to know where Al was then they would have let me go, I think. I looked around inside the car without moving my head. A swivel eye scan. His mobile phone lay on the glove shelf. I doubted if any mental thought process could get it to ring 999. I didn't even know how to switch it on. Green light or red? I needed to go on a course.

He'd found what he wanted, the show-room key in the ruin. So why did he need me? I was nothing, no one, except that he had told me too much.

We were bumping down some farm lane, the wheels jolting over ruts. I had no idea where we were. The fields were empty, old buildings stood gathering decay and dereliction. Another farm gone bust. He drove past the farmyard and up another narrow lane. The mud was inches thick. He stopped, choosing a spot where overhanging branches would disguise the shape of the car.

'Thought we'd go to church,' he said. 'The perfect place for a confession. Good for the soul.'

'My soul is already in great shape. Nothing on my conscience,' I said.

'Get out,' he said, using the knife on the side of my neck. The blade was lethal.

I had to go with him. My feet squelched into the mud. My toes registered the cold. The mud enclosed my feet as if they were bare. We were in a valley, the Downs stretching in all directions, gorse and rabbits and unshorn grass. No one came here.

Yet a single storeyed stone building stood halfway up the hill, clusters of gravestones on the slopes. It had been there a long, long time, the centuries etched on its walls like graffiti.

It was the oldest church in Sussex, built by the Saxons on a Roman site sometime in the twelfth century, the nave widened by the Normans, every century changing windows and doors, serving a slowly diminishing farming community. I wondered if they still held services.

Leslie Fairbrother herded me up the hill, pricking the back of my neck with the knife. I wondered how he planned to kill me. He'd already done burning and glueing. Perhaps he was going to starve me to death, a martyr's death.

None of the graves had flowers. They were all neglected. The headstones were fallen or broken. Weeds climbed over crosses and recumbent angels with crushed noses. Positive thinking: grab a headstone, hit abductor on head, escape. Plan success rate: zero.

'Don't even think of making a run for it,' he said. Are my thoughts so transparent? 'I've got the keys to the car.'

The church door was unlocked. It felt used inside, revered, not neglected. If the circumstances had been different, I would have enjoyed being there, among the thousands of souls who had prayed on their knees in the worn pews.

Gutted candles stood on the altar. Kneelers lay askew in the pews. There was no stale smell, only the fading scent of flowers.

'They still have services here, once a month. Beautiful, isn't it?' he said. 'Look at the vaulted ceilings and the scraps of medieval paintings still on the walls. You can see them better if you block out the direct light from the windows.'

'Really.'

'The windows and doors have been changed a dozen times. Bigger, smaller, higher or lower. The trefoil-headed windows are fourteenth century. And on the floor ... all these marble floorslabs. They're impossible to read, the dates and names half worn away. And see this tiny door in the wall? A hermit used to live behind there. A hermit's cell. Amazing, isn't it? I love history. I ought to have been a historian instead of a bank manager.'

He was showing me round like a guide. Yet he was on the point of killing me. It was bizarre.

'I need to go to the bathroom,' I said. Nearly true.

'Sorry, no such facility in the church. Still, it won't be a problem for long. Let's get this over with. Sit in a pew and we'll write this confession.'

'I'm not writing any confession.'

'Oh yes you are. I can inflict quite a bit of pain with this knife. Such an unpleasant distraction.' Leslie had a pad of A4 lined paper. He pushed me down on to a pew and handed me a pen. 'Now write "I, Jordan Lacey", or whatever your full name is.'

I scribbled Help, Help, HELP all over the page. For a moment he looked angry and then he laughed. He tore the page off, crunched it up and threw the ball on the floor.

'Very funny, let's try again,' he said. '"I, Jordan Lacey, being of sound mind, do confess to the murder of Councillor Adrian Lacey."'

I wrote very slowly. I put being of unsound mind. I spelt councillor incorrectly. He did not seem to notice the mistakes. It was getting cold in the old church with the door open. The Downs were blowing a winter wind. My feet were slowly turning to ice. Perhaps I was going to freeze to death.

'"I also confess to receiving six thousand pounds from Pippa Shaw as a bribe. I confess to starting the showroom fire with petrol—"'

'And with a candle in a waste bin?' I interrupted.

'That's very good. I like that. Add candle in a waste bin.'

I spelt waste 'waist' and added an extra nought to the blood money. He was very careless for a bank manager. But I felt impotent. My handwriting was barely recognisable. A drop of blood was running down my neck. He had nicked the skin.

343

'"And after locking the showroom door, I threw the key in the sea."'

I spelt sea 'see'. 'But I didn't,' I said. 'You've got the key.'

'Don't argue. Now sign it. Your full name.'

I signed. I put Jordan MacLacey. Mac the Knife. Someone might get the connection. Someone with a few brain cells.

'Well done,' he said. He did not spot the errors in the dim light of the church. 'Didn't know you were Scottish.'

'On my mother's side.'

'I'll pop it into the post, addressed to West Sussex police. They should get it tomorrow or the next day. DI James will be pleased to have one less case to deal with.'

'He'll get you for your wife's death.'

'Never. I disappeared weeks ago. I could be in South America by now.'

He unlocked the hermit's door with a large iron key someone had left in the lock and opened it. Stale air flooded out. It was total darkness inside. Just a hole in the hillside.

Leslie Fairbrother caught my arms, my sleeves, the lobe of my ear. He had ten hands, pushing me inside. I fell, off balance, and the door slammed shut behind me. I heard the key turn.

'Time for meditation on your sins,' he said. 'No hurry. You've plenty of time. 'Bye, Jordan. Nice meeting you. I'll think of you when I'm sunning in Spain by my pool, maybe.'

'Let me out! Don't go!' I screamed. 'Don't leave me. This isn't fair. I haven't done anything.'

'Sorry, Jordan. I've other things on my mind.'

I heard him leave, the door to the church shut.

It was the inky blackness of no light whatsoever. And it was small. The hermit must have been a midget or perhaps he shrank with time. The floor was hard earth, flattened by centuries. I made myself activate my senses. At the back were several piles of books. From the uniform size and thin pages, I guessed they were hymn books. The hermit's hole was used as a store. I felt around some more and found several boxes of waxy sticks – altar candles. Wonderful. I could have a sing-song.

In my pocket was the trawl of Waz's kitchen counter top: I had gathered paper clips, a plastic wallet, a cork, a tube of wine gums and, glory hallelujah, a full box of matches. Note to self: always carry matches.

I made a makeshift candlestick holder out of the clips, plastic wallet and cork, my fingers clumsy with haste. The contraption held a candle firmly enough to light. The match flared happily and took hold of the waxen wick. Lo, we had light.

A soft light wavered round the hole. The light cheered me. I lit a second candle and held it aloft. Now I could see that the hermit's cell had been dug out of the hill with two sides supported by walls of rough stones, holding back the earth. It was too low for me to stand. I could hardly dig out the back wall. A mile through the South Downs? There were no communion biscuits or wine. I'd have to survive on the gums.

I had got to get out of this. No way was I going to let Leslie Fairbrother wash his hands all the way to Spain. I thought about burning down the door but it was inches thick and would no doubt kill me in the process. Surely someone would come to dust, water the flowers, straighten the kneelers, replenish the guide leaflets by the door. Perhaps.

Or I would die. The timeless boredom before death was more of a worry. How long would it take? No food, no drink, not much air...

I thumbed through a hymn book, peering closely at the print. I knew several of the hymns from childhood. The words were comforting.

'All things bright and beautiful,' I began singing, 'all creatures great and small. All things wise and wonderful, the Good Lord made them all.'

# Twenty-Three

It was an endless vacuum of time that hung like an old sepia print. I couldn't remember how long an hour felt like. Shopping list: buy a watch. No, delete that. I wouldn't be needing a watch by tomorrow.

I sat, knees hunched up, in the cramped hole, surrounded by stubs of candles, some burning, some gutted. I saw no point in being economical. I needed light and a flicker of warmth. My feet were beyond feeling. At the end of every verse I rubbed them. Terry Waite had exercised regularly for muscle tone.

High-level dread was eating into my resilience, weakening my normal sturdy defences. This old church was miles off the beaten track. No one would find me for weeks.

I was so cold it was hard not to doze off. I knew I must not sleep. It would be my last sleep if I did. My mind was slipping away. I was walking the pier in a kind of fog. Happy Birthday, Pier. As I strolled the decking, I realised what was wrong with one of those photographs in the exhibition. The negative had been printed the wrong way round. The east side of the pier appeared to be on the right; the view of the west side was portrayed on the left. A simple error. I knew east was towards Brighton, the Seven Sisters and Beachy Head which I could vaguely see; the west was towards Cornwall which I could not.

No one had noticed. It was like my recent cases. No one had noticed that they were the wrong way round. What appeared to be on the right, was actually on the left. And vice versa.

Terence Lucan appeared to be the victim with his stolen water lilies, but he was actually the villain with his insurance fraud. Mrs Drury and her WI appeared the victims of vandalism, but she was the villain, getting free publicity deviously manufactured by herself. And Mrs Fenwick ... she might appear a victim, her cake being stolen which in fact it was, but then it was no ordinary brandy-laced wedding cake.

Pippa Shaw looked like a villain, framing me for crimes I didn't do, but she was a victim, being blackmailed all along the line. I tried to think about Waz Fairbrother, decide what she was ... but my brain cells were sounding Whiskey Alpha Zulu, drifting back to panda-car days of long ago. I shook myself awake.

Lacey's eleven most loved hymns of Latching were on their eighteenth airing when I heard a faint noise outside. Hallelujah. I wasn't sure if it was rats or ghosts or Leslie Fairbrother coming back to finish me off. Maybe it was a Holocene ghost, from the rock period. Ten thousand years ago. After all I was holed up in the South Downs. I don't know where I picked up this useless bit of information. If it was a rat, I could try making a pet of it.

I thought I heard a light being switched on. Yes, there was light, a glimmer under the door. Or was it angels with shimmering wings come to fetch me?

I managed to call out, banged on the door with a hymn book till it slipped from my hand. I was so stiff I could hardly move. That hermit must have been a cripple.

'Jordan! Jordan! Where are you?'

I was hallucinating, of course. That voice. More dreams. It was the voice that I would die hearing. James ... James ... my James. Not my trumpeter because he was a fantasy figure and belonged to another woman. His music succoured my soul but he had no place in my life, in my bed, in my arms...

'I'm here ... in the hermit's hole.'

'God! Why doesn't the woman talk sense! This is no time for jokes, Jordan.' He sounded angry. I heard footsteps pacing the church, stamping over the floorslabs. They were making more noise than I was. It reverberated like half an army.

I banged feebly on the door, sobbing. 'Here ... here ... here.'

'The banging seems to be coming from this tiny door in the wall, sir. It's locked.'

Bless his size-ten cotton socks. Some barely shaving rookie constable had noticed the door. He sounded about fourteen.

'Move back! We're going to break down the door,' DI James shouted.

'You can't!' I cried. 'It's centuries old.'

'Move back, you idiot!'

'I can't. There's no room.'

'OK. Then you'll have to stay there until you are thin enough to slide under the door.'

'Break it down,' I said.

It was a tough old door. Splinters of wood showered round me. They were using an axe. I covered my face. A shaft of light flooded in and I looked up. They had destroyed the area around the lock and the door swung open harmlessly. DI James stared in with a flange of faces behind him. They looked startled. I suppose I did look odd.

I was so stiff, I couldn't move. Someone blew out the candles. DI James hauled me into the transept of the church. I couldn't stand properly. My legs had departed this earth.

'Are you all right?' he asked roughly, letting me lean on him.

I nodded. 'Want a wine gum?' I asked, offering him the last in the pack.

Somehow we got down the hillside to his car. It was dark now. The gloom was enveloping. He slid me into the front passenger seat, holding my head down in normal police procedure. My brain was thawing slowly. I was not going to die but I might lose my toes.

He took off the mud-caked plastic hospital issue and began rubbing my feet.

'You should get yourself some proper shoes, Jordan,' he said. 'There are lots of shoe shops in Latching. Or you could buy a pair of trainers in a discount store.'

'Yes,' I said. I was beginning to tremble.

Then he did something amazing. He took off his shoes and socks, and put his own still warm socks on my feet. I could have died then from the sheer pleasure.

He put his shoes back on his bare feet and turned on the car heater.

'Who was it, Jordan? Feel like talking? Who locked you in?'

'Yes,' I said. 'It was Leslie Fairbrother, the bank manager. I think he's planning to go to Spain. Maybe by ferry to France then driving down to Spain. He has a new Ford Fiesta, red. Didn't get the registration number, but it's this year's. You'd better hurry if you are going to catch him.'

'I'll radio through to the ferry ports and Gatwick airport, see if they can pick him up.'

'And he looks different now. Greyish beard, trimmer build, well dressed, no glasses. He's had a makeover. And he's always washing his hands, creepy.'

'Nothing like the photograph?'

'No. How did you know it was me in the church?'

'We didn't at first. Someone spotted your spotted car outside number eighteen Tarrant Close.' DI James didn't know he had said something funny. His face was set. 'We decided that was shorthand for calling on number twelve.'

'But the church ... it was miles away.'

'A woman walking her dog heard this strange singing coming from the church. She knew it wasn't choir rehearsal night so she called the police.'

'But you still didn't know it was me in there.'

DI James handed me a crumpled sheet of A4 paper. It had help, help, HELP WRITTEN ALL OVER IT.

'You really must improve your writing,' he said.

It was VIP treatment at Latching police

station. Sergeant Rawlings fussed about with a blanket and I got the same armchair. A WPC whipped out to Safeways and came back with a wrapped shrimp and mayonnaise sandwich and a packet of sour-cream crisps. DI James produced the Chardonnay although I knew it was against the rules. It was cool and oaky and slid down my throat like silk. I read the label. It was from Australia and was good with salads and meat and fish dishes. He recorded a statement from me and I told him all I knew. It took a long time because I was tired.

'We can't charge him just on this,' he said. 'You could be making it all up.'

'Sure, and I locked myself into the hermit's cell just to lose weight and meditate for a couple of days. It's up to you to find the evidence. I'm giving you the background and the motive for both deaths.'

He held up his hands in submission. 'I believe you, Jordan. But any good defence lawyer could shred this statement to pieces in court. No one can verify a word. No witnesses. Leslie Fairbrother would deny every word, say you were freaked out of your mind, deny he had even met you, never been anywhere near the church.'

'Mud on his car wheels, from the farmyard, from the lane,' I said. I was really into forensic. 'Get a match.'

'He's probably been to a car wash on his

353

way to the ferry, hosed down the wheels.'

I yawned. The wine was making me sleepy. My legs and feet had a degree of returned life in them. I needed a walk but even the few yards to the bleak station loo and back was hard going. It would be nice to sleep stretched out on a comfortable bed in a warm room, surrounded by hot-water bottles.

'I want to go home,' I said.

'Sorry, Jordan,' DI James. 'But we can't let you go home. We'll make arrangements for you to stay in a hotel, one of our safe havens. WPC Patel will accompany you. We'll get some clean clothes for you and anything else that you might need. You can't go back to your flat or your shop until Leslie Fairbrother is safely behind bars. He's a dangerous man.'

'That's what Adrian Fenwick was trying to tell me when he phoned before the fire,' I said. 'Remember, he said something about being in danger?'

'You're probably right. We'll never know.'

They caught Leslie Fairbrother in the act of throwing two keys into the Channel while on the Dover–Calais ferry. Perhaps he wanted to give my confession some validity. The keys caught in some deck superstructure and fell on to a passenger's foot. They were identified as the keys to the hermit's door and the FFH office key.

He denied handling the keys but a party of French students on deck had witnessed the event and gave evidence several times, volubly and in several languages. The police sergeant got a severe headache.

As soon as he was in custody I was allowed to go home. Not that I hadn't enjoyed my few days as a pampered hotel guest but the novelty soon wore off and I wanted to get out and go off. Seawards. They let me keep the jeans and sweatshirt kindly provided out of some fund. The sweatshirt was a mildewy green, not my colour at all. It went in the props box.

My flat said hello, hello, hello, despite the shut-in-air feeling. I opened windows, touched things, sat around, reminded myself that I paid the rent. As soon as I put on a jazz tape and turned up the volume, then it was all mine again and the drums rolled and the trumpets blazed. The Saints Came Marching In.

It didn't surprise me when DI James turned up on my doorstep, carrying a pair of trainers. I had left them at No 12, parked tidily behind the kitchen door. He looked drawn and tired. They work him too hard.

First I sat him down, gave him a bowl of freshly made carrot and orange soup at which he turned up his nose but managed to down two bowlfuls. There were granary rolls and garlic butter to mop up any spaces.

'Don't ask for tomato sauce because you're not getting any.'

'I wouldn't dream of putting it on garlic butter but the soup could do with spicing up.'

'Is this a social call?' I asked as he settled down with a cup of my best coffee. He was stretched out on my moral chair, all long arms and legs, hardly statement-taking, intimidating police stance.

'Just a few gaps to fill in. I want to hear your side of things, Jordan, get the full picture. Could we start with Terence Lucan?'

'I've solved that case,' I said grandly. 'I found his water lilies.'

'Where?'

'Ah ... they had been mislaid.'

'You can't mislay a dozen ponds of lilies. Come on, Jordan, where were they?'

'I'm not sure where they are now,' I said carefully. Burnt, decomposed, returning to Sussex mould? 'But Mr Lucan was reunited and he dropped the case, didn't he?' I didn't want the poor man to be charged with wasting police time.

'What about Mrs Edith Drury?'

'Nothing to do with the police,' I said promptly. 'She didn't call in the police.'

'I read about it in the newspapers. Did you find the vandals?'

'Yes.' I put the soup bowls in the sink and

started washing up with a lot of sudsy noise.

'But they were never charged?'

'The perpetrators were punished enough,' I said, remembering Mrs Drury's desperate trotting to the bathroom. 'It won't happen again.'

'Are you sure?'

'I'm sure.'

'We'd better send you some of our criminals. See if you can work the same magic on them.'

I didn't answer. This was just a warm-up. Now he was going for the jugular.

'What were you doing in number twelve?'

'Leroy Anderson gave me the key. She wanted me to look round and see if the police had missed anything. She thought I stood a better chance of finding a lead. Her sister was someone very special to her.'

'What did you find?'

'Leslie Fairbrother. Who had slept there since his wife was found murdered. A man who looked different, was no henpecked husband, a man with pound signs in his eyes.'

'How does Pippa Shaw figure in this? Tell me all you know about her.'

'You know as much as me. She is/was engaged to some pop impresario and Leslie Fairbrother was blackmailing her. He knew her affair with her father-in-law would not go down well with her fiancé who liked to keep a squeaky clean image. His company sells to teeny-boppers. So he got her to do the bike-riding and money-dropping in an appalling red wig, nothing like my hair at all.'

James nodded in agreement. He was actually looking at my hair. I had just washed it and it was all fire.

'I'm surprised people were taken in,' I added. 'Did Leslie Fairbrother admit this?'

'Leslie Fairbrother has said nothing. He got a lawyer straightaway. But Pippa Shaw has made a full statement on condition she won't have to go to court. I think this can be arranged. She admits to putting sleeping pills in Adrian Fenwick's flask but this cannot be considered chargeable. Leslie Fairbrother probably went to see Adrian Fenwick that evening to talk him out of backing away from their scheme, found Adrian Fenwick in a dozy state, shredding and burning the evidence. He saw his opportunity and returned with a can of petrol, splashed it about a bit and then locked Adrian into the office.'

I shuddered. 'How cold-blooded.'

'He'd watched you for days; earlier he'd broken the chain on your bike and forced Pippa to ride it past the showroom with a can of petrol, then park it nearby. He thought he would set you up, get her to pay money into your bank account.'

'Watched me for days? What a nerve!'

'You do it all the time.'

'It's called surveillance. I'm paid to do it. Are you going to charge him?'

'Of course. We have on both counts of murder. We don't know how Mrs Fairbrother found out about him locking Adrian into the fire, but she did and that was enough to make her a problem. A problem that Leslie Fairbrother had to remove.'

'I'm emotionally involved in this,' I groaned. 'Get me out, please, James. Do you know what Leroy Anderson was doing in Pippa Shaw's flat?'

'She doesn't really know herself. She knew that Pippa Shaw was involved with Adrian Fenwick and that he was involved with her brother-in-law. She thought there might be some link with her sister's death and as she had a key to number five Horizon Views, she went along to have a look. She admitted it straightaway, took nothing, found nothing. She left when she heard someone opening the front door.'

'Me.'

'And panicked. She tipped a drawer of things on the floor and hoped Pippa would think a burglar had got in.'

'She was very convincing,' I said.

'By the way, Jordan,' James leaned back easily as if he was made for my chair; he was made for my chair, every inch of him, my flat, my car, my bed. 'We arrested two Italians earlier today. They were going to blow up a Latching garage. An observant attendant saw them setting the fuses, called us immediately. We had to evacuate the area and get the bomb squad in.'

'They were looking for Al Lubliganio,' I sighed. I had told the brothers that Al Lubliganio worked at a local garage. People could have been killed ... and I would have been responsible.

'So they said, once we'd got an interpreter in. I thought you might be relieved to know that they are being sent back to Italy, pronto. They are wanted for a string of offences. They'll be put away for a long, long time. Unless, of course, you want me to detain them here on charges of abduction and threatening behaviour?'

'No, thank you. Send them back,' I said firmly. 'The further, the better.'

'I thought you might say that. Thanks for the soup, strange though it was. I'll let you get some rest.' James got up, stretching, searched around for his jacket. He'd left it hanging on the back of the door.

I didn't want any rest. I wanted him to stay and talk about other things. You know, anything, state of the world, UK economics, foreign policy, flower-arranging.

'I got an invitation from Pippa Shaw

today,' I said. 'To the party after her wedding. A sort of knees-up following the reception. It said to bring a friend. Do you want to come?'

'Might as well,' he said.

# Twenty-Four

In the days before the wedding, I sorted out a few things that had been troubling me. I removed the cardboard boxes from the Grecian temple in Mrs Drury's garden and threw them in the sea. After checking the contents, of course.

Another irksome enigma was that Lancaster bomber and the skeleton of a woman found aboard, a silver bracelet around her wrist. I wanted to know who she was. Not exactly a crime and no one was paying me.

I went round to Pippa Shaw to thank her for clearing me in her statement and for the invitation. I had accepted the invitation, not believing that I would ever get there.

It was all very strange because I had always thought of her as unapproachable. But this time she was amiable and offered me a glass of wine and to sit down on her white leather sofa. My jeans were clean. The whole episode had obviously knocked some corners off her and she was more human, less sharp-edged. Being blackmailed had been a nasty experience.

'It's been a really harrowing time for us all,' I said, the wine loosening my tongue. 'I've never been framed before and I don't suppose you've been blackmailed before.'

'It was a nightmare,' she agreed with a deep sigh. 'And then I had my grandmother to think of as well.'

'Your grandmother?' I blanked out. I tried to draw her back on track. But she wanted to tell me.

'I was trying to protect her. Linda Keates was my grandmother,' she said after another gin and tonic. I could see a certain problem on its way here. 'That's why Adrian was so against the raising of the wreck. He knew I would be upset.'

'That was your grandmother, found on the bomber?'

'Yes, I knew she was down there. Hoped she would stay there but they found incendiaries on the beach and thought the wreck had become dangerous.'

'But why object? Then you could have a proper funeral for your grandmother. It can't be much fun being at the end of the pier, all those kids being sick after brawls at the nightclub.'

Tacky but true. Pippa offered me another glass of wine so it showed she did not mind.

'My grandmother was separated from her husband, and my mother, only a child then,

363

was staying with relatives while Linda worked at Patcham House. She saw a chance of making money for them both. There was a burglary one night and a lot of valuable silver was taken. In the confusion afterwards, she took this rare ivory group from the Tokyo School from the Patcham House collection. OK, it was stealing but she was desperate. It was quite small, illustrating Japanese life, but superbly carved with great sensitivity, and something for which a German collector would pay a great deal of money.'

'How do you know this?'

'She left a letter for my mother, explaining everything. That's how I know. In case something happened to her.'

'And something did happen.'

'She was going to be dropped over occupied France, parachute down with the ivory, contact a German dealer who was willing to buy, get back somehow. It was a crazy plan. I think the pilot must have been sweet on her. But the Lancaster developed engine trouble and crashed into the beach at Latching instead.'

'And the ivory group?'

'The police divers found the bundle in the wreck and it has been returned to the owners of Patcham House. It's still in reasonable condition despite being wrapped in sacking and under water for fifty years.

It's worth a lot of money now. The sale of it will solve a lot of their financial problems. They are very happy and not taking any action. Just glad to have it back.'

'And Linda Keates?'

'I'm going to have her funeral the day before my wedding. It seems right, a private service. My mother is still alive, quite old but spritely, runs her own business. I'm glad you can come to the party. I feel I owe you a lot. You've sorted out my life. Have you got something nice to wear?'

'Not yet. As you can see, I'm not into dresses.'

'Do you mind if I ask you something?'

'Ask away.'

'All that money. The cash that Leslie Fairbrother made me pay into your account, impersonating you. What happens to that?'

I was thrown. Did she want it back? But it wasn't hers. Leslie Fairbrother had drawn it from his own account and had had it put into mine.

'It was a problem,' I said. 'You see, the bank manager told me that the only way to get rid of it was for me to draw it out. And only I could withdraw it.'

'And...?' Her face had gone a shade pale.

'So I did. I sent half of it to the Children of Chernobyl fund and half to a Save the Seals sanctuary in the Orkneys. I'm sure Leslie Fairbrother would approve of this charitable distribution of his money. Anyway, it's too late now. I've sent it.'

Leroy Anderson came to my rescue. She lent me her blue chiffon dress. It had a swirling skirt, draped bodice and shoelace shoulder straps. I had to buy sheer tights and a pair of strappy sandals. I hardly recognised myself in the mirror and I couldn't walk. I looked like a lampshade on stilts. She also did my hair and make-up.

'You deserve a party,' she said, pinning my hair up into a bird's nest. 'Forget everything and have fun.'

She and Blackie had moved in with the friends who had been giving her shelter. No 12 was waiting to be sold. Leroy was practically running FFH and Mrs Fenwick was delighted with the ways things were going. They had become friends, more like mother and daughter, good for each other. They shared grief and that was bonding.

Pippa's wedding was pretty posh, women in fancy clothes and men in brocade waistcoats. The evening party was in Latching's top hotel. They had taken over the whole of the ground floor and a band was playing in the ballroom. I could hear the subdued beat. There were white flowers everywhere, lilies and carnations and roses. The scent was heady.

'I don't know anyone here,' I said as we

went into the crowded reception hall. Pippa and her new husband were standing in line to greet their guests. She was in white parchment satin, stiff and reed-slim, elegant as a lily herself. She had an old silver bracelet dangling on her wrist. But she was radiant, smiling and laughing.

'You know me,' said James.

He was in a dark grey suit, a black shirt and ice-blue tie. Mafia gear, Latching style. Our blues toned. He was so good-looking, I didn't want Pippa to see him in case she changed her mind. The man lit a sunshine window in my heart.

But I wished I was at home or on the beach or walking the pier, wanting fresh air and pounding waves, anywhere but here in this overheated crowd. A waiter offered me a glass of champagne, golden bubbles spilling like temptation. James also took a glass. He toasted me and smiled gravely.

'We might as well enjoy the party,' he said. 'At least we're not working. It beats paperwork.'

I had to ask. 'Do I look all right?'

He surveyed my appearance. 'I didn't know you had legs,' he said.

MICMD. 8/02

H

n finished

savoy